# Calculated Concealment

By Doug Hollidge

Published by MVP June 2009

© Doug Hollidge 2008

Doug Hollidge asserts the moral right to
be identified as the author of this work

All rights reserved. No portion of this book may be used or reproduced in any manner whatsoever, except for brief quotations in critical reviews or articles, without prior written permission of the publisher.

Cover design: South East Design

ISBN 978-0-9554692-5-1

Dedication

To a long suffering, but very precious family

In the writer's knowledge, Titian's protrait of the Vendramin family has only once left the National Gallery. That was a year after the portrait was acquired for the National Collection. For a brief time, during 1930, it was at the Royal Academy. It can currently be seen in all its splendour in Room 9 of the West Wing at the National Gallery.

# Prologue

Terry Berrysford's first viewing of the Zimmermann Treasures 'B' List turned out sadly to have fatal consequences. Terry was not to know that Heinrich Zimmermann held very forthright views about those who failed to cooperate with the advancement of his plans.

The Zimmermann Treasures 'B' List was closely guarded and discretely hidden from public view. This breathtaking collection was for strictly private pleasure only. The man's wealth was beyond calculation. But Terry was beginning to believe that Zimmermann's passion to possess the treasures of history veiled a greed fed desire that travelled, and more than occasionally crossed, the fine edge of legitimacy and legality. If it were possible to possess via mere monetary means, no trouble, money was no object. But if it were not possible, then Zimmermann had other methods.

The trade knew Zimmermann to be a collector of prodigious proportion. He graced the sale rooms of the world. His agents acted on his behalf, and spent his money with a degree of flambuoyance that bordered on the vulgar.

Terry had seen the process at first hand on many occasions. Once, and only once, Terry had battled against him openly in the bidding, going way beyond his own prudently set and sometimes too cautiously set limit. Zimmermann had been present himself and, quite unlike him, had stood up and searched the sale room with an ice cold stare attempting to identify the owner of the young voice seemingly intent on robbing him of his purchase. Terry had smiled when finally their eyes met.

Unbeknown to Terry it was as a direct result of that first contact that he was now being head hunted to join Zimmermann's employ.

Terry was on the edge of an experience that few others in his line of business had shared.

The invitation had been quite formal. "Heinrich Zimmermann extends with great pleasure a most cordial invitation to Mr Terence Berrysford to attend a viewing of the renowned Zimmermann Treasures 'B' List."

Date and time were affixed. A reply of acceptance was asked for by return.

Terry, more than just a little intrigued, accepted.

As a consequence he travelled to the stated destination, Zimmermann's London office, from where he was driven a further hours journey in a Daimler limousine with curtained windows and non see through screen separating him from the driver. This, he was told, was to ensure the secrecy of the location. It was all very elegant. The drinks cabinet in the Daimler was very well stocked, and the man who accompanied him was

extremely polite. But not so polite as to reveal anything about the destination to which they travelled.
The journey ended in an underground car park, from where a lift was taken to a venue that was still deeper underground.
The man who had travelled with Terry led him into a waiting area that was coldly clinical in its appointment.
Nothing there to suggest the expected opulence.
Heinrich Zimmermann entered and extended his hand to a much amazed Terence Berrysford.

"I'm so glad you could come. I know our meeting will be of mutual benefit.
I want you to become a member of my organisation. I know a great deal about you, Terence. Take a look at this."

He handed a folder to Terry. The printed title stated. 'Terence Berrysford.'
Terry perused it for a moment, and was very quick to understand that the dossier on his life; for that is what it was, was all too worryingly complete in every detail, even down to his present salary.

"Don't worry about all that," Zimmermann said after a few minutes, "I'm very thorough in my preparations, and I expect an equal thoroughness from all my employees. There are rich rewards for everyone. I'm offering you a place on my staff. Would you care to see my private collection?"

The Zimmermann Treasures 'B' List was very close at hand.

Without waiting for any reply from Terry, Zimmermann walked out of the door and turned down a well lit corridor.
No one in Terry's position could have resisted such an accomplished act of self belief.
Terry followed without hesitation.
At the end of the corridor there were huge bronze doors. Zimmermann punched in a code on a wall panel, and the doors slowly opened.

In the enthralling hour that followed, Terry viewed in wide eyed amazement as the Aladdin's cave was explored.
The collection was indeed outstanding.
But during the progress of it all Terry made two dreadful mistakes.
Terry's own particular speciality was $17^{th}$ and $18^{th}$ century furniture. He took in with great delight everything that was on view, but when he saw

one particular piece of cabinet work, that he knew very well indeed, his eyebrows raised with a sense of disbelief.

His first mistake.

Zimmermann, who was watching Terry's every response, noted Terry's reaction, but said nothing.
Terry's raised eyebrow was an innocent over-reaction, but Terry knew that the particular piece of furniture had been stolen five months before.

What was it doing on the 'B' List?

With equal innocence, after viewing some priceless Chinese porcelain that had actually passed through his own family's firm eighteen months before, he had said that he hadn't realised that Lady Charnley had sold the stuff again.
She hadn't.
Terry's memory for absolute detail and his retention of the intricacies of the business had caused him to make his second mistake.

Zimmermann had made no comment.
When the private viewing was over, Zimmermann made an offer of employment to Terry that had he accepted would have trebled his salary. Terry made no mistake. His reply was cautious. That he would let Zimmermann know.
With that, the visit was concluded.

The same elaborate procedures were gone through on Terry's departure and he was finally reunited with his own car and was soon on his way back home.

Five days later he was back in the company of Heinrich Zimmermann, but this time there was no love lost between them.
Terry had been abducted in a sort of way.

Zimmermann was anxious for a reply. He must have it now. No one had ever delayed in giving an affirmative answer when Heinrich Zimmermann was the man employing.
Zimmermann's command of English was excellent but he was in an agitated mood and his words sounded more guttural and clipped.

"What is your answer Mr. Berrysford?"

"I'm afraid my answer is no. I am quite content to be working for my father."

"You will not change your mind?"

"No, and that is definite. But thank you for your belief in me. I am very honoured."

"Mr. Berrysford. You have made your third mistake. I will not tolerate it."

"Third mistake?"

"Your simple honesty will be your downfall Mr. Berrysford. The cabinet... you knew it to be stolen... didn't you? The porcelain... you doubted my acquisition. And now you refuse to join me. Three mistakes that I cannot tolerate. Your knowledge places me in jeopardy. I'm so sorry Mr. Berrysford, but I cannot allow you to shame me in such a way. No-one treats me in such a fashion. We must say goodbye!"

Two other men had entered the room.

Before Terry had chance to react in any defencible way, the two men had grabbed him, and pinned his arms making it impossible for him to move. Zimmermann opened a small wall safe and took out, what Terry could see as, a small stainless steel box. From it he withdrew a syringe. Adeptly he filled the syringe from a glass phial, and in a coldly clinical and unfeeling way proceeded to inject the contents of the syringe into Terry's arm.
Terry's struggle and his shouts of defiance went unheeded.
"Goodbye Mr. Berrysford."

The effects were not immediate. Terry could feel his legs and his arms going cold. It was as if he was being frozen slowly and surely. He tried to speak, but couldn't. The words were locked in his throat. His mind was still active, he thought of Faye, his wife. He thought of his father, his mother. He looked at Zimmermann. The cold unfeeling eyes looked back without any sense of remorse. The freezing sensation had reached his stomach. He vomited, and was somehow pleased to see that he had caused Zimmermann some distress.
But now he was finding it hard to keep his mind focussed. His eyes could no longer see. The cold had reached his pounding heart. He couldn't remember where he was. Who he was?

The end came finally. Terry Berrysford was history.

# Calculated Concealment

# I

"Aaaaaatishooreshoo."
It was one of those, back of the throat aching, down the nose gushing, lights behind the eyes exploding, brain nearly bursting sneezes, that always shook me so convulsively. Driving was almost impossible when this well rehearsed routine started.
"It will be the death of me one day," I thought to myself.
"A photosensitive allergic reaction to sudden bright sunlight, namely a photic sneeze" a medic friend had told me ages ago, "a very small percentage of people suffer with it, you may grow out of it."
I never did. I was, sadly, one of this privileged small percentage?
I'd be driving along minding my own business; alert to the rage making stupidities of other drivers, and blithely unaware, or perhaps very forgiving of my own. I'd turn a corner into bright sunlight; and 'wham' my head would turn inside out. The force of it would occasionally demand my stopping very quickly, in order for gradual recovery to take place.
This was one of those occasions. I stopped as quickly as was prudent, finding, fortunately, a space at the kerbside just large enough for my newly washed, electric blue, Transit executive K reg. bus. At the very last second of this forced parking manoeuvre I managed, through tear filled, slightly out of focus eyes, to make out an object in the kerb. And, by applying instinctive extra pressure on the braking system (thank goodness for ABS) just managed to avoid smashing into it.

A car had driven out of this space at quite some pace - no signals!
"Typical," I shouted aloud, with a sense of driver superiority.
Then of course came the involuntary volcanic eruption in my head followed by my speedy dash for the now vacant slot. No signals! But I was excused,
of course, by force of necessity.
The blaring horn, and the less than charming invective issuing from the car that had been following didn't exactly please me, and the raised fist from its driver, as she sped away, aroused an unusual sense of anger in me.
I had stopped. "Just cool it," I thought.
Knowing that a breath of fresh air would improve my well-being, I climbed over gear stick, brake and passenger seat and exited from the nearside, and then saw what it was that I had so narrowly missed.
I picked it up.
Only twice in my life had I made kerbside 'pick ups' of any importance.

The first time it had been a great deal of money. And the second time; separated from the first by only a few months, it had been a young woman!
Both occasions had been during my student life, now well receding into a distant past.
I remember them both vividly but for very different reasons.
As far as the money was concerned – my virtue remained intact – I handed it in to the nearest police station.
As far as the young woman was concerned – well all that I can say is that the second 'pick up' was less than virtuous!
I was taught invaluable lessons from both experiences.

It was a wooden box; ornate, inlaid with mother of pearl, swirls of flowers and dragons, a hinged lid, locked, with no apparent keyhole, and yes, quite beautiful, well handled, deep honey toned polish, worn with age. I looked around, there was no obvious owner in sight.
In fact there was no one in sight at all.

Traffic passing, but no people. Parked cars, but no one returning.

The road I had turned into was part of a diversion I had been following for some time. I was a stranger to the area and was unsure now of what my next move should be.
Where exactly was I? Nowhere in particular it seemed, just on the way to somewhere else.
I stood for a while, box in hand, wondering what next I should do. Moments later I climbed back on board, placed the box securely on the seat behind me, and prepared to drive away, decision made.
Mirror; nothing coming.
Signal; text book correctness.
Look behind, everything safe.
I drew away, slowly, deliberately, a faultless manoeuvre.

Why doesn't the human body give you clearer signals to alert you to hidden dangers? Why don't we have some inbuilt video screen somewhere in our mind; that would be prompted to display warning signs in response to stupid decisions we make?

All I was feeling was a sense of mild intrigue.

My now clearing head, my now easing throat, my now seeing eyes were all contributing to a state of well being that enabled me to map the way

ahead quite plainly. My decision, of course, was to hand the box in at a police station, let them deal with it.
My decision, correctly made; no, virtuously made, was to make sure an owner could be found.
And I was sure to pass a police station on my way, wasn't I?

I still had a good few miles to travel before I would reach my destination.

My journey had been forced upon me by circumstances way out of my control. You know how it is.
A friend asks you to get involved in a situation.

'Have you got a couple of days spare? Could you please come? It won't take long,' you are assured.

But already I had been on the road for two and a half hours.
Traffic had been bad leaving London, as usual.
Why did I always go round the North Circular? I knew that it would try my patience. The chaos and the constant grind of traffic always did.
Why did I always say to myself, "maybe it will be better today!"
Would I never learn?
I did have lots of time, however. A calculated career move had gone disastrously wrong and I was now out of work.
The designers job I had taken had folded almost as soon as it had started.
I had felt very let down and was just getting over that 'I'm feeling sorry for myself' state that usually encouraged lengthening inactivity. But unusually for me, I was alert and mindful of the necessity to put myself about in order to secure new employment somewhere.
That was partly the reason why I had readily agreed to visit John. We had studied together, kept in touch, over the years, albeit infrequently.
He'd kept me informed of his increasing family.
I was Godfather to his son Michael (not a responsibility I had taken all that seriously at the time, I have to admit) And I was now halfway nearing his new home, from which, he had told me on the phone, he ran his new design company.

Was this the opportunity I was waiting for?

As there was absolutely nothing in my diary, there was no reason for me not to respond to his quite urgently repeated request.
'Would I please make some time.'

I prided myself on being the sort of person who could detect unspoken sensitivities in conversations, but he would not elaborate, and I did not press him further on the phone.

I was never all that good with diversions; my wife was the one who had had directional awareness, always maintaining a cool appreciation of where next we should be.

I had obviously missed a turning and was now on a road going out of Chelmsford. Chelmsford had been my choice for a stop over lunch.
There was no point in turning back so I headed on towards, yes, the sign said Braintree, that would do, perhaps another fifteen minutes or so. I could then turn east and head towards Colchester and be back on track.

Chatham Green, Great Leighs, then the Essex Show ground,
Young's End and on towards Braintree.
I journeyed with little thought save that of finding somewhere for a good lunch. My sometimes titillatingly perverse mind misread a sign. I thought it read Bonking! No it was Bocking. Shame, what an amazing address to write, if only! My mind wandered for just a moment, it had been a long time...

Braintree was a pleasant enough Essex town and the Nag's Head provided an excellent lunch. It was Wednesday, obviously market day, the place was filled with 'County types.'
Overheard conversations were of humorous self importance, local politics, family dilemmas; I heard hardly a comment on the national scene at all.
There is an obvious warmth in relationships that are truly parochial in nature.
Such a contrast with my, inner city, London life.

I rejoined the A12 at Marks Tey and made good time round Colchester and was soon off in the direction of Ipswich.
And there beyond, a reunion with a friend, who had been very much a part of my life.

I continued the journey without incident.
My thoughts, however, were deep into the unspoken urgencies that I had sensed in the conversation I had had with John.
John, my senior in college, had always been so positive in attitude. Sometimes so brusquely assertive, encouraging all of us to make the future happen. Our friendship, which had started with a fair amount of

suspicion on my part, quickly became a strongly bonded thing with few rules. We knew many of each other's secrets and found a delight in the exploration of the new ideas forced upon us, as we became the receptors of new knowledge.

When college life was over, promises were made; strange, binding things, that had possessive energies with almost a religious fervour attached.

He had quickly married Stella, a girl of stunning beauty he had known from before his college life had begun. Their energy for life founded a strong and growing union that deepened in its passion and sheer beauty.

All thoughts that it would never last were quickly dispelled. I checked this out on the numerous occasions I met up with them in those first heady days. Their first child was born on April 23rd St George's Day, Samantha Georgina. Then two years later, a boy, and the request was made for my presence and my willingness to take on the role of godfather. Without hesitation I complied. And on visiting them at their then London flat, I was dramatically introduced.

'Michael, meet Michael,' they had said in unison.

Of course I was flattered, and yes, it was in my honour that they had chosen the name. Poor boy I thought, what a role model.

'But only Michael,' I had replied, with a wry grin on my face.

'Yes,' they replied, with equally knowing looks.

One of the many secrets we had shared in college was my middle name, and the awful memories it often provoked within me as I recalled the many times I had been abused in my younger years in my junior school when in one dreadful moment, through an unfortunate and definitely accidental happening, I became the butt of all sorts of cruelties.

I had been christened Michael Titian Grantsman.
The middle name was hopelessly pedantic. Why parents do it who knows? Why my parents did it?
Well, they said simply, they just liked the artist's name, so why not?
And anyway I didn't have to use it if I really felt aggrieved.

And the happening?
At the junior school I had been sent to, each boy and girl was chosen on a daily basis to write on the blackboard the information relating to that

days events. You would write your full name on the board in block capitals. Underneath; the date.
Then the timetable of events, any changes and alterations, etc..
My turn came. And so I began to write. MICHAEL TITI...then the chalk broke and I was scrabbling around on the floor trying to find the larger of the two pieces in order to finish my name. But it was definitely too late.
The awful chant started. MICHAEL TITI... MICHAEL TITI... It changed to TITI MICHAEL. Even though I had now completed MICHAEL TITIAN GRANTSMAN, and the teacher had secured order in the class, my shame was complete.
I continued with my task but definitely without any sense of joy, tears were not far away. But I refused to give in to those feelings of desperation, feelings that I had never ever felt before. It made such a mark, one that took many months to live down. I still feel a sense of undeserved abuse as I recall the hurt. Some in the class made sure that the incident was heard around the school, and so the inevitable continuation of my felt shame was etched into the folklore of the school for the years to come.

But that was the past.

When invited now for my name, I always insist on being Michael, not Mic, not Mike. No abbreviations, no foreshortening, no nicknames...Michael. Michael Grantsman!

I know the reason why I am so insistent, and it sometimes annoys me that I am made aware of the cause all too often.
And as for the Titian!

Strangely, and perhaps ironically, I had become quite a good artist at a very young age, and my course in life was seemingly set in that direction, not particularly the fine art route that might have been suggested by the noble name I bore, but rather that of art and design, a direction that I had been exploiting very successfully in recent years.

'Prescriptively prophetic, and powerfully poetic' John had said, in a typically verbose manner, when he first understood my feelings on the subject of my middle name.
But then he was always wordy, sometimes to a point of annoyance.

John and Stella's new home was just outside Southwold, an area I had known and loved and fully explored as a child on holiday with my parents.
Memories of the place were filled with childish innocence and wide-eyed mystery, joyous times of discovery. Calm seas, raging seas, sunshine, rain, and even deep snow on one occasion. The lighthouse, the beach-huts, the leather brown face of the ferryman in his rowing boat, who battled against incoming or outgoing tides on the way over to Walberswick, and the awful smell of Adnams Brewery (mind you that's what I thought at the time - fortunately my 'nose' has improved somewhat in that direction!)
Fish and chips right on the beach at Dunwich with local fishing boats still bringing in their catch, the collapsing cliff edge, music and art at Snape and Aldeburgh. Then to the north, Lowestoft, Great Yarmouth, and days of sailing and swimming on the Norfolk Broads, the low arched bridge at Potter Heigham, and the countless moments of watching and waiting, dearly wanting inexperienced helmsmen to fail in their progress through it.
Norwich, Cathedral and market, egg and bacon rolls just dripping with fat.

Blythburgh came, its solid foursquare church dominating the skyline for a while. The tide was in.
A simple turn to the right, and I turned towards the coast.
I stopped just before the town began, in order to check the exact address.
My briefcase was on the seat behind me.
The box!
"Grief!" I said aloud, with obvious annoyance in my voice.
I had completely forgotten that I had placed it there. I had completely forgotten my virtuous intention of turning it in at a convenient police station.
Well I hadn't seen one, had I?
Maybe it was the nature of the journey, the thought provoking process evoked by the recall of times past. Or maybe the nature of my unavoidable sense of concern for those whose home I would soon be in.
I would have to make a further opportunity to deliver the box to the relevant authority. On the way back home. I decided. That would be alright. It would only be in a couple of days time. Two extra days wouldn't matter.
I checked the address, and found that the house was not in Southwold itself but back towards Wangford.

I turned through Reydon and soon was at a standstill before a most imposing house. Solid built, Georgian style, double-fronted, impressive driveway, well kept lawns. Gravel drive.
The loud bark of a dog. My arrival would not go unnoticed. Both John and Stella appeared. Ahead of the pair of them, a large dog.
But for their smiles of reassurance I may have been slightly unnerved by the size and speed of the animal. A stern command from John, and the dog stopped at my feet.

What a welcome!
"Michael." John said.
"John." I replied.
"Stella." We embraced.
My voice betrayed an emotion that was sensed by all.
It was so good to be there.

It had been over five years since we had met. That last occasion brought back such difficult memories, memories of Lara. The dreadful accident, her lingering death. The funeral, a desperate sadness overshadowing everyone. John and Stella had both been there, a tower of strength to me. They had brought the children as well, Michael and Sam, both of whom had said that they just had to be there. In their own way they had given so much of love, their full-flow tears at the grave side had near broken my heart again.
Though not related to us in any way at all, Michael and Sam had called us uncle and aunt from their earliest years, and still did, and they were as much ours as anybody's, or so we felt. No children of our own, we doted on them and spoiled them at regular intervals with a sort of compulsion that was difficult to understand.
We had spent so much time together over the years, and we had seen them grow into glowing examples of rugged individualism.
Michael, then at seventeen, on the threshold of a university course, a brilliant inquiring mind filled with a sharpness in his decision making abilities that was certain to set him apart in whatever his future held, yet with a goodness and gentleness that was so endearing and somewhat old-fashioned. There was much of his mother in him.
And Sam, nineteen, so filled with the exuberance of life, her long blond hair flying out behind her wherever she went. Her life was lived at such speed. Yet for all of that she had a perceptive sensitivity. And, if you could catch her for a moment in a quieter mood, a reflective quality that allowed you to see deeper and more tranquil pools of inner reserve. She was the only one in our extended family for whom a foreshortened name had any relevance.

Though christened Samantha, she was definitely a Sam.

We had loved them both so much.

I loved them still.

Five years. So much had happened. It had only been my work that had kept my life together, or so I thought. I made myself be busy. Taking every contract that came my way, finding myself in far flung countries.
The business boomed. New art, new design. I was very rarely at home. Giving myself no real time to think, and little time to maintain that most precious thing called friendship. I had hoped that they would understand.
I hoped that they would see that it was my way of dealing with those unnerving feelings that can so easily destroy.
Nothing seemed to have changed. No reserve. No sense of judgment.
The warmth of their embrace had conveyed everything to me.
Friends meeting once again and finding remembered richness almost beyond their deserving.
We had not yet entered the house, and indeed before that became a possibility there was a screeching of tyres, flying gravel, and squealing brakes.
The dog barked a well rehearsed greeting.
And out of a smart green mini Cooper tumbled a smart....

"Uncle Michael! Dad just said that you would come."

She kissed me and hugged me and danced around me, bumping into the dog who was definitely keen to get into the act as well.
It was Sam. And still with long blond hair.

"Hold on Sam," John said, "Michael has only just arrived, let's get him into the house. Here, help him with his bags."

I opened the back of the transit and reached for my case. Sam took that.
I shut and locked the back. Then I went to the still open drivers door and reached over for my briefcase. Noticing the box on the seat. I said.
"Perhaps you wouldn't mind bringing that as well."
Stella led me through the very impressive hallway into a large and welcoming kitchen, the gentle touch of her hand on my arm felt reassuring. I'd glanced here and there on my way and couldn't help noticing what had to be a lovely Georgian mahogany display cabinet

with contents that looked alarmingly like Rene Lalique glassware. I knew that I would enjoy discovering the delight of this well appointed household, hoping beyond hope that they had managed to maintain the sense of warmth and security that their very first London flat had evoked. Everyone who had visited them then in those early days experienced 'welcome' writ large.

John and Sam had disappeared with my case, and my briefcase, and the box, taking them, I found out later, to a most expansive bedroom on the first floor; en suite bathroom as well.

They returned to the kitchen.

"Black coffee, two sugars?" John knowingly asked.

"Fine," I replied, "but I've given up the two sugars."

Once again the pain of the past swept into my consciousness.
Sweetness had gone out of my life five years ago.
How strange that it had had its effect on my coffee drinking habits as well.
To tell the truth, I had given up sugar the day after the funeral, preferring in its place a more bitter taste.
Over these recent, globe trotting years I had come to like it, and now felt nauseous at the very thought of two sugars in anything.

The kitchen exuded comfort wherever I looked.
A huge pine table and six chairs, four of the places set for a meal (they had been sure that I would come) a dresser littered with newspapers and magazines, an Aga cooker spreading its generous warmth, the clutter of a lived in space.

And in the corner; the dog, watching me.
I wondered if in the two or three days I might be there, whether the dog would accept me as a friend. I hoped that it wasn't suspicion I could detect in his look!

We sat in the kitchen playing that time absorbing game of 'catch up.'
And the years of separation slipped away.
John and Sam showed me over the house.

Behind the simple notice declaring 'John's den - Keep out' there was a veritable studio of delights. High tech stuff supporting what obviously was a busy life in design.
Print, graphics of all sorts, video, computers, TVs, lay out boards.
It was my life as well, I recognised much of what I saw.

As we left the room, Sam declared, "Dad should take that notice down because I do most of the work in here now."

"That's right," John agreed. "She's my right hand man now."

"Right hand person," Sam quickly corrected.

I wondered what it must be like for him to have his daughter working in the space that once had been for him so private, and all of his creation in such recent years. Some of the posters on the walls told of newer, younger ownership now.
Her mark could be seen almost everywhere. There were large paper flowers, straw hats and CDs definitely not belonging to the John that I knew.

"Dinner's ready." Stella called.

We joined her at a now well stocked table and the conversation kept flowing over a tasty lasagna, fresh salad, warm bread and red wine. The innocence of reunion and joyful acceptance of renewed acquaintance.
And no hint, for the moment, at least, of anything untoward.
Perhaps I had been wrong.
We finished with fresh fruit.

"Biscuits, brie, and coffee," we were informed by Sam, "would be served in the lounge, after the washing up."
Still the conversation was unceasing.
All four of us attempted the washing up, the drying up, the putting away.
No one wanted to miss out on any snippet of information. I found myself quietly mentioning Lara's name without the usual sense of guilt.
There was a lot of 'do you remember when?'
We adjourned to the lounge.
John opened up a bottle of Port, and we all settled down to continue what we thought would be a gentle ending to a precious and unplanned feast of wonderful reminiscence.

One of those lulls occurred. Not because we had run out of things to say, but simply because we all felt so comfortable in each others company.

"Michael.......... it's Michael," John said.

There was a noticeably quieter emphasis in his voice.

"What's the young blighter been up to?" I replied, "Is he about to take over the whole of the City of London with his computer wizardry?"

I realised then that though his name had been mentioned in a passing fashion, we had not talked at any depth about him. I had seen his room; quite tidy, obviously ready for him if ever he should visit home. (He did after all have his own place in London). They had told me that he had got a good degree. And I already new that he had this very good job in the City.
He, himself, had proudly sent me his card a couple of years ago.

"No, it's Michael. We think he is in some sort of trouble."

John's voice had changed, no longer buoyant.
An inner fear appearing on his face.
Sam's smile became a fixed and staring thing.
Stella moved quickly from where she sat, and took John's hand as she sat down beside him.
I had never seen him cry before.
Deep inward groans that made his body shake convulsively.
I moved towards the pair of them and sort of knelt before them hardly knowing what next I should do.

"Oh Dad!" Sam whispered, "I thought you were going to wait till tomorrow before you told uncle Michael."

She too started a gentle weeping that soon became a flood of tears.
Stella, as strong as ever, quickly found tissues and moved between the pair of them with love and devotion.
She had always been so strong.

Nothing was said for quite some while. The moment was too filled with conscious grief and deep foreboding. I comforted as best I could. But at this moment I felt so out of it. The story was yet to be told. All their obvious and inward pain was gradually surfacing and it was some while

before the weeping ceased. They seemed to have found a moment of release in my presence. Trusting me with their grief was a totally new experience for me.
The last time we had met I had trusted them with mine.
My thoughts raced within me. Was he ill? Was the job no more?
Neither of these questions seemed so bad as to evoke such reaction in them.
It must be something more.
Was there a girl on the scene? Had he done something wrong?
Were the police involved? I had no idea of what it could be.
John recovered some composure, wiped his eyes, and slumped forward, head in hands.
He looked so vulnerable.
This was the John, who in years gone by had told us all, 'to make the future happen.' His brokenness made him look so frail, all his power and strength and forcefulness had disappeared completely. After dreadful moments of obvious inward distress he was able, at last to speak.

"Michael did not come home for Stella's birthday."

John's voice was almost a whisper.

"He's never missed his mother's birthday."

The emphasis on the word 'never' was explosive, and I could see an anger in John's eyes. His voice broke again, and the tears started once more. Here was a man, I thought, who was near a moment of collapse. I poured a glass of port for him and he sadly made a sort of smile of thanks as he took it and downed it in one deliberate head back swallow.
"He's never missed his mother's birthday, all through university he came home, the day was always... so... special."

This time the emphasis was on the words 'always.... so.... special.'
He said the words separately, with great feeling, pausing between each, as though remembering the good times of the past. He fell quiet once more and I could sense the tension in all three of them. There had got to be more than this, I was grasping for some angle on any deeper issue.
My thoughts were interrupted as John continued.

"That was the last straw. Everything that has happened over these last few months points to something seriously wrong.

He's just not the same anymore."

It was as though flood gates had been opened, he spoke quickly now with deep and measured feeling in all his words.

"Telephone calls are no longer instigated by him. That's most unlike him. He's always been so quick to tell us of some new experience. There has been such joy in sharing it all with us. He describes things so vividly, it is as though you are in the experience with him. And when we phone him now, his conversation is so cold and reserved, off-putting really.
Not even Sam can get through to him, and they have always been so close. Stella and I have marvelled at the bond that they have built up over the years, all that early competition stuff has turned into a depth of relationship that has been truly beautiful to watch. Their trust in one another has been so special. We have been so privileged.
We've even started to write letters to him, something we have never had to do before, it's always been the 'one to one' stuff on the phone. His replies to letters have simply been cryptic notes conveying no real information at all. We feel that he is trying to sever all connections with us, and it hurts so much to believe that it is our son who is doing this.
It is impossible to believe that it is happening.

We can't get through to him.
Sam was due to go down to London for one of her regular shopping trips.
She always stays with him. 'No he wouldn't be in' he told her, 'and no would she please not bother him again, and why did she have to spend so much money on clothes anyway!'
She was so upset, and she is even blaming herself that maybe she has taken him too much for granted over the years."

The torrent of words stopped. He slumped forward once again.

" O h             D a d ! "                               S a m said.

"What can we do Michael?" John pleaded. "Can you think of anything that we can do? We are desperate to discover what has gone wrong. Maybe he's in trouble. We want to help him if we can"

All of John's assertiveness and forthrightness had seemingly vanished.

He now appeared so diminished in stature, there was an emptiness about him that was quite frightening to perceive. There he was, clutching at the support his womenfolk provided so lovingly. Stella, tribute to the years they had spent together, strong, unwavering, their love was true, and unreserved. And Sam, tearful, yet so full of tender compassion for her father. I guessed that she had never ever seen him so distressed.
'What could they do?' he had asked. 'What indeed,' I thought to myself.

I knew that I would have to get involved in some way, but how?

"I'll go and see him." I said after a while, voicing my thoughts as soon as they came into my head. "No," I corrected myself. "That would be too confrontational. I'll write him a note saying that I'm back in town, and could we meet up. It would be good to chat after all these years"

"O uncle Michael, would you?" Sam said.

She left her father's side and hugged me with such a forceful passion.
So different to the simple uninhibited greeting she had offered when first we had met. This time there was a feeling of relief that I could sense.
She started crying once more, gentle sobbing tears. Maybe she had hopes beyond my capability of delivering. Maybe she was seeing answers where I was still seeing imponderable questions. Maybe her belief in my abilities was five years out of date. Could I achieve anything for these folks, whose friendship I had so abused in recent years?

Damn it, I thought, I'm going to try.

It is strange how moods can change so quickly. It was as though I had given them the wisdom of Solomon in my simple suggestion. John got up and shook my hand. Sam disentangled herself.
And Stella started clearing away the plates.

"Yes, that would be a good idea," John agreed, " perhaps a casual approach from you will bring about some change."

He was dabbing at his eyes, almost as if he were embarrassed at the show of emotion that had been released.

"I must let the dog out," he said.

He put away the bottle of Port, picked up the empty glasses and went out to the kitchen. He was determined to control himself once more.
I looked at my watch. Twelve thirty five. It had been a long day.
It would be good to sleep, if that were possible.
The red wine and the Port, I hoped, could be trusted to help in that respect.
I too went to the kitchen, helped in the final clearing up, and waited for the dog to come back in.
Rhodesian Ridgeback, yes... it was a Ridgeback, I hadn't taken all that notice of it when I first arrived, my hands and heart, after all, were full of greetings for those for whom I had such warm regard.
I hadn't seen a Ridgeback for years. When was it? My memories had been jolted into action more than once already and it was now less painful to recall times when, with Lara, we had all been together.
It had been on a holiday that Lara and I had shared with John and Stella when the children were quite small, Michael about twelve and Sam, I suppose, fourteen. It was on a beach on the South Cornish coast. We had been on an early morning walk and were just descending a somewhat overgrown pathway that led down to a vast expanse of shimmering sand. The tide had gone out. The two children, already far ahead of us, were running madly about, as always.

Around the headland, and very fast into its stride came this animal. A huge dog; hungrily, or so we all imagined, after the children. John and I leapt passed the girls and raced towards what we could only think of as an impending disaster, of horrendous proportion.
The dog's owner came into view, and with one shout of a command, stopped the dog in its tracks. We were suitably impressed and not a little relieved. Michael and Sam were still playing their own games, completely unaware of the developing situation.
That was our introduction to Rhodesian Ridgebacks. Magnificent dogs. 'Could run forever, and wouldn't hurt a fly', its owner had said. John and I had found his absolute conviction a little difficult to believe.

"What's his name?" I asked, as the dog came bounding in.

"Brown Mystery the third," John replied. "We call him Canute. He just loves to stand at the water's edge barking at the waves. We'll walk him tomorrow morning nice and early. Do you think you can make it? We can all go. OK Stella, OK Sam? We'll leave about seven. Not too early for you? O, and by the way, Michael...thankyou."
He touched me on my arm, and looked at me for a moment, thoughtfully.

The unreal and sombre foreboding of the late evening had been replaced, and the pressing needs of life, right now, came more to the forefront of all our minds. Time for bed.

"Good night." We chorused.

The box was still on the bed, where either John or Sam had placed it. I picked it up again and found it to be a little heavier than I had remembered. I shook it. No noise whatsoever from inside. I still couldn't open the lid. O well, tomorrow. Tomorrow!

I slept fitfully, and woke before six. Showered, dressed, and descended to the mouth watering aroma and sizzling sound of bacon frying in a pan.
Sam was in the kitchen.

"Want some?" she inquired. "Mum and Dad have had theirs already. It's a bit of a ritual before we walk Canny on the beach."

"Yes, that would be so good, thank you Sam."

Stella and John came in togged up in old boots and walking gear and asked if I had any decent footwear, did I need a hat, what about something round my neck for it was pretty chilly out there, and could we go in my bus as I was parked in front of their garage.

"Yes. No. Not needed. And of course."
I think I answered everything correctly.

We all piled into the bus.
Canute just a little wary of boarding something new.

There is something so refreshing and so renewing about travelling in the early morning light of an early spring day. We journeyed the few brief miles in silence for most of the way. They were surprised that I knew the route, and were intrigued to learn that I had spent many a holiday in this area.
We crossed Buss Creek, I turned left and finally stopped on the front at Sole Bay. Ahead of season, and this early, parking was no problem.

"Which way? The Bavents or Gunhill Cliffs?"

But the dog had already made up our minds.
The beach, the sea, and endless running to and fro. There was surf to be chased, and gulls to be dispersed. Seaweed to chew and plastic bottles to be found and buried.

After a while we cut back up through the town, heading for the golf course. Canny had a nose for the new direction we were going in, instead of gulls it would be rabbits.
We passed the water towers and made our leisurely way on towards the river . A couple of not so early morning golfers turned in ahead of us, parking their cars at the modest clubhouse. The road was dead straight to the river, about a half a mile away. Canny was away, diving through the hedges, and plunging into the dikes that controlled the water level in the marshes, birds scattered as he rushed by in full flight.

"What about a quick half at the Harbour Inn?" John shouted to the girls.

But Stella and Sam had other things in mind, and certainly a very different venue. Though windblown and rosy faced, we were all so relaxed. The day was working its gentle magic. The tense awareness of what had been shared the previous evening had been replaced, for the moment, by the beauties of this quiet place.
All sense of threat had been put to the back of our minds, thankfully.

"No!" said Sam and Stella, almost in unison. "We want to have coffee and cake at the Parish Lantern in Walberswick."

They had been walking ahead us, and had obviously been plotting for some time. It would only add about a mile. Turn right instead of left when we got to the river. Up towards the sluice, and cross the Blyth by the bridge before the windmill, and walk back down the river bank.

As a growing boy enjoying holiday adventures in the past, I had done this trip so many times before. I fancied that I could do it with my eyes shut. But you could never shut your eyes to the fascination that was all about. The boats, the business of the sea. True there had been great decline in all of it, but still there appeared to be some activity.
The occasional small fishing boat returning to a mooring. The sounds were special too. Wind playing tunes in the masthead rigging of yachts not yet ready for a summer's sailing.
Gulls screeching annoyance at anything and everything. The sound of water lapping at the sides of craft of all shapes and sizes, some floating

free at the extent of mooring ropes, trying to escape, and others, some decaying, still locked fast in gripping, oozing mud.

As a boy, in this very place, I had conjured up fantastic stories about smugglers and pirates, gun runners and drug dealers. I knew the reasons for the decay, where treasure could be found, where dead men's bones were buried. I had told my parents endless stories about why, and how, and when, and where. This place, for me, held memories. The skeletons of once proud craft still gave me deep feelings of sadness.
What could have been? I wondered.

The coffee shop was just the same, the crafts, the garden, the homemade scones. The warmth.

We walked back, passing the swings and things. Sam flung herself down the slide as though she were an eight year old. We laughed a lot. The ferryman was there, different to the one I had known. We climbed aboard, with Canny wanting dearly to jump in the water rather than stay in the boat. John had difficulty in restraining him. We landed, paid our money, and walked on, eventually passing the same old beach huts with those wonderful names.
Up passed the cannons on Gunhill Cliff. And on, hurrying now, for light rain was falling. We reached the bus, boarded, and made for Wangford, and home. We journeyed in an afterglow of comfort, trust, and renewed friendship.

As with the outward journey, so with the homeward, hardly a word was spoken. I looked back on occasions, as we drove, to see each of them deep in thought, enjoying the intimacy of their own space, each with a broadening smile, that seemed to suggest security.
The morning had been so good.

We cleaned ourselves up. The dog found his own spot in the garden, beneath an early flowering rhododendron, out of the rain, and settled down to sleep a well deserved sleep. Sam told us that she would do the lunch, and that it would be ready in thirty minutes or so. John went to his office, not the studio, to check the fax. And Stella busied herself with the post that had arrived whilst we had been out.
So I went up to my room, knowing that I had a difficult letter to write to Michael, I wondered what tone it should contain.
Fairly lighthearted and easy...... yes.
I took some notepaper from my briefcase.

I'd always had this thing about hotel stationery, I considered it one of the few perks from my globe trotting way of life. I never helped myself to much, just two or three sheets of headed notepaper and a couple of envelopes.
My vices were not after all, excessive! It amused my business colleagues, at times, to receive communications from what might be suggested as far flung places, even though they knew me to be still in England. It was a trivial thing.

Beneath a heavily embossed Sheraton, Chicago, I wrote.

> My dear Michael,
> I know I have not been in touch for some while, but I am back in England now, and business will keep me here for a while.
> Is there any possibility that we might meet up for a chat.
> I have one or two business projects that are in the pipeline.
> Your advice would be invaluable.
> It's worth a good meal! Can I tempt you?
>
> > Yours as ever
> > Uncle Michael.

I signed it and stuck it in an equally impressive Sheraton envelope.
Then it dawned on me that I should not post it from Southwold. That would be a stupid give away. I must be careful at every level, to be sure that Michael would see the communication to be an innocent one.
I put it carefully into my briefcase and wondered to myself what sort of response I might get.

The box was where I had placed it the night before.
A good conversation piece, I took it down stairs with me. It was indeed a lot heavier than I had first thought, and on looking a little closer I saw that there was brass inlay work as well as the mother of pearl that I had recognised before. It was well made.

I placed it on the kitchen dresser, answering the curious looks from all of them with the one word, "later!"

We lunched on cold chicken pie, pickles and mashed potatoes. The plates were piled high, we were all starving. Sam's appetite was as good as the rest of us, and she did the serving. She reassured us that there was plenty more where that came from. John produced a good bottle of red, as he had done the previous night, reminding us all that it was good for our hearts.

The expected strain from the years of parting had completely disappeared, we felt a comfort in each others presence. The lunch was excellent as well.
The light rain had turned to a more persistent downpour. Any thought of outdoor activity was put from our minds, so I went to the dresser, picked up the box, and placed it on the table.

"What do you think of that?" I asked.

I first told them the story. My journey up. The detour. The sneeze. The rapid parking in the newly available space. The last second avoidance action.

I was in full flow, but something stopped me.
I paused in the telling of the sequence of events.
I had remembered the make of the car that had sped away in front of me, the 'no signals' car that had vacated the space.

A chill went through my body, a hideous memory came to the forefront of my mind. It was a Jaguar Sovereign, a silver grey Jaguar Sovereign, two aerials at the back (one on the right, for radio, the other on the left, for telephone) It had been such a car, driven by some maniac joyrider that had ploughed into Lara's car. She stood no chance. Coming home late one night after one of her meetings. Both cars had been written off. The boy died outright, but my Lara lingered in her dying.

A Jaguar Sovereign! I had vowed to myself that I would never forget the make and model. It was an intense drag back to the painful past.

They all noticed that something had happened but with real resolve I kept it from them. It was, after all, my agenda, not theirs.

Theirs was pressing enough as it was.

"Sorry," I said, and continued the remainder of the story. "And there at the kerbside was this box, and no one about to claim it,"

I had composed myself sufficiently to complete the tale. I told them of my resolve to hand it into a police station somewhere on the route, and of my subsequent failure and further intention now to do so on my return.

"O uncle Michael," said Sam, "how intriguing, and... how virtuous of you!"

We looked at the box. Noted all the obvious features, The dragons, the swirls of flowers. Tried in vain to open it. The lid was obviously in two halves, but the fit was so expertly crafted, there was positively no gap, and no one dare suggest we take some screwdriver to it. It was not a question of forcing it open. The box was a sort of enigma.
There to be opened. But how?

"The two dragons on this side are very different in size," stated Stella, with a sort of triumph in her voice, as though she might have found some clue.

We all tried to see what she had discovered. We turned the box slowly round and saw in fact, that from the smallest dragon on the side that Stella had seen, they increased in size all the way round the box.
There were two on each side. Sam, in a mocking childish voice, deliberately counted them. One, two, three....

"Hey! The tail on this one is loose," she proudly stated.
On closer inspection, it wasn't that it was loose, rather that it appeared to be quite deliberate. You could depress the whole of the tail section of the dragon. Indeed, you could do it to all of the dragons. Their tails could be pushed back slightly into the sides of the box. The detailing was so fine. There was a thin brass edging outline to all of them.

"They aren't really dragons, are they," John said. His question was intriguing.

"No, they've only got two legs."
Sam spoke, affirming what her father had said.

She startled us all by leaping out of her chair and making her way noisily upstairs. We placed the box back on the table. And each in turn prodded and poked it, hoping that something might magically happen.
After a few minutes Sam noisily and proudly returned, waving in her hand a print out from the computer.

"They are Wyverns." She was speaking in a funny lecturer like voice, and could hardly contain her sense of triumph. She continued, "A Wyvern, An heraldic beast. An imaginary animal with the forepart of a dragon, the legs of an eagle, and a coiled, barbed tail, and wings expanded."

From the many resource discs she had in the studio she had remembered that there was one that contained a library of heraldic designs including pictures of heraldic animals. It was there that she had discovered the information.

"And here's the picture to prove it, and in glorious Technicolour."

We clapped. Congratulating her on her studious endeavour.

"But where does that get us?" I asked. "What can this Dragon bird with a twist in its barbed tail tell us?"

"Maybe the twist IS in the tail." John murmured thoughtfully.

We all looked again at the box on the table, and all agreed that the imaginary dragon-like animals looked remarkably like those in the picture that Sam was showing us.
But pressing in the tails in any sort of order, did absolutely nothing.
"The tails can be pressed in," said John.
"So let's press them all in.... together!"

There were eight dragons. And between the four of us we had eight hands.
To get the right pressure we had to press the tails of dragons on opposite sides of the box.
We contorted ourselves into such a position to allow equal pressure to be applied to all of the tails at one and the same time. Had anyone looked in through the kitchen window they would have been sure to think that some weird magical rite was being enacted. There we were with arms interlocking, each gripping the sides of the box. Stella started giggling, and that finished us for a moment. We sorted ourselves out once more.

"On the count of three," John said. "One...Two...Three"

We pressed. We held our breath. There was a satisfying click. On either side of the lid, part of the brass inlay now protruded. We dared to let go our hold. John lifted the lid.

The box appeared empty. The sides of the box were quite thick, obviously housing the locking mechanism. You could see that four brass barrels had become depressed into the sides and that there were corresponding holes in both the hinged sections of the lid. Overlaid around the edge of the box was some fine tracery work, in brass, the detail was exquisite. On looking much closer you could make out an inscription. It was written along one edge.

"ARTIS EST CELARE ARTEM"

"Something about art?" John suggested.

"Nuttall's!" Sam exclaimed. And dashed upstairs again.

She returned this time with a large, red covered book in her hands. It turned out to be Nuttall's Standard Dictionary of the English Language.

"It will be in here," she positively proclaimed. "Dear old Nuttall's has got a section on Latin mottoes. I've used it before."

And sure enough there it was.

ARTIS EST CELARE ARTEM –
THE PERFECTION OF ART IS TO CONCEAL ART

'The perfection of art is to conceal art.'
What a tribute to the maker of the box.
What wonderful craftsmanship to produce such a thing of beauty.
We wondered if we could close and open it again. We shut the two halves of the lid and pressed home the protruding inlays. A similar click, the box was shut once more. We intertwined our arms again, found the dragons' tails with our fingers, pressed together, and yes...the click. The lid opened once more. We did it with countless satisfaction a number of times.
The box was no longer an enigma. We had unlocked its secret.
No mere box, we all agreed. And I was well advised by all three present to make sure I returned it as soon as possible to the police, who would perhaps be able to find its owner.

"I will tomorrow," I said.

"Tomorrow?" Sam questioned. "Do you have to go so soon. Can't you stay for a couple more days at least?" There was almost a pleading in her voice.

In the process of discovering what the renewal of our friendship meant and through the silly diversion provided by the box we had put aside the underlying reason for my visit for a while. A more sombre note was sounded. Our feelings chilled by several degrees. Not that our friendship had cooled. No, that was now on a most warm and secure footing, as secure and trusted as ever it was. But we all sensibly realised that I had a delicate job to do, that I could only do back in London. I told them that I had written the letter to Michael already, and that I would post it as soon as I was home.
Tomorrow it would be.
I left straight after breakfast. The goodbyes were warm, but we all knew of the hidden agenda that was mine. Knowing looks were exchanged as though each was unable to voice the deeper things that spoke of their fears.
They wished me well, and would I let them know as soon as possible if I found out anything, and do not forget the box.

I travelled uneventfully, the A12 at this time on a Friday morning was refreshingly clear. I made excellent progress. I had decided to retrace my route around Chelmsford in order to get the necessary details of road names and junctions so that I could inform the police of exactly where I had found the box. There were no longer any diversion signs up, but when I turned into the road that I knew I had taken, and approached the spot where the incident had occurred, I saw ahead of me that police were stopping all the traffic.
They appeared to be asking questions of all the drivers.

I had expected that the road would be full of parked cars as before, but no, not a single car was parked. Police cordon tapes had prevented this from happening. I considered it a bit of a nuisance that I couldn't park to find out the information I needed, but on the other hand I would very easily be able to ask them where the nearest police station was. Each vehicle ahead of me was only being stopped for a brief moment, each driver asked, so I imagined, one question. It had always pleased me that from the higher vantage point of the driver's position in the Transit that you could see so much more of what was happening on the road in front.

"Excuse me, Sir, you didn't happen to be driving on this road last Wednesday."

The officer's question quite threw me.
Surprise must have been seen on my face as I stuttered my reply.

"Well yes, I was. It was part of a diversion that I had taken."

"You wouldn't mind pulling in over there, would you Sir," the policeman pointed to a further cordoned off area. "We would like to ask you a few questions, that's if you don't mind Sir."

I drew into the spot that he had indicated, and waited. A driver ahead of me was just being told that he could be on his way. So then it was my turn.
My adrenalin kicked in, suggesting to me that I was aware of some strange coincidence about what was happening. I had been planning to find the police for my own purposes, now they had found me, obviously for some reason of their own.

A youngish guy in plain clothes approached me, showed his identification, and politely started.

"You were in this neck of the woods last Wednesday then were you Sir. What time would that have been, Sir? And what was the reason for your being on this route?"
"Yes. It was around lunchtime that I was here." I heard myself speaking the words quite deliberately. "It was part of a diversion. I was going in the other direction. And I actually stopped for a while, over there, I think."
I pointed to an area of the road just ahead on the other side.

"And why did you stop, Sir?"

I sensed a real sniff of interest in his voice.

"I had to stop, because I had sneezed rather violently, and needed some time to recover." It sounded such a weak reason. Already I felt a little intimidated.

"Would you mind getting out of your bus, Sir. I'd like to take your details."

He took me to where a police car was parked, and invited me to get in the back. Inside the vehicle he produced clipboard, paper, and pen, and proceeded to question me.

"Name, Sir?"

"Michael Grantsman."

"Would that be your full name, Sir?"

"Michael Titian Grantsman."

"How do you spell that, Sir?"

"T...I...T...I...A...N." When asked, I always spelled the name most deliberately. He would never ever know why!
"It's strange that you have stopped me," I went on quickly, desperately trying to move away from the name business, "I was actually on my way now to the police station to deliver something I found over there,"
I pointed right opposite, "It was a box that had been left in the kerb."

"But this is not the way to the police station, Sir. You're way off the track. And why didn't you hand this box in last Wednesday, when you found it?"

His words sounded like an accusation to me. I was beginning to feel quite defensive of my position. I struggled on hoping that I wouldn't put myself;
in his thinking, in a very suspicious category. Already I could see that his interest in me had increased considerably.

"I think we should go to the police station, Sir. We can deal with everything more easily there. Could I have the keys to your bus, Sir. One of my officers will drive it. You can come with me, Sir. You don't mind that, Sir, do you?"

All this 'Sir' stuff was beginning to annoy me intensely. I hoped beyond hope that he would not sense my change of approach to him. I gave him the keys. He left me in the car, and spoke with another officer, who went directly to my bus. I knew what would happen next. I was locked inside the police car, and it was too late now to do anything about it.

The alarm system I had had installed was very sophisticated. The insurance company had insisted on it because on occasions I carried some pretty expensive stuff around with me.

I could see that the officer had seen his way through the door opening procedures, but as soon as he tried to start the engine, the alarm went off, and what an alarm it was, earsplitting to say the least. I was prepared for it, the officer on board was not.

If it were not for the fact that I knew that it would put me deeper in trouble, the incident was very funny, I tried to stop myself from laughing outright.

They both moved amazingly quickly, fearing the worst. The driver exited the bus and ran for cover. The officer who had been interviewing me rushed back to where I was, still in his car. Nothing blew up, only nerves were shattered.

"That wasn't very clever, Sir, was it?" he sarcastically said.
" Would Sir like to do something about it.?"

"If you will let me out and give me my keys... I will." I replied, trying to be careful of my tone of voice.

The situation was quickly dealt with. The silence was bliss. But I now had two very annoyed policemen making noises of protest concerning my apparent total lack of cooperation. I could hear in my mind, cell doors clanging shut.

I was locked in the back of the police car once again, and immediately the two vehicles left the scene, in convoy.

We drove up the road passed the junction, where, just two days before, I had turned, and to my horror I saw by the side of the road, the burnt out shells of, one, two, three.... no, five vehicles.

Any humour in the situation disappeared very rapidly indeed.

"Good grief," I said, still looking back at the devastation, "what on earth happened there? It looks like world war three."

The driver continued on in absolute silence. I could see the tightening in his neck muscles. I decided to be silent myself, awaiting developments in another place and at another time.

At the police station I was bundled into a cold, and somewhat clinical, office. I remained there on my own for a few minutes.

Two officers came in carrying my case and my briefcase, and the box.

"These are your things, Sir? Is this all there was in your bus, Sir?" one inquired, "and this is the box?"

It all seemed fairly obvious to me, of course they were my things, and of course it was the box. I was beginning to wonder what sort of situation I had driven into, so unwittingly, at lunchtime on Wednesday.

"Could I have my keys? I asked.

"We'll hold on to them for a while, Sir, if you don't mind."

They left the room, taking my things with them, and shut the door on me.


I was left on my own for what felt like an interminable length of time. Finally after, and I checked it on my watch, precisely twenty five minutes, someone, of much more senior rank, swept in with a whole entourage of others in his wake.

"Michael Titian Grantsman?" his questioning voice was cold and terse, "we need you to answer a lot of questions, so be prepared for a long stay."

"I beg your pardon, but what is this all about?" I asked in a most naive tone.

"Excuse me, Sir. We'll ask the questions if you don't mind."

There followed some ninety minutes of quick fire questions. But to whoever did the asking, my answers were straightforward and consistent.
My story was so simple
I had been travelling on the diversion... I had turned into the sunlight... I had sneezed... I had managed to stop safely in a space just vacated by another car...I had got out of my bus...I had seen the box...I had picked up the box...
I had not seen anybody around....I had decided to hand it in to a police station on my way... I had not passed a police station...I unfortunately forgot about the box...I had lunched at Braintree...I could show them my Visa bill if they wanted...I had journeyed on to my friends on the east coast...I had discovered the box again...and I had decided to deliver it to a police station on my way back to London...so here I was with the box!

It went on for some time still. But there was no other story to tell. In the end there appeared to be a grudging acceptance of my story. The overnight things in my case convinced them, I think, of my two day delay. The business bits and bobs in my briefcase helped with the innocence of my journey.
There was nothing to incriminate me in whatever business they were on about. The somewhat hostile approach changed, and at last I was able to ask questions about what had happened to make them so interested in me.

It appeared that just after I had left the scene on Wednesday, a car parked on that same road had burst into flames, causing four others to be destroyed in the aftermath of the incident. That was not the most disturbing factor. The badly incinerated body of a young man had been found in the back seat of one of the cars, he had died in the flames before the fire brigade had arrived on the scene. Motorists who had been forced to stop by the ferocity of the fire had described to the police the agony of seeing the body there, but no-one had been able to do anything about it. It was being treated as a murder inquiry now as it had been discovered that the young man's ankles had been tied together. Local reporters, quick on the scene, had witnessed the cutting free of the body. Yesterdays papers had been full of it. I had to admit that with all that I had shared in the two days I had been away, that I had seen neither newspaper or television. The body had not yet been identified.

The police were now more interested in the car that had driven away at speed just before I had parked. Could I describe it in any way. I explained about the sneeze once again, and my obvious focus problem, but that yes I could definitely tell them that it was a silver grey Jaguar Sovereign. I did not, however, tell them why I had been so sure.
And the box, possibly antique, they told me. And no they couldn't get it open. No noise when shaken, so obviously empty. (I did not feel inclined to tell them of the success that we had had in that direction - let it remain for them an enigma - I hoped that they wouldn't try to force it open). They told me that they would make inquiries of local antique dealers to see if anyone reported anything missing.
It may be a totally innocent event, or on the other hand, it may just be the lead that they were after. They would keep in touch with me, and let me know if anything turned up. The box, after all, might become mine if no one claimed it after the required time. They had my name and my address in London. And yes, I would not be going away in the next few days. And here are your keys, thankyou, Sir.

I left them, somewhat bemused by what had happened. Wouldn't John, Stella and Sam be fascinated when I told them, I thought to myself.

I journeyed on, deciding not to stop, even though I was feeling very hungry.
I wanted to get back to the security of my own place. There had been more than enough packed into the last few days, my mind was reeling, I needed some space to gather my thoughts. I inadvertently missed the M25 turn off, and found myself later back on the good old North Circular, on a Friday, in the rush hour. No! I would never learn. Two hours later I finally pulled up outside my West London home. I parked, removed my things from the bus, opened my front door, and collapsed into my favourite chair.
I fell asleep straight away.

At three thirty three in the morning, I awoke to an aching hunger that just had to be satisfied. I knew which 'Take away' would still be open, and so found myself ten minutes later, eating what was, I convinced myself, the best kebab I had ever tasted! I slept again, this time in my bed, and finally got up at ten forty. I was rested and ready… but ready for what?

## II

I had been away since Wednesday, it was now Saturday, I needed to buy foodstuffs and some other bits and pieces. There was Michael's letter to put in the post. I went into the room that I called my office, found my address book, and wrote out Michael's address on that posh Sheraton envelope. Before sealing the envelope I re-read the letter, it was very brief and to the point and I wondered whether it would do the trick.
Whatever it was that was going on as far as Michael was concerned it had to be his choice. I settled for the simple approach.
An hour and a half later I had finished all that was required of me and I was back at home, settling down to a quickly micro-waved meal for one and an excellent beer. It would be an afternoon of relaxation. A little sport on the box, maybe another beer or two, an early evening bath, and then maybe an hour or so at the gym. I was currently out of work, no deadlines to meet.
My time was my own.

Amongst the post I usually received was the general run of adverts, circulars, free offers, trade magazines, business letters of all sorts, inquiries after my services, the occasional cheque in payment of completed contracts (always pleasing to receive those - thankfully I wasn't owed too much by clients - my sort of approach had more often than not encouraged prompt payment, I don't know why!) but very few personal letters.

To receive personal letters, you have to initiate the correspondence.
I rarely wrote personal letters these days.

Life for these five years gone had been a race to make my business successful. My contacts were business contacts. I was more than happy with those sort of relationships. If you are clever enough you can keep those relationships neatly boxed. It had been Lara who had maintained things at the more personal level. And since her death, the personal side of my life, whatever is meant by that phrase, had really not progressed at all.
It may have been as a result of a self pity, or a blocking off of the grief of bereavement, who knows? John and Stella had tried in the early days to maintain the contact, but even they gave up after a while. I was never around, the hunger for business success had to be satisfied.
Business success had come, but a strange hunger for something still existed. These last few days had stirred things to a dramatic degree. I realised that I had starved myself of relationships that had any depth at

all. Though lean and fit in business terms, I felt somewhat undernourished in the personal relationship department. Maybe things were at a point of change.

I well knew that moment in business terms, when with all the facts in front of you, you have to say to yourself, 'go for it.'

The moment of commitment to a future project was always for me a moment of exhilaration, a moment that I relished.

My post Monday to Thursday of the week following my return from Southwold, was of the business variety.

Amongst that of Friday was a hand written letter addressed to,
'Mr Michael T. Grantsman.'

Hand written letters were the absolute rarity. I put it on one side, and dealt with the other correspondence as efficiently as possible. I binned a great deal of it, and filed, in relevant places, the rest of it.

There were two cheques to be banked.

The hand written letter I took to the kitchen. I surprised myself by calmly and deliberately making myself a cup of coffee before sitting down to open it.

I was encouraged to find that it was from Michael.
It read.

>Dear Uncle Mike,
>
>Thank you for your letter.
>I don't think it will be possible
>for me to help you at the moment.
>I am very busy with things at work.
>But thank you for your letter
>Good to hear from you.
>
>Yours as ever
>
>Michael

My hand was shaking as I read the note. I felt a chill go right through my body. I now realised that something was seriously wrong. My letter to him had been simple and to the point. His reply was equally simple and answered my inquiry directly, if not tersely. Should I have expected anything more? Maybe he was making a different life for himself.

Maybe he was trying to distance himself even from me. But the reason for my sense of fear was hand written at the very start of his letter.

Dear Uncle MIKE.

It was a very profound and disturbing signal.

I knew from that moment that there could only be real, disturbing, awful trouble somewhere. Without telling me in words, he had shouted out a distress signal that he knew only I would understand.
What could I do? He of all people knew how I would react to that foreshortened rendition of my name.
As a child he had gradually understood the reason for my insistence on always being Michael. Out of growing love and, I hope, respect, he had even adopted the rule for himself.
He had proudly corrected others who called him Mike. I can hear his young voice saying, 'my name is Michael, thank you very much!' This foolish name thing had always provided an unbreakable bonding between us.

For a moment I doubted my understanding of the issue.
Was he trying in an oblique way to be deliberately hurtful to me?
Was he dispensing with the former friendship in this calculated fashion?
Was he saying 'get out of my life?'

For reasons, perhaps unknown, I decided that my initial 'gut reaction' was the only justifiable understanding of his cryptic non spoken message.
I even felt like a betrayer of his trust, for even imagining another possible conclusion. But that made it no easier for me to begin to fathom out what I could do.

I must somehow see him. Talk to him.
Share with him his family's deep concern.
He wouldn't know that I had been in touch with them. He wouldn't know just how much he had broken their hearts by his seeming coldness. He wouldn't know that in fact his hidden signals to them had caused them to get in touch with me after all these years. He wouldn't know that they loved him so much, and wanted to help him, whatever the cost. I must find a way to get to him. But there was an obvious need for caution. The note had convincingly shouted NO! How on earth could I change that?

How could I discover what this was all about?

My immediate task was to let John, Stella and Sam know that my communication with Michael had brought a result of sorts. I phoned them. Sam's voice answered in cheery mood, but it turned out to be one of her answerphone specialities, she did that sort of thing when she was a youngster, and she obviously still enjoyed the prank. I foolishly thought for a moment that I was actually speaking to her. It took a while before the tone allowed me space to put my brief message to them.

'Michael has replied to my letter.

I feel an anxiety for him, so will try to see him as soon as possible. Michael.'

I didn't think that I could spell out the depths of my fear as a cold message on their machine, so I simply implied some progress...a sort of 'watch this space' message. Now the hard part.

What was I to do?

I must try and make physical contact. I needed to see him face to face.

I was beginning to understand one thing. He could not be openly truthful either in spoken words on the phone, or in written words in letter form. The first had been confirmed by his father in the cold off putting calls that he had made to him.

The second was definitely confirmed by the letter that I had received.

Was he being watched all the time? Was he afraid that his phone was bugged? Was someone with him whom he could not trust?

My mind was racing into all manner of cloak and dagger stuff, that on the face of it seemed stupid, but the more I thought around the subject, the more possible even the most fantastic thoughts were becoming.

I must remain calm about this. I must try and make rational decisions.

Well...it seemed rational to me!

Tomorrow, Saturday, I would go 'cold calling' down his street, as if I were selling something. But what?

In my office I had cartons of print run examples of merchandise that I had been involved with, (designers are unusually arrogant about keeping examples of their work, I was no different). Might there be something there that I could 'sell.' There would have to be enough of the 'bumph' to work a whole street, just in case his place was being watched. I hoped beyond hope that Michael's road wouldn't turn out to be impossibly long.

Michael was distraught. He could say no more. He slumped with his head in his hands. I had seen a similar broken man only days before. Father and son in sorrow were very much the same. My own heart was filled with anguish as well. Surely I was way out of my depth in thinking that I might be able to help. It must be a job for the police. We could never handle it on our own.
A moment of crystal clear thinking broke in on my own distress.
How long had I been inside Michael's home? I checked my watch.
It had been at least twenty minutes. If the house were under any sort of surveillance... what might someone be thinking, if they were watching right
now? I must complete my stupid cover. I must continue to deliver my leaflets and knock at doors.

"Michael." My voice was perhaps unnecessarily abrupt.
"I must continue on down the road to deliver these leaflets, just in case someone is watching the house."

I had noticed that the picture of the two of them leaving the house had been taken from a high level, certainly not from street level. Either it had been shot from the first floor of one of the houses opposite, or it had been shot with a long lens from somewhere that overlooked Herstwick Gardens.
Had whoever taken that picture been around just at Christmas time or were they still around now?

"Michael, tell me where we can meet up again. I must leave your house now." I was trying to sound convincing, as though I was in control of the situation. Another moment of inspiration came. "I'll give you my personal mobile, you can use it to contact me on my business number at home. Ring me tomorrow about eleven. Think of somewhere safe that we can meet."
I was quickly writing down the numbers of the phones. If the house was being watched then maybe his phone was being listened to as well.
A deepening sense of urgency was making itself known.
Life was getting a little scary.
He agreed to think of a venue for our meeting. I left to complete my task.

I tried to apply myself to the job in hand of being as inconspicuous as possible, adopting a casual air. I even started whistling as I went down the path. I could see that Herstwick Gardens was overlooked by a large

I left a message for him one day, asking to see him. He came to my office and assured me that it would be worth my while to complete the task as he had directed. He gave me the impression that I wasn't to question the reason for the work. 'Just get on with it' he told me. 'There is a deadline to meet.'
The next day I found an envelope in my post tray, just a photograph inside.
Hold on a minute I'll get it for you right now.
There were others, I'll get them all"

He left me in the kitchen and I could hear him going upstairs.
He returned a few moments later with several photographs in his hand.
As he looked at the photographs I could see that he was in even more distress. He handed them to me. They were photographs of Sam and him.
One obviously of the pair of them leaving this very house. Another of the two of them walking together in a busy London street. The third, and last, of both of them again, this time in a restaurant eating a meal together. As I looked at each of the photographs in turn, I was horrified to see that each had been disfigured in some way. The one of them leaving the house showed Sam with her head circled in red marker. The one of them in the London street had Sam's legs roughly torn off. And the third, the one in the restaurant, had one single cut across half the picture, just below Sam's neck.
Michael continued his story with increasing difficulty.
I could tell that he was on the edge of some deep emotional abyss.

"On three successive days I received each of these. They were delivered, in plain envelopes. They all arrived in my office before I got in." He paused, exhausted, trembling. He sat down alongside me. "Uncle Michael," he cried, "I don't know what I have got myself into. I am so scared."

"When, and by whom, were the photographs taken?" I asked.

"Sam came down to stay with me just after Christmas, to do some shopping in the sales. She loves her visits. We had a great time," he sobbed, " I don't know who took the pictures. She stayed three days and then went back home. She's in terrible danger. And it is all my fault. What can I do Uncle Michael? Tell me, what can I d o ? "

"O Uncle Michael!" he gasped, " I knew somehow that you would come."
He held out his hand and grasping mine, he dragged me inside, with a forceful determination that took me by surprise.
"What's up old chum? I asked, in an almost lighthearted fashion, as he guided me into his kitchen. I was immediately annoyed with myself at my flippant tone. I could see that by the look on his face that all that I was fearing about his situation was true. There was something very seriously wrong.

He sat me down, and even though he was obviously on edge he asked if I would like a coffee.

To my reply of 'yes, that would be nice.'
He said, "black with two sugars."
It wasn't a question. He had remembered.

My reply, 'that I took it straight now,' quite surprised him.
I didn't explain the change.

He made the coffee in silence, obviously thinking deeply as to how he should tell me whatever it was that was on his mind. He gave me my coffee and began to pace around the kitchen.

"Three months ago one of our overseas managers came into my office and asked to have a word with me. He had heard, so he told me, that I was the new computer boffin in the firm and would I do something for him. I told him that if I could, I would. What was it? ....'Just a little programme that I would like you to set up for me on the firm's system,' he said.
I handle all that side of things for the firm.

He gave me some papers with some very detailed explanation as to what the programme was about. Then he left, telling me that he would be in touch in the not too distant future.
As I went through the papers he had given me I realised that he was asking me to create a sort of secret system that would be hidden deep within the firm's accounting procedures that would enable anyone who was in control of that system to bury all manner of financial stuff in a sort of 'black hole.'
The more I worked at it, the more I got concerned. But he had directed me to deal only with him, that is, if I had any questions about it. 'Only with him.' He had been most insistent .

His address was 16 Herstwick Gardens. The 16 was hopeful... only a few before... who knows what might follow....Gardens...that need not be too long.
I was grasping at straws, and why should I stupidly believe that he would be at home when I chose to call.
For the first time in a long, long time, I actually found myself praying to God that he would be in.

That was how it was that at ten o'clock, the next day, I could have been seen by any casual onlooker, knocking on doors in Herstwick Gardens, trying to interest the residents of said 'Gardens' in the wonders of 'The Bookmaster Club.' The Bookmaster Club had been a successful insert in a national magazine some months before, so I thought I could get away with trying it out as a 'cold call' experiment. If anyone turned out to be really interested in the product they would find that the information on the leaflet was still relevant.
I turned myself into a dreaded 'survey person.' Clipboard and leaflets in hand, I worked Herstwick Gardens like a professional.
I confidently expected that at ten o'clock on a Saturday morning there would be few who would be interested. I wasn't going to wait too long on doorsteps. If no one answered, I popped a leaflet through the letter box and made my way to the next unsuspecting customer.
At number 8 the door was answered by a scantily clad young lady, who I think was expecting someone else! We were both rather embarrassed. I left the leaflet and went on. My heart beat was racing out of control. Would he be in?

There had been no answer at numbers 2, 4, and 6. The' vision of delight' had appeared at number 8. An elderly gentleman at number 10 told me that his wife dealt with all that sort of thing but that she was shopping. There was no reply at number 12. There was a shouted 'go away' from number 14.

I walked up the pathway of number 16 with my heart thumping even more.
I knocked. I waited. I knocked again, and rang the bell and waited even longer. I was beginning to think that if anyone was watching they would surely see that I was spending far longer at this door than at any other.
I was just about to put a leaflet through the letter box and go away, when the door was opened.
It was a rather concerned faced Michael who appeared.

office complex but that it was a fair way away. If the picture was taken from there it would have been an extremely sophisticated set up.
Who might we be dealing with?
No reply from number 18. 'Why on earth do you do this on a Saturday morning?' from number 20, who begrudgingly took the leaflet.
No replies from 22, 24, and 26. I was thankful for the non-contact for my mind certainly was not on 'The Bookmaster Club.'
Number 28 was in his front garden, he took the leaflet, and then deposited it straight into his dustbin, without a single word being spoken.
Number 30 was the last house on the evens side. No reply.
I crossed the road and started the return journey. A dog started barking so loudly when I rang the bell at 31. I convinced myself that the whole household would be angrily at the door at any moment and that the dog would be let out at a run to see off whoever it was who had dared to disrupt their Saturday. No one came. The dog continued barking. I put a leaflet through the door. The dog still went on, same old bark. It dawned on me then. Clever stuff. It was a security device. Ringing the bell, tripped a relay that started some sort of continuous tape or electronic chip. I wondered as I left, what may have happened had I knocked at the door instead; a loud cat, or a hissing snake maybe. But this was definitely not the time for foolish thinking. My nervous humour made me understand something of the importance of what I was involved in.
29, no reply, 27, no reply, 25, no reply. My hands were beginning to sweat so much that I had to stop at the door of 23 and get them dried off a bit. I got some more leaflets out and knocked at the door.

"How was Michael then? Has he bought whatever it is you're selling? How long did you stay with him? I couldn't help noticing when you went in. I was just getting up and was looking through my bedroom window. Saw you coming down the road"

My mind instantly froze, and I only just prevented myself from innocently saying 'O Michael's fine.' I realised in a split second that I could entrap myself if I were not careful with my words, I must not acknowledge in any way that I knew Michael.
Was this the house? Could this, seemingly mild mannered young man, be Michael's vicious enemy? Was this the household where plots were being hatched? Was it from a bedroom upstairs that photographs had been taken? Was Sam in danger from this man? My mind was quickly out of its frozen state and was now racing out of control. Was I in danger from him? Were there others with him?

"You saw Julie at number 8 then?" the young man went on, not giving me time to answer any of his earlier questions."She's a girl! A new fella every other week. I'm surprised you didn't go in. Didn't she look lovely in the blue? And old Joe at number 28 didn't say much did he? He never speaks to anyone.  Now what's this all about?" He took my arm, and led me into the hallway of his house. " What have you got to show me?"

"I'm just doing a survey for 'The Bookmaster Club,'" I said. "Introducing their new offer....and we're not allowed to discuss any of our dealings with potential customers...you may have seen their advertising a little while ago it was in a number of national magazines....I only need to leave a leaflet...if you are interested you can fill in the form."

I heard myself speaking at such a nervous rate. I wasn't too sure as to whether or not  I may  be at this very moment being propositioned for something very different. It was most confusing. In my line of work I had met all sorts.

I had always tried to be non-judgemental.

It took some pretty imaginative thinking on my part to enable me to find a way of leaving number 23 Herstwick Gardens. My made up patter about

'The Bookmaster Club,' almost convinced me that I should join.


I did not ring or knock on the doors of any of the remaining houses, I posted the leaflets and left as quickly as I possibly could.

I glanced over at number 16 as I passed, and wondered whether Michael had watched any of my progress. Would we ever know if my cover had been required or not? But I had thought that it was better not to take any chances.

I turned the corner at the end of the road, got back into my bus and breathed a sigh of relief that it was all over. Well, not all over. How stupid of me to think that!  It was only just beginning.

I awoke early on Sunday morning and waited somewhat impatiently for Michael to make contact. At exactly eleven  the phone rang.

"Uncle Michael is that you?"

"Yes."

"I've thought of a place where we could meet."

"Where?" Why was I being so coldly monosyllabic?

"How about Kensington Gardens and Hyde Park? It looks as if it will remain fine today. I'll meet you at Lancaster Gate Tube Station about two. Will that be alright?"

"Of course it will Michael." At last I had found my tongue. "Don't worry, I'll be there."

And there I was, and there he was, just as arranged, prompt at two. We headed for the path that takes you down the western side of The Long Water for half a mile or so, then turns along the southern side of The Serpentine. We were nearing the statue of Peter Pan before he began to speak.

"I've been terrible to Mum and Dad and Sam. But I just can't allow them to get involved in any of this," he said defensively. "It frightens me so much to think that Sam's life may be in danger. I was so rude to her the last time she phoned. She may never forgive me for what I said to her."

I broke in at that point saying, "I know Michael, they got in touch with me a couple of weeks ago. So I went up and stayed with them until last Friday.
My note to you was the only way I could think of that might help us get in touch. They are very very anxious for you. They are at a loss to understand what has happened. Can you tell me more so that I can let them know something at least?"

"No! Uncle Michael. We mustn't let them get involved. They must never, never be involved!" It was obvious that he was deliberately attempting to put space between himself and his family.
"For their safety, they must never be involved."

"But Michael!"

"No! I would never forgive myself if anything happened to any of them. Uncle Michael, you must promise me that you will not tell them. They must not come down to see me. They must keep out of the way, completely"

That area of discussion was definitely closed for him, at least for the moment.

- 55 -

After a moment or two of consideration I promised him that I would not break his trust. And I hoped to God that a way would be found for all of this mess to be cleared up.

"Michael, what does your firm do?" I needed to understand so much more.
At this point in time I knew nothing that made any sense.

"I work for Smettons Smartway Security and also their subsidiary which is Smettons Smartway Destinations.
We are a sort of high class parcel delivery firm really.
But when I say 'high class' I mean discreet, top of the range. And when I say 'parcel' I mean top security stuff, bonded items, precious metals, money, antiques, you name it, and if it has a million dollar price tag attached, we ship it. Anywhere any time. We will deliver a single diamond or a bottle of wine or a huge container of antiques and we will do it on time and at a good price, a very good price.

My job is to make sure that the computer systems are maintained at a very secure level. I am constantly updating and changing codes, creating new systems. There is an incredible level of secrecy even between departments within the organisation. I provide encoding systems that maintain that security, and it works simply because other managers of other departments are required to add their own codewords in order for the secrecy to be kept tight. That means that the various bits of work completed will always be under the firm's strict level of security at all times.
I am accountable to the Smetton's directors. It is a family firm, there are three of them, with one extra member of the board, who is not family, making four in all. I supply the updated codes to the directors on a regular basis, who in turn make sure that the managers of the departments maintain a regular code change for those departments. It works very smoothly, and up till now there has been no problem.

My fear is that I am being used to create a sophisticated programme that will give someone somewhere, a way of challenging the security of the system.
And because I have questioned the one who asked me to do it, Sam's life now appears to be at considerable risk.

Whoever it is behind it has provided me with the bones of a most intriguing system. But what started off for me as an exercise to test my creative abilities, has now turned into something very dark indeed. I can see now the potential of this 'secret system.'

It is not so much to do with top level super security, it is more to do with avoidance of disclosure. It will give someone a great deal of power.
I am sure that the Overseas Manager who asked me to do it is not the brains behind it. I think he is just somebody else's messenger.
I have my own way of discovering how much folk know about my part of the business. You know the sort of thing...I trail a few ideas in general conversation and then just sit back and listen...I soon find out who knows and who doesn't know what I am talking about. I get a great deal of satisfaction in discovering those whose pride wont allow them to say to me, 'Michael I don't know what you mean, could you please explain.' In my field there are no end of middle and upper management people who have been left completely behind in their knowledge of computing. A little knowledge in the hands of some arrogant 'know it all' can be extremely dangerous. It can cause all sorts of problems. I am quite often discreetly employed to get someone out of trouble, someone who may have inadvertently erased some very important data. I've had the occasional quite good bottle of wine from one or two who have been thankful, not only for my skills, but also for my discretion.
I have also developed some pretty smart technology for the security of containers 'en route' to and from destinations. It is no good having secure office systems if you lose the stuff when it leaves some port or other. There's plenty of carriers who have been embarrassed when their containers finally turn up after weeks of searching only to discover that they had been lost due to bad routing procedures."

He stopped, not only in what he was saying, but also in his walking. He stared out over the water. Deep in thought still. His reply had been so full, he had hardly taken a breath. He turned once again to face me this time.

"Uncle Michael. I signed all manner of secrecy clauses when I was given my contract. I think in these brief moments with you that I've broken all of them, but we must find a way of preventing whatever it is that is about to happen.

This next week will see my work on this project completed. I have been told to communicate with the Overseas Manager as soon as I am ready. He has already spoken of 'deadlines' so maybe there is a particularly

big overseas shipment of something or other that someone wants to make disappear.
Or maybe it's a money transaction that somebody wants to cover up.

It can't be an ongoing scam because the system that I have been working on will only 'open' at a coded time and then it will 'close' at another coded time. Once 'closed' the whole process can never be traced. I have quite excelled myself in the fine detail of this. But it horrifies me to think that I have become involved in something that has the potential of ruination for the firm and the possibility of a life threatening outcome for members of my family. At this moment in time I have no idea what is at stake. I don't see the daily manifests on movements of goods, because I don't need to. Neither do I see any future directives about jobs in hand, again because I don't need to. Mind you I could easily begin to take that information from other departments.
You don't after all make locks for doors that you can't open yourself if you need to in the future.
The directors agreed with me that I should have complete access to the firm's full international system but also that I should have a completely secure back up for myself alone, so that I can test out my own inventive schemes, without anybody else being able to snoop. I have designed a programme for my own secure system that will innocently tell me if anyone has tried to enter it without my permission. At 'start up' I have digitally installed a picture of my own face, now there's vanity for you! Every morning I am greeted by my machine smiling at me and saying, 'good morning.' Now that is not very new. There are loads of gimmicks like that around. But if my face 'winks' at me. I know that someone has entered my computer without my knowledge and run some programme or other. I then simply have to key in an instruction and my computer will trace back what has been illegally viewed. Uncle Michael, that was one of my more imaginative programmes. I might sell it on sometime as the ultimate security checking programme. It could make a bob or two.

So what shall we do, Uncle Michael? Tell me, what shall we do?"

"What shall we do indeed?" I replied. "What the hell can we do?"

It was painfully obvious from what Michael had told me that everything was in 'start up' mode. The 'something,' whatever it was, could only happen, as and when the system was complete. The system, so Michael had stated, would be complete in this coming week. Events were becoming serious, not only serious, but imminent.

"What shall we do indeed?" This time I said the words with a tone of resignation. I paused, then slowly continued, the beginnings of a plan coming to mind, "You must complete the system. It would appear that Sam is in some sort of danger if you don't. Although that has not been spelt out in words, it is your deep feeling that that would be the outcome of your failure to comply. So you must complete the system. You must also find out what might be coming up in the days ahead with regard some large and extremely valuable shipment, or maybe the movement of a huge sum of money. Tap in to the departmental information. Keep your eyes and ears open for anything that may appear trivial on the face of things but that may be a clue to some illicit behaviour. See who is talking to who. You have to find out more information. Without the information we can't go to the police."

"No! Uncle Michael we must not go to the police," he shouted out the words, oblivious of the fact that we were in the open air and being passed, on occasions, by all manner of people.

Startled by his outburst, I looked around to see if anyone was in earshot. Fortunately we were just out of range of a group of shutter clicking tourists who thankfully for us were very loud in their appreciation of The Serpentine. If only they knew what was being discussed under their noses.

"OK, Michael," I replied, attempting, at the same time, to quieten him down. He had become very animated at the mention of the police. "OK, for the moment we will not go to the police.
It must be an option at some future time, though. This whole thing has the smell of something out of the ordinary. We don't know how dangerous things really are as yet. But we must try to make mature decisions about what we do. We are hardly equipped to handle this on our own!"

Sunday afternoons for me had always been times of relaxation. The 'wind down' awaiting the 'wind up' of the week to come. This particular Sunday afternoon's activity threatened to change my lifestyle completely. And this was some 'wind up!'
I could not afford to be relaxed or clumsy in my thinking, too much rested on clarity of thought and clear decision making. People's lives were possibly at risk. People for whom I had such a deep love and respect.
This young man who walked by my side was expecting so much of me.

I could not let him down.

"Right now, Michael. You must go to work on Monday morning and act as per normal.

You will naturally be aware of the increasing stress but you must try to be your usual self. Try and give yourself as much time as possible to find out other information. Put off the completion of the dodgy programme until Friday morning at least. Is there some secure way that you can use to let me know of your progress?"

"Are you 'online,' fax, printer and all that stuff?" he asked, with an obvious way through that particular difficulty already in his mind. On my expected reply of 'yes' he went on without hesitation. "If I keep your personal mobile I will be able to leave messages on your business answerphone," he paused. "Have you got an answerphone on your personal number as well?" and again with my answer of 'yes' he continued without a break in his thought. "You can use your business phone to call your personal number and leave messages for me on that. If you are not in when I call your business number, I can call up the personal number's answerphone, and discover what you might have to say to me, that way we will be able to keep everything secure. I can fax information to you from an outside agency, and the firm will be none the wiser. I can transfer all the documentation I find that might be relevant, so that both of us can search for possible clues."

That seemed a brilliant idea and we settled on that as the way ahead.
With my mobile still in his possession he had a secure form of communicating with me at all times, plus with the fax link, a way of allowing me to do a lot of the searching for clues. He had, after all to maintain his position at work as though nothing were wrong.
His was going to be the hardest part.

How strong was the head on his young shoulders?
How resolute could he be?
How carefully could he disguise his actions?
How discerning of the evil intentions of others?
That he was brilliantly creative at his job was beyond dispute.
It was this very brilliance that had got him into this dangerous position.
I looked at him again as we were walking on. He had withdrawn inside of his own thinking for a while, but there appeared to be much more resolve about him. His step quickened almost as if he had found some small, but certain security in the plan that had been decided upon.

For myself, there was still so much doubt about our ability to achieve anything at all, but I knew that I must never transfer my self-doubt to him.
We had said all that we needed to say, for the moment at least, as far as the proposed activity for the week ahead was concerned. He seemed to be content that there was nothing more that was essential that we should do. So our conversation changed direction.
So did we. We left The Serpentine behind. and made our way out of the park. sensing another hunger that needed to be satisfied in both of us.

"Where shall we eat?" I casually inquired.

It broke the mood immediately.
"What about an anonymous McD's? There's one in Oxford Street," he replied.

I had to remember that he was only twenty two, so why not McD's?

We ate, and talked of more innocent things, amazing ourselves that the mind could switch from the absolutely crucial to the almost banal in a matter of moments. Oxford Street on a Sunday afternoon was as cosmopolitan as ever. The world wide flavour of it all still gave me a buzz. I told him of my time with his folks, and how important that had been for me quite apart from the actual reason behind it. I could see his sense of relief.
I realised that whatever it was that our two families had had in the past was as strong as ever right now. But the thought of the testing that was ahead of us all made me aware of the possible vulnerability to which we would be exposed in the coming days. He especially would be a lonely figure, with a dangerous task ahead of him.
My phone rang...in his pocket...weird! or what?
'Michael?' the caller said. 'Yes,' he replied, mimicking my voice. He handed the phone over and I answered a jovial inquiry from Harry, a business acquaintance of mine about the possibility of a game of squash that night. That arrangement made. I gave him back the phone.
We both agreed that it might be best if he kept it switched off and only use the phone to make calls rather than receive them as well. He might stir up all sorts of hornets in my private life, such as it was, if he answered for me.
And I would never know for sure whose company he might be in.

We wished each other well, and went our separate ways.

I was woken early Monday morning.
A caller from the Chelmsford police.

"Mr Grantsman, hello," the voice was in no way as demanding as the last time I had heard it. I knew it to be that of one of my interrogators. "Good morning, Sir, sorry to call you so early," this time there was no undue sarcastic emphasis on the word, 'Sir,' and his manner was easy.
"Mr Grantsman," he went on. "My inspector has asked me to get in touch to see if you could possibly come up to Chelmsford to help us further with our inquiries. There have been some new developments.
We have found the owner of the box you left with us.
He says that he would like to see you to thank you in person.
But there are other complications. It would really help us if you could come."

With all that pleading in his voice, how could I refuse?

I was sure that Michael would not be able to process any of the information we would be looking for, at least not till Tuesday at the earliest.
That decided, I told the officer that I could be with him later on in the morning, and that I would set off straight away. I had to be back home in London for the rest of the week so it was best to get it done with as soon as possible. He thanked me for my cooperation and asked if I would let them give me lunch.

With my mind definitely on my driving I actually succeeded in avoiding the North Circular Road, and was more than surprised to find myself on the A12, and passing Brentwood, just after 10 o'clock.
Another thirty minutes and I would be there.

It was precisely twenty eight minutes later that I found the police station; parked, and went in to discover what the 'new developments' were all about. So different from the last time.... 'journey alright?...would I like a cup of something?...and thanks very much for coming so promptly.'

I was shown into a pleasant office style interview room. Different from the last occasion entirely. I did not feel threatened in any way at all. My black coffee arrived at the hand of a smiling, young, police woman, who also asked after my health. I was beginning to wonder what this complete reversal of attitude was all about, when a rather tall grey haired man arrived.

"John Treddick, CID. Pleased to meet you Mr Grantsman."
He stretched out his hand and greeted me warmly. "A very strange twist in the story has occurred in the last few days. It is a bit of a delicate affair.
One of my officers took that box of yours around to a number of the town's antique dealers. No one recognised it as theirs. So he spread the net a bit and went further afield. Outside of town on the Danbury Road there is a well established antique business by name of Bantock, Berrysford and Brownsmoor. Known by everyone in the trade as 'Treeby's,' which is short for 'The Three Bs.'
Old man Berrysford was there and happily surprised my officer by telling him that the box belonged to his son, and why had the policeman got it?
My officer explained to him the circumstances that you described and where you had found it. Old man Berrysford went on to say that the box was part of a collection his son was putting together for an overseas customer who was fond of that sort of mystery box. Why the box was on the road at that particular part of town was a mystery to him. They're called enigma boxes actually. And anyway, he told my officer, his son was still away, building the collection up. When he comes back I'll phone him and let you know.
His son would sort it out.
Well that was at the beginning of last week. Old man Berrysford got in touch on Thursday and he was obviously worried. His son, who lived some way away, had been due home on Tuesday afternoon from the trip, but had not turned up. His son's wife had phoned her father-in-law and told him that her husband had not come home, and that she was very concerned for him.

Mr Grantsman. You must know that the main activity here at the station is to do with the burning of the cars and the murder of the young man.
Up until Thursday we had not identified the body. It was when old man Berrysford was giving us a description of his son; you know the form; height, weight , build, age etc, that one of my junior officers took me aside and said to me, 'sounds like the body in the car.'

Now this is where the very sad connection was made. Berrysford was asked if he would take a look at the body just in case, this he did on Friday. And, would you believe it. The body in the car was the body of his boy.

Although the body was very badly burned, old man Berrysford recognised a ring that was on his son's right hand. The ring had been given him by his grandmother. The lad had never ever taken it off. You can imagine the shock of it. But the car was not the boy's car!
The forensic boys are still at work on the body, checking dental records, just to make sure.
Mr Grantsman, there must be a connection between the box and the young man's death. Where you found it...the car that sped away?
We need to ask you some more questions to see if you can remember anything else at all.
And, if you remember, I told you it was a bit delicate, old man Berrysford would like to see you. He says he wants to thank you.
Although the news has put them all in a dreadful state of shock, he still wants to thank you. He told us that without the box turning up as it did they may never have known what had happened to his son. The whole family are out at 'Treeby's' now waiting for us. So would you mind?"
"Would I mind?" I blurted it out, coughing and half choking myself at the same time.
W h a t     h a d     m y     w o r l d     t u r n e d     i n t o ?


He drove me out of town for some way; and I could see immediately, as we neared Danbury, where the antique business was. A uniformed policeman was at the roadside preventing any unnecessary traffic from entering the impressive entrance into which we turned.
What was I going to say to this man? Would the young man's wife be there? Who were the 'whole family' who would be there?
My mind was in a turmoil.

Bantock, Berrysford and Brownsmoor, Fine Art Dealers. So the highly polished plaque on the double doors informed me.
We entered into a huge hallway all laid out with some very expensive furniture. They were obviously the sort of high class establishment that laid out their wares in state room style. Potential customers would view as if the furniture were in a natural setting.
The first impression was staggeringly beautiful.

There was certainly some very expensive stuff on show.

We were taken through to a private room towards the back of the house. There were quite a number of people present. Most were dressed in 'bible black' out of respect, with one exception.

A middle aged woman in a dress of flame red, holding between the fingers of her left hand a monstrously long cigarette holder, that in turn held something of Turkish origin. The smell was unmistakable.

A tired eyed elderly gentleman with rather noble features got up from his chair as we were shown in. Treddick moved towards him and said to him.

"I've brought Mr Grantsman to see you Mr Berrysford. You said that you would like to see him." Treddick spoke with a comforting firmness. I admired him for that.

I was impressed by his approach to the situation, the two together looked the part in this fine house.
Tall grey haired Treddick, and the noble featured Berrysford.

"Thank you for coming... Mr Grantsman." Berrysford spoke quietly as he came towards me.

He remembered my name.The tired eyed furniture salesman knew that names were important. His eyes met mine in acknowledgement and there was a depth to the look that I immediately sensed as genuine. Remembering names was something that I had tried to cultivate in my own work life also. Greeting someone by name could be very disarming especially in difficult moments.

"Would you fancy a drink?" he inquired, "I have a fine sherry over there on the dresser, you won't find a better one, not too sweet."

He had all the courtesies you would expect of a man in this setting, but to see them all in place, at this particular time was truly amazing.

"No, no thank you," I replied.

He took my hand in his, his grip was strong.
We stood there for a moment or two with nothing said.

"I'm Jack Berrysford. Let me introduce you to the family."
He led me towards the assembled group. The first to rise was a young woman, in a smart black suit. Her face was flushed with crying. "This is Faye, Terry's wife." We nodded a sort of greeting. "This is Bertie Bantock my partner." Bertie did not get up from his chair. He was a rounded sort of man in a pinstriped suit of charcoal grey.

"And here is Moira Brownsmoor, the widow of Fred, my former partner in the business." Moira was the middle aged lady in the flame red dress. "And over there," he said pointing towards the window, "is Alan Marsters, my accountant." Alan Marsters was looking out of the window, he did not turn to greet me.

A most elegant woman came into the room with a trayful of cups of coffee, the aroma went before her.

"And this is Joanna, my wife. Thank you my dear. You will have coffee won't you?" He took a cup off the tray and handed it to me. "Sugar?"

"No thank you," I replied.

"Mr Grantsman, I did so much want to thank you... O this dreadful thing... We may never have known what had happened to Terry... You were close... Did you see anything strange?... Where did you actually find the box?...
Terry had been collecting these things for months.... He had shown me that particular one only a few weeks back... He was pleased with that purchase... He said that he had been able to get the price down because the fellow he bought it from did not know how to open it.... You usually buy them with the original maker's instructions complete... They were sometimes the product of craft apprentices who were completing their time... The best ones show exquisite workmanship... the time involved... they are always so beautiful... the police have still got it... fingerprints you know." He paused.

I told him quietly and, I hope, sympathetically all that I had seen. I told him that I was dreadfully sorry that I had become involved in his family tragedy; and when was the funeral?

His daughter in law, who had been listening all this time, got up out of her chair and came over to us.

"We've not been able to arrange things yet. The police wont release Terry's body," her voice was calm. She put her arm round her father in law's waist. "O Dad, don't go on" she pleaded.
She turned and looked at me straight in the face, "Who would want my Terry dead? Everybody loved him. He wouldn't do anyone a bad turn."

In the next half hour I learned a lot about the firm, Terry's place, or rather, former place within it. I spoke with all of them. It seemed that

each of them was reaching out to me in some way trying to catch a final closeness with the young man.
Moira Brownsmoor was the strangest of the group. And Alan Marsters was the coldest of the group. She spoke of Terry's inexperience and that she had always doubted Jack Berrysford's confidence in his son. And he could only speak of the bad publicity that would inevitably come their way when all this came out.
As this was going on I could occasionally hear that Treddick was using the time to ask more probing questions, about the young man's life style, contacts, personal finances. He was fortunately causing no offence with his questioning and for this I was very grateful. Even in grief these folk were keen to talk.
I supposed my Lara had also been murdered in some cruel way. I found at the time that I could not speak about the event for any length of time at all without getting very angry, and hostile even to my few friends who dared to probe my feelings. Death in cruel circumstances leaves scars that remain deep. I had buried mine deeper still. Only in these last few days had I spoken of her in such a different way.
These grand folk in this grand place were all going through the same sort of experience right now. The tragedy for them was that it appeared that some evil person had deliberately set out to destroy their Terry.

Treddick made the move to close the conversations by saying to Joanna and Jack Berrysford that he had a lunchtime appointment and that we must now regretfully be on our way. He told them that he would be talking with them again and that he hoped to get to the bottom of the dreadful affair as soon as possible. Thanking them for the promise of their full cooperation he signalled his intention to be on his way.
Berrysford thanked me once again and led us out through the impressive showrooms towards the main door, and then to the waiting car.

Experiencing an unusual hunger, I asked if I was Treddick's stated lunch time appointment. I found I was to be his guest, but only at the station canteen.

The beef and beer pie was extremely palatable, the vegetables nicely done.
I dined on canteen food without complaint. Steamed treacle pudding followed. Then came the coffee.
Whilst eating, Treddick needed to hear the details of my story once again.
He asked if I could really concentrate on every small part of it.

The slightest piece of information might be crucial in their unravelling of this gruesome murder.
Well of course I knew that, but it was increasingly more difficult to remember anything else other than that I had told them already.
Could I recall how many people were in the car that raced off? Had I seen anyone in the back seat of the car? Were there any badges, or logos of any sort, on the back of the car? or in the rear windscreen? The prompts to my memory seemed endless, but at last proved of some worth.

"There... was.... a person in the back of the car, I think I saw a face that had turned to look at me. But it is just a blur in my memory..... Yes..... It was a woman's face"

I felt quite pleased with myself. Though It was obvious that Treddick was less than enthusiastic about my effort .

"More than one person. At least one of them a woman," he dryly commented.

I had to confess that said as coldly as that, my slender piece of information was not that helpful.

"Do remember that it was a Jaguar Sovereign," I said. "There can't be too many of those around. Won't Swansea be able to help with possible owners?" I was trying to improve things slightly. My reasons for remembering that detail still brought bad memories. "A silver grey Jaguar Sovereign.... It was a 4.2.... Now that IS worth a bit. The 4.2 is not made any more. And it did have two aerials... right hand side, radio.... left hand side, telephone."

"That's more like it, Mr Grantsman," Treddick commented with real enthusiasm in his voice this time. "You're well up on Jaguars then.
What makes you so sure that it was a 4.2?"

Dare I tell this stranger the whole truth about my knowledge of Jaguar Sovereigns of the 4.2 variety.
Dare I? Hell no! It was neither the time nor the occasion to relive those dark, dark memories. How could Treddick appreciate the reasons for my all too intimate knowledge of that particular triumph of engineering.
I would recall the shape, the styling, forever; the size, the power,
the awesome speed, forever.
O Lara....Lara!

I could still see the hospital ward to which I had been called. The quiet efficiency. The frightening technology. The dimmed lights. The green traces on darkened screens. The sometimes reassuring blips that spoke of life's frail timing. But intensive care at its best had not been enough... she had lingered... but she was dead! The staff had been so kind... the boy's mother had come... I refused to talk to her... her son was dead... serve him right... how dare she seek to share my grief.

I was quiet for a while.
"Mr Grantsman! I asked you what made you so sure it was a 4.2?"
He wanted more. There was an insistence in his voice.
"Oh! It is a car I know quite well. Believe me. It was a 4.2."

I fiercely determined not to parade what I knew would lead me to a point of grief beyond his comprehension. Five years ago it may have been.
But it always felt like yesterday when I was forced to remember.

Our extended lunchtime came to an end. He inquired about the box, had anyone else handled it? To my reply of 'yes, three of my friends,' he confirmed the necessity for fingerprints to be taken. The arrangement would be made by the police in Southwold, and, if you don't mind we'll take yours before you go, and could I fill in the form that might get me my expenses for the travel I had incurred.

I left Chelmsford just after three o'clock and was back home at six thirty.

I discovered to my relief that there were no messages or faxes from Michael, or anyone. But what tomorrow, Tuesday might hold? Another question entirely.
I made myself a toasted ham sandwich, covered it with English mustard. Made, and poured myself a coffee, sat down in front of the TV to enjoy another lonely supper. Whatever the Southwold visit was bringing into my life I didn't rightly know, there was a growing feeling of trepidation as I thought of all that had gone on in these last few days. Michael's situation.
His family. And now this thing in Chelmsford.
One thing I did know, that the need for me to rebuild the friendship was increasingly more important.

The revelation that the police had now found out the name of the murdered young man in the burned out car in Chelmsford actually made for a story on the news. Old news, I thought to myself.

The poor Berrysford family had only been protected from prying eyes for a couple of days. What price their privacy now?
There was no further detail given and no mention of the box.

There was nothing more that I could do, bed called. I answered the call and was, quite unlike me, in bed and all too soon dreaming strange, nightmarish dreams all through the night, dreams that featured Michael, Sam and Lara.   I hated it when my dreams told me untrue things. I hated it when passion was thwarted in the sweat of failure. I hated it when my hold on her was loosed and she slipped away again.
I hated it when I awoke to find that I alone was there and that memories were simply tricks of light and shade. I hated it.... how I hated it.

Monday morning it had been the Chelmsford police that had called.
Tuesday it was Michael, and very early indeed.
Six fifteen was early for me. Too early!

"What on earth do you want at this time in the morning?" was my somewhat abrupt reply to Michael's all too cheery greeting.

"Have you got enough paper in your fax machine? Because I brought a fair amount of information home with me last night, and I want to send it through to you this morning before I get to work, there is a fax agency at the station.
I just wanted to warn you that it was on its way, I didn't want to scare you with the noise of your machine churning it out.
I am going in to work now to do a bit before the crowd arrives, there's nothing like the quiet of an empty office to inspire the sleuthing skills."

To my mind he was sounding far too buoyant. I couldn't believe that conversations that we had had in the last few days were responsible for this change of outlook. He was actually sounding confident, and eager to get at the task in hand. How could he have forgotten those feelings of desperation that until so recently had sent him on a downward spiral of despair?

"Yes, there is paper in the machine," I replied sarcastically. "And just be careful. Do you hear me?" It was said to him as he was saying his goodbye.

At six thirty eight the machine sprang into life. I found myself over breakfast reading the contents of twenty four A4 copies of, manifests of movements of goods, and projected customer requirements for the next two weeks.

There were the names of customers. Descriptions of goods. Where the goods were to be picked up. What level of security to be employed. The final destination. The amount of goods. The weight of the goods. The value of the goods in transit. What level of insurance that the customer had agreed to. What sort of carrier to be used. Courier, light van or container.
The categories seemed endless.
I decided to help myself by making my own lists. Values, in descending order. Types of goods in transit. Were there any common destinations? High insurance? Did the same customer feature more than once?
It surprised me to find that some very large quantities of cash were being picked up and delivered to all sorts of places, on a regular basis. There were containers filled with the contents of the houses of wealthy customers moving here and there in Britain and overseas as well. There were some sensitive cargoes. A small consignment of day old chicks was to be transported to a destination marked as 'category A,' no address was given for this. Precious metals. Jewels of differing quality and value. A consignment of classic cars to be delivered to a collector in the States.
I scrutinised the lists time and time again, there was nothing that caught my attention. There was a consistency in the Carrier name for furniture of any worth. The initials SSSD, I presumed stood for Smettons Smartway Security and Destinations. Those initials appeared alongside high value containerised goods being shipped overseas.
It was staggering to add up the values of business in any week.
Smettons certainly had a grip on a considerable amount of the high value market. Although how was I to know for certain, it was all so new to me.
I recognised some of the names of auction houses from which goods were to be picked up. Sotheby's, Christie's, Phillips, they were all there alongside others I did not know.
The more I looked, the more I was sure that there was nothing irregular to be detected in any of these lists.
It seemed as though a high class security firm was simply going about its usual daily business, and doing it very successfully.

What was Michael's fear? What did he believe his new computer programme would be able to achieve? He had told me that the potential of it was all to do with the possibility of 'opening a black hole, putting something in the black hole, then closing the black hole and that nobody would know that anything had happened.' He had suggested either large transfers of money, or high value goods.

Smettons seemed to be dealing with things in those categories every day of their business lives. Where was the unusual?

The security employed seemed, on the face of it, to be very efficient.

The programme would give someone time before detection. I therefore reasoned that it could not be the electronic transfer of money, because that could be done at the touch of a button on a computer terminal. A good number of lives had been ruined in falling to that temptation. But what about the collection and delivery of actual cash. In those circumstances the security was usually intensive and very high profile. I gave that idea up as well.

The programme would give time... why was time important? Time?

At this stage in my deliberations a thought struck that caused me to break from my perusal of the paperwork. I went to my office and wrote the word TIME on my computer. I highlighted it and asked for the thesaurus to do its job on the word.

Instant intelligence followed the touch of a button.        TIME

| | |
|---|---|
| OCCASION | Instant, moment |
| TERM | Duration, hold, interval, length, occupancy, tenure |
| RHYTHM | Beat, cadence, cycle, lilt, pulse, rate, tempo, |
| OPPORTUNITY | Chance, break, crack, gap, occasion, opening shot, show, stroke of luck |
| TERM | Period, cycle, duration, interval, season, span spell, stage, stretch |
| PERIOD | Era, aeon, age, cycle, decade, epoch, eternity, forever, long time, millennium, reign, span, stage, years. |

Duration, interval, length, gap, period, stroke of luck, long time.

All these words began to contribute to a simple process of thought.

I returned to the kitchen where the paperwork was still spread out amongst my breakfast things.

What, of all these items of considerable value, took TIME to arrive. Things collected and stored, to be delivered elsewhere, maybe not in this country. Not the items that were to be under the scrutiny of an

owner, or a guard, but the items that were shut up over a period of time, left somewhere in store awaiting the routing to be completed. Those items that could be put into the 'black hole', could wait in the 'black hole', and then disappear from the 'black hole' at a convenient moment. Of the items in this category the choice was between two groups of things.
People's personal belongings in transit due to their removal to a new address.
I did not favour that.
Or purchased goods awaiting collection and delivery.
Now that was a possibility.
I had noticed on the manifests, the delivery of the classic cars, which appeared to be a 'one off.' And very desirable.
And the constant collection and delivery of high value collectables, silver, furniture etc. There were several possibles in that category.
Might the programme have been commissioned by someone who wanted to make off with the cars?
Or was it to do with high value antique furniture?
Gold, silver. Or fine art? I decided I must go through the lists yet again, this time with a fine tooth comb.

The fax machine started up. I could hear it from where I was in the kitchen.
It stopped after a brief while. I thought to myself that Michael was risking it a bit doing it at this time in the morning. But in checking my watch to see what time it was I was surprised to find that it was already twelve forty five. He must have slipped out in his lunch hour to send me more information. I had been at it longer than I thought. Didn't time fly when you.... I did not finish my silly thought.

I could see at a glance that the second wad of faxes gave me similar information as the first, but now extending the time scale…
right to the end of April.

A sandwich first, I thought.
I had been in the kitchen all morning, the debris of my early breakfast was still on the table. Make more mess? Or clear up first? It was the single person's daily dilemma. I had prided myself in the early months following Lara's death that she would have been proud of my ability to cope. There had been lapses since, when self-pity made inroads into my routines. But sensing a need to be disciplined in the matter, I washed up and cleared things away before thinking of what I should eat. Knowing

that a good pub lunch was only round the corner, just five minutes away, I made an easy decision.
A change of atmosphere would be of real benefit.
I gathered up the papers, locked up the house, and was on my way, already looking forward to 'Today's Special' which being Tuesday I knew would be 'Ken's Chicken and Leek Pie.' The lunchtime regulars always expressed a certain ribald humour at anything on Ken's menu that said '.... and Leek' asking him whether or not it was an order that they must obey! Doubtless I would enter into the same spirit of things when I arrived. 'Boddingtons, Chicken and Leek in that order,' I would say, it was a well rehearsed opener that led to a grin and, depending on how Ken was feeling, a somewhat caustic reply that inferred that those 'prostate years,' were rapidly approaching.
It was innocent enough, and the pie was always good.
There was a table available, so with my order placed, and laughter shared,
I sat down to peruse the paperwork that I had brought. The new information that Michael had sent through was similar in content to the first that I had been looking at all morning. I asked myself the same questions as before. Was there a pattern as far as customers were concerned? Was there a similarity in what was being carried? Were there items of extreme high value going to similar destinations?

The container depot at Felixstowe featured often in the lists, but then as a great many of the final destinations were in Northern Europe, why should I query that? But there did appear to be a build up of containerised goods at Felixstowe, due to be waiting for forward shipment.
Forward transit date 'to be specified.'
'To be specified.' That caused a flicker of interest... date to be specified? There was an unknown 'TIME' factor in that statement, something waiting to be decided.
Had I hit on something?
Boddingtons, Chicken and Leek came and went. A second Boddingtons and then the inevitable visit elsewhere... which if Ken had seen me, would have been quickly accompanied with his comment of 'I told you so.' I gathered up my paperwork and on this occasion was saved the mild embarrassment, for Ken was busy at the other end of the bar and failed to see my exit.

Back at home I settled to the task of further analysis of the situation.
What type of goods would be waiting at Felixstowe?
What was the value of goods that would be waiting at Felixstowe?

Was there a customer name that appeared more than once?
Was there a common destination for these goods in transit?
What carrier firms were being employed?

The first question concerning 'goods waiting' had a simple answer. Antiques.
The second concerning 'value' produced a staggering bit of arithmetic. Even without my calculator I estimated that goods to a value of well over twenty three million pounds would be waiting for that 'time to be specified' order before their onward shipment could take place.
Of the 'customer names' there were several. Some were obviously code names of regular customers. There were sets of initials, amongst which SOTH appeared ten times. I presumed that meant Sotheby's. TREB appeared seven times, I had no clue as to who they were. CHRI, presumably Christie's, appeared three times.

Forward transit on arrival in Hamburg would be to several different places.
Smettons was itself the carrier container provider.
I needed to ask questions of Michael.
When might he ring again? Should I use the system he had devised that entailed me leaving a message on the answerphone of my personal number?
I decided that I must do just that.
Although it would seem odd, it needed to be done.

I wondered if he might contact me once more in the early morning hours. This had been successful already. Why hadn't we thought of this as the established way of communicating?
Without that it would be a natural phone call, one to one, I needed to be very explicit in my asking of the questions. A little time was therefore required to work out what it was that I wanted to know. I had, up until now, only asked him for forward information. We could be on the tail end of a build up of goods already waiting at Felixstowe.
From my business phone I rang my personal number, hoping that Michael had remembered to switch the mobile off. When the number rang right there in my room I had to fight off the urge to answer it and then had to wait whilst my pre-recorded tape ran its course.
At the tone I began...

Michael it's Michael! Question. Can you back track in the firm's records to find out how many containers may be waiting at Felixstowe for onward transit on a date 'to be specified?'

Question. Can you let me know what the various sets of initials mean under customer names? Who are some of these customers?

Question. I presume that the firm has knowledge of what is in the containers. Can you run the manifest lists for those containers that are due to be waiting at Felixstowe for the date 'to be specified' onward transit?

Question. How close are you to completion?

I put the phone down, realising that I was feeling unnerved by the whole exercise. An idea of what may be in hand was beginning to be formulated in my mind. Michael was being asked to provide the system by which the legal routing and delivery of containerised goods might be changed and then hidden forever.

Whoever it was who was masterminding this whole affair must be seeking to steal a massive collection of antiques, getting them delivered to a new destination, by some means or other, and then losing from all the records any detail of the transactions. I was sure that I had hit on the truth of things.

## III

My knowledge of this form of container transport was very limited indeed. Though I was not completely ignorant of some of the basic procedures, after all in my own business I had often had to arrange delivery to some foreign part, of some of the products I had designed. Some of the work that I had produced could be seen in some very exotic places. And indeed all that
'Bookmaster 'stuff had involved me in designing a set of bookshelves that you could easily expand as your collection of books grew, I had been pleased with that. A container full had gone to France.
That was all there on the leaflets I had delivered in Herstwick Gardens.
It did me no good whatsoever to remember that that little episode was only last week.

I needed to know more about the container transport business.
My squash playing pal could tell me all about that. Yes, Harry could put me in the picture. I had met him at the local where I could often be seen attempting to drown my sorrows after Lara died. Harry was a genuine help when times were bad. He had often seen me safely home in those early days. A former docker of no mean intelligence who enjoyed a game of squash on occasions. Our lifestyles were nowhere near the same but we enjoyed each other's company.
And when we played squash, each played to win.
Harry ran a little delivery business now that he was 'retired' from the docks.
I had used his services often when I needed bulkier things taken from 'A' to 'B.'
We had played some hectic games just last Sunday and he had asked then when next we could play.
I phoned him. He wasn't in. I left a message with his wife. Would he like a game or two tonight? She said that he would phone as soon as he was in.

Five forty five. The phone rang. It was Harry.

"Harry! What about a game tonight? There's a court available at eight thirty."

"What? You want to get your own back for the drubbing I gave you on Sunday. You were right off form. OK then. May is going round to her Mum's. I'll be there. You might win tonight, I was on the road at the crack of dawn this morning, and I've only just got in."

He rang off.
Why was this man always so cheerful?
Eight fifteen saw us both parking at the club... eight thirty and we were on court.... nine fifteen, five games later, he had easily beaten me again... a rap at the door... next booking arriving dead on time... nine twenty five, exhausted, we're in the showers... nine forty eight and we are in the bar, both unashamedly drinking grapefruit juice and lemonade.

"I got you again," he said, with a note of surprise in his voice. "You must have something on your mind. You were beating hell out of the ball all the time. Not your usual finesse. What's up chum?"
I had trusted this man before, when my own life was in a state, why shouldn't I trust him again right now ?

"Harry... " I paused for a while. "Harry... something has come up in these last couple of weeks... something that could become pretty messy."

In the next fifteen minutes I unfolded the bones of the story, I spoke without interruption. He listened intently to every word I said.

".... so I need to know something about the world of large containers, security procedures, customs and excise, how shipments are handled, and all that stuff," adding, as I finished.... "would you care for another drink?"

"Good grief!" he replied. "What sort of world do you live in?"

He declined the offered drink. But continued with real interest and genuine concern as I asked him question after question.
He readily gave me answer after answer.

"Could anyone tamper with the contents of a container, whilst it was waiting at a dockside depot?"

"Not really. Not without a number of people being involved. It's the way the boxes are parked up. The containers only have doors at one end and for security purposes they are parked so that you never see the doors.
The first one in the line is the only one that you could get at.

But as soon as the second box is put down, doors to doors, no one can get in at all.

You see what I mean?"
He was busy arranging beer mats to put me in the picture. He carried on.

"No! There would have to be someone in the office involved. They are the only ones who know where the numbered containers are stacked. A crane driver would have to be involved if you wanted to lift a box. Security would have to be involved. The seal on the doors would have to be cut. It takes a couple of people to lift some of the bolt cutters that are used for that purpose. No! I should say it would be very difficult indeed. Customs are the ones who have the right to open anything up, at any time. For anybody else they would have to have all the right paperwork. At the container depots and on board ship they are pretty secure. It's when they are on the road that they might be vulnerable."


I took in all that he told me with a great deal of interest. It was the hard world that he had been a part of for many years. His stories, in between my questions, were full of a passion that was to do with comradeship and manliness and dignity, of dock workers supporting their brothers in time of trouble. He told of times way back when wives could be seen at dock gates waiting for their men folk, demanding that they hand over the wage packet before pubs and betting shops could be visited. He spoke of honour and integrity and solidarity at times when docks were strike bound. I could see just why I had a liking for this man. There was true honour in him, a man of depth and character.

My questions answered; his ongoing support promised.
We left to go our homeward way.
Whatever this series of events was doing to me, I didn't fully know, but what I was beginning to discover was that I was being drawn closer to two totally different people. Michael so vulnerable. Harry so strong.
I realised just how much I had missed out on the friendship front over these recent years.

In my office, when I returned, the business answerphone was winking its little red light at me. There were two messages, both from Michael.

"Uncle Michael. It's Michael." It was our standard greeting. " Sorry you're not in. I'll phone you tomorrow morning at six thirty. Is that all

right? Just to say that somebody winked at me when I got back from lunch today.
Tell you about it tomorrow."

"Uncle Michael, it's me again. I have listened to your message.
I will try for the answers to your first three sometime tomorrow.
The answer to the fourth question is that I am a day away from completion.
I'll be in touch."


There was a definite edge to his voice, I could feel the anxiety in his words. Things were heading towards some sort of climax. I wondered to myself how much control we might have over the unknown events that may be ahead of us. I was even more glad that I had trusted Harry with the story. I knew that he would help if things got out of hand. I wiped all messages from both machines and made my way to bed.

He was eager to be in touch, so much so that the phone woke me at six fifteen, a full quarter of an hour before schedule.

"I have not slept much, I've been worrying all night." There was a desperate tone to his voice, in his anxiety he carried straight on without giving me time even to greet him. "Just after I finished faxing that stuff to you yesterday lunchtime I met up with a young girl who works at our place. She's in the Overseas Manager's office. She had been out doing a bit of shopping in her lunch hour. As we were walking back to the office together we were talking quite casually, when out of the blue she told me that her boss had asked her that morning whether she knew the name of my girlfriend, 'the one who was with him at Christmas time,' he had said to her. She went on to tell me that she had told her boss that 'no, the girl wasn't Michael's girl friend, no, that was his sister Sam.'

Well Uncle Michael, I tell you straight, I went cold .
We got back to the office and I was in a bit of a state. It was when I switched on my computer that I felt even more afraid.
For the very first time my 'start up' face winked at me.
I quickly ran my search programme to discover what had been looked for.

Whoever it was had gone for my personal addresses file. Entry is barred until you put in a code word. So there was no joy there. But then a 'find it' file was entered. I saw Sam's name come up. There it was on screen

'Searching for Sam or Samantha Trevough.' I was shaking by this time. What came up then was my Christmas card list of addresses, I had forgotten to wipe them off after printing the envelope labels. I always send a separate card to Sam. Uncle Michael," his voice was trembling now, "they've got the address, they know where she lives, Uncle Michael, what are we going to do? Sam could be in real danger now." He was almost hysterical.

I was finding it extremely difficult to think of what to say to try and reassure him, especially because I too was shaking with a sense of foreboding and anger that any such thing could happen to these people I loved so much.

"Michael! Listen to me now... Michael! Are you still there? Michael!."
I heard a sob on the other end of the line. "Now Michael try and calm down. You know that whatever it is can't be done until you have finished the programming and you know that whoever it is who is using you in this way can't carry things out until you have explained to them how to work the programme. You will find out sooner or later who it is. You still have the upper hand for the moment at least. Do you understand that?" There was a muted grunt on the other end of the line. "Michael, you must go into work as usual, find out that information. I think it may give us a clue."

"O Uncle Michael, I don't think I can carry on. If anything happens to Sam. I'll never forgive myself."

Michael was completely unaware of the fact that I was now beginning to believe that his life was also in serious danger. The police must be informed, the crucial question was, when?

We finished our conversation with difficulty but he agreed in the end to carry out the tasks for the day, agreeing also, but very reluctantly, that we would have to involve the police at some time in the very near future. 'But not just yet' he pleaded as he said goodbye.
I was now very much awake and very angry indeed. But what now?

I tried to settle myself to some of the routine tasks of home. It was no good. The post came earlier than usual. I did as best I could to put my mind to the task of binning the rubbish, filing the pending, and reading the necessary.
It was still no good.

At eleven the fax sprang to life. He's taking risks now, I thought to myself. Please be careful Michael. Please, please be careful.

The answers to my questions were plainly laid out.
There were two containers already at Felixstowe with that 'to be specified' time written on their transit notes. There were the twenty that we knew would be arriving there and waiting over the next few days.
All were Smetton's containers.
There was a long list of expanded initials giving full names of customers, in alphabetical order.
And as far as the last question. The manifests containing the lists of contents. They would take a little longer.

The address from which the faxes had been sent really horrified me.
Michael had sent them straight from work. He certainly was taking risks.

I began the task of reading through the customer name list.

I was right, CHRI was Christie's. SOTH was Sotheby's.
And TREB was TREEBY'S....THREE Bs....
BANTOCK, BERRYSFORD and BROWNSMOOR

My heart started racing, I went ice cold. I stared in horror at the paper. What sort of ghastly coincidence was this? There was a young man dead already. I made my decision. Treddick must be informed, immediately.
I got through to Chelmsford straight away.

"Mr Treddick please. Tell him it is Michael Grantsman."

"John Treddick here. What can I do for you Mr. Grantsman?"

There was a genuine warmth in his voice. How I needed this man to be responsive to my needs right now. How I needed him to discern the urgency of response to what I was about to tell him. How I needed him to say 'yes Mr. Grantsman, of course I will Mr. Grantsman.'

"Mr Treddick..." I paused.... I started again. "Mr Treddick, I think I can provide a major clue for you in respect of the death of Terry Berrysford. There is a strange connection between my finding of the box and the people I had been with, prior to that event, and a further series of alarming events of which I am a part right now. In my understanding of

things there are other people, close to me, who may be in danger of serious harm. Would you be prepared to come and see me to discuss things?"
I tried to make myself say all this in a cold and calculating fashion, not wanting my real fear to be transferred. But he was obviously far more discerning than I had thought, for he immediately replied.

"Mr Grantsman, are you saying that you would like me to come down to London right away to see you? Do I get the feeling that you are understating the situation? Are you saying that your need of my help is urgent?"

"Yes! Yes! and Yes!" I said, feeling relieved to have expressed things in such a way as to have made him understand the gravity of my predicament
"And is there any chance that it could be today?"

His affirmative response quietened me down considerably.
He must have sensed that also. For he went on to say.

"Mr Grantsman, or can I call you Michael?"

My quiet, 'of course' allowed him to continue.

"Michael, are you OK? Should I get the London Force involved or are you saying that you want to see me on my own?"

"No! Just you, if that's possible," I replied, reasoning to myself that I would not be completely betraying Michael's trust in me if I simply got the Chelmsford police involved regarding their need for information concerning the Berrysford death.
That was surely the right thing to do.

John Treddick informed me that he would try to be with me by three o'clock. He took my address again, asked for my wisdom on the route that he should take once in London, and then said his goodbye. 'Fancy asking my advice about routes to take in London,' I thought, 'he's a copper, he should know!'

Although things had not changed one little bit. I was beginning to feel that with Harry in on the story and promising his help, and with John Treddick on his way, that there was a stronger base to my activity. I left

a message on my answerphone, just in case Michael made contact. The message thanked him for his speedy bit of faxing. I told him that I might be on to something and that would he please be careful. And that I was just popping out to post some business letters that I had actually managed to write.
And phone me at that unearthly hour of six thirty tomorrow if there was need.
I gathered up the letters for posting, and went out.

My brisk, short walk to and from the post box, took all of fifteen minutes.
I returned, invigorated by the chill wind of early April, having planned what
I would do for my lunch, and what I would do whilst waiting for John Treddick to arrive.

My plans were immediately put on hold.
There were three messages on the answerphone, two of which completely shattered any sense of my improving confidence.
The first was my message for Michael.
The second was a message from Sam.

"Uncle Michael, sorry you're not in. I just want to tell you that I received a letter by special delivery this morning, from Michael, saying that he wanted to see me. It was very important. And I mustn't tell Mum or Dad. Could I meet him in Southwold by the golf club at one thirty. Mum and Dad wont be in till late, so I thought I'd just let you know. Isn't it great? I'm just getting ready to go now. I'll let you know when I get back."

The third was from Michael, obviously out of his mind with worry.

"Uncle Michael," his voice was almost out of control, "I've just listened to your message on tape, and then realised that there was more, and that it was Sam. Uncle Michael it wasn't me who wrote to her. It wasn't me. They're going to get her. They've set a trap for her. O God! Uncle Michael. If anything happens to her. I'll never forgive myself. I could only have missed her by a matter of moments. If only I had your mobile switched on I might have been able to speak to her and stop her going. Where are you? Why weren't you at home? I'll come to your place straight from work. Make sure you're in, please, please make sure you're in."

His sobbing voice stopped. I was stunned to silence.
I was impotent to do anything.

Two appointments waited. Treddick at three. Michael probably at six.
I sincerely hoped that the first would in some way help with the second.
And as for Sam! Where on earth was Sam?

I quickly dialled the Trevough household hoping beyond hope that she may not have left.

It was Sam's cheery voice that answered all right, but only on answerphone.

I was too late.
I left a terse message. 'John, Stella ring me as soon as you get in. Michael.'

What would I tell them when they phoned? How could I explain the delay in getting the police involved? Was there anything more that I could have done? I was beside myself with worry.

All I could do was wait.

The police connection had to be Treddick, he would be here around three.
Please let the roads be clear. In my thinking I was pinning my hopes more and more on Treddick. I must not confuse the issue by dialling the local police. It would take far too long to put them in the picture.

We hadn't got time.
Sam hadn't got time.

Why? I don't know, but I found myself remembering a time when a well loved friend of our family had gone missing. I was very young at the time.
I had gone out into our garden and started calling his name, as though he would be able to hear and answer.

At this very moment I felt like shouting out Sam's name to the sky. Where was she now? Surely they wouldn't harm her? I tried to convince myself that the key to her safety was still in Michael's possession. Whoever it was who was masterminding this whole thing still needed Michael.

How I waited for three o'clock I will never know. I was there at the window watching the road for Treddick's arrival.
He was as good as his word.
Three minutes after three and his unmarked car drew up. I was at the door waiting to greet him.
He realised as soon as he saw me that something drastic had happened.

"Mr Grantsman... Michael," he corrected himself. "I came as fast as I could."
"Thank you so much," I was gripping his hand and ushering him in at the same time, "even more has happened whilst you have been on your way here. I don't know where to start. Sam could be in real trouble."
I blurted out that last statement, and as I did, my stomach turned over making me wretch with fear.

"Michael," he now gripped my hand with reassuring strength and deliberately carried on. "Michael, please try to calm down. Tell me what this is all about. Who is Sam? And why might he be in real trouble?"

"Sam Trevough. You know, the daughter of the family up in Southwold where I stayed for those few days. You know, where I had taken the box. You've taken all their fingerprints. Sam! Sam Trevough! She might have been kidnapped!"

"Michael, sit down, and just stop for a moment. You need a drink, let me make one for you. What will it be?"

We were in the kitchen. He took command of the situation.
My weak reply of 'coffee, black' was soon attended to.

"Now from the beginning."   At least John Treddick was calm.

I drank half of the coffee before attempting to get underway with my story.
I was trying desperately to put things into some order in my mind. The journey to Southwold had been but two weeks ago. How was it possible for life to be so interrupted and changed round in such a short time?
How was it possible for so many lives to be put in jeopardy?
Beyond a hesitant start, I became an ardent teller of the story so far.

I covered every aspect of what had happened in as much detail as I could remember, beginning with the reason for the first journey.

"My friends, John, Stella and Sam Trevough live just outside Southwold. I was visiting them because, one, they had asked me to, and two, because I had sensed in John's conversation with me a hidden problem that he would not divulge on the phone, and I was keen to find out what that might be. On the journey up I had to stop... the sneeze... the box... well you know that part of the story. I arrived on that Wednesday to a great welcome but in the evening they told me the real reason why they had asked me to see them. They were beginning to believe that their son Michael was in some sort of trouble. Michael works for a high class security shipping firm here in London, he is the firm's computer wizard. Since Christmas he was showing real indifference towards his parents and was obviously putting distance between himself and them, even his sister Sam. They were very hurt by this, and could see no reason at all for it to have occurred. Could I help in some way as I was in London? I agreed to do something. I would try to get in touch with him.

I left them on the Friday, and on the journey back I was caught up in our first somewhat indelicate contact as I tried to hand the box in to the police.

I heard from the police the story of the burned out cars and the murder. I remember that very well indeed.

I got back home, and on the Saturday posted a brief note to Michael, hoping that he would respond. I heard nothing from him until late in the following week. By the manner of his reply to me I felt, or rather knew, that he must be in some deep, deep trouble."

"Excuse me, Michael." Treddick interrupted me. "How was it that you knew that he was in deep, deep trouble simply by the way he replied?"

I told him as quickly as possible the reason why, and then continued with a shortened version of how I had eventually met up with Michael at his home and of how he had told me of his worry over the photographs of him and Sam, that he had received at work, and of the computer programme that he had been asked to supply to the Overseas Manager... I told him of our acceptance of what the 'black hole' might achieve... I told him of the meeting in Hyde Park on Sunday... the decision to find out more about the forward business activity of his firm... the plan to fax me the information.. the mobile... I told John Treddick everything.

"Alright Michael, I know about Monday, because you came up to Chelmsford to see me. I told you of the development in the case of the box, and that the body in the car was Berrysford's son. We went to see Berrysford. We met the Directors and family. You told me all you knew about the car that you had seen driving away fast on the previous Wednesday. The 4.2 Jaguar Sovereign.

I'm still intrigued about how you were so sure that it was that particular car, maybe you will tell me that some time.

Then you travelled back, presumably to your home here.

So what happened Tuesday?"

"Michael phoned me early to warn me that some faxes would be arriving. They arrived... I worked on them as best I could... more arrived... I took them to my local pub, and over lunch came to the conclusion that there were a number of containers of very high value goods either waiting or due to be waiting in the next two or three weeks at Felixstowe container depot for a 'time to be specified' for forward transit."

"Felixstowe, you say. That is interesting." Treddick interrupted me again. "We've just found and identified Terry Berrysford's car. It was burnt out on a bit of waste land near the docks at Felixstowe. Carry on."

"On Tuesday night I played squash with a business pal of mine who used to work in the docks, and found out from him, a good deal about the container business and the sort of security that is involved at dockside depots.

I came home to find a message on my answerphone from Michael.

That message suggested that something had happened at work that had stepped up the fear aspect of all of this, and that he would phone me early Wednesday morning.

He called me very early Wednesday morning... this morning... telling me that he had found out that the Overseas Manager had inquired of another friend of his at work whether Sam was Michael's girlfriend. This friend had unwittingly said that Sam was Michael's sister, not his girlfriend.

And that was not all... Michael's personal computer at work had been started up and that whoever it was who had done it had found out Sam's address."

"How could he be sure that Sam's address had been found?" Treddick asked.

"Quite easily," I replied, and I went on to tell Treddick of Michael's secret search programme, and how that it had shown the path by which the information had been found, and how Sam's address had been located.

I told John Treddick of Michael's increasing sense of fear for Sam's life. I told him that Michael had agreed to try and carry on at work and complete the task in hand.

I told him of my request to find out who the customer initials referred to, and of my horror, when Michael's mid morning faxes arrived, in discovering that Bantock Berrysford and Brownsmoor... Treeby's was involved.

"That was when I phoned you, knowing that you must be told of that particular development. You agreed to come straight away... I want to thank you for being available so quickly.

But even whilst you have been on your way events have turned nasty, really nasty. After I phoned you I went out to post some business letters I had written. When I returned home here I discovered that there were two messages on my answerphone." My voice faltered once again, I paused, reliving that dreadful moment. "It would be best if you came through to my office and listened to them yourself."

I was getting to a level of anxiety that I was finding difficult to control. Treddick sensed this and held out his hand to me as we got up to go the office. I played back the messages without further comment.

Hearing the first buoyant Sam and then the despairing Michael caused me to gasp for breath. I was glad that Treddick was with me, I needed his strength.

"I phoned the Trevough household straight after hearing the messages, but the house was empty, there was no reply, Sam had gone. I left a message for John and Stella to contact me... Mr Treddick! What can we do?"

"Well first I must make contact with my lads at Chelmsford. Can I use your phone?"

He dialled the number, got through, and I heard him asking whether they could find out who the officer was who had gone to the Trevough household with the fingerprint guys from Southwold. He waited... they were very rapidly back on line with the information. The name given.

He inquired whether the officer was on duty now. To the answer which was obviously yes, he replied that he wanted to speak with him right away... that it was urgent. He waited... the officer was quickly on the line. Treddick came to the point immediately. As he began to speak he looked round at me and nodded that I should come closer. He switched on the conference facility on my phone. His voice, asking his first question, filled the room.

"Peters! How well do you remember your visit to the Trevough household?"

"You mean when I took the prints guys from Southwold?" his distant voice boomed out into the room. "Pretty well, Sir, it was only yesterday."

"Do you remember Sam Trevough?"

"O yes! Sir."
His tone betrayed the fact that Sam was definitely worth remembering.
"Do you think you would recognise her again if you saw her?"

"O yes! Sir, definitely Sir!" His voice changed. "What's this all about, Sir?"

Treddick went on to tell the young officer just what was in hand.
That he should take a couple of other plain clothes officers with him.
He named them, including a female officer as well. And that the three of them should go to Southwold and see if they could find Sam's whereabouts, but to be very careful indeed. They must not be noticed. They must go immediately. Her life was in danger. He turned to me and asked whether I knew what car Sam drove.

"A green mini Cooper" I replied.

"Peters! Did you hear that?"

"Yes Sir, a green mini Cooper."

"Peters you are to go now. Keep in touch with me at this number until further notice. That is, when you get there, and then every fifteen minutes.
And Peters, please be very careful."

He finished the conversation by reading out my number.

Listening to him giving these orders made me aware of the gravity of the situation once again. I wanted to go to Southwold myself. I wanted to try and find Sam. But I knew that that was impossible at least for the moment.
We had to wait for Michael and see what the update was concerning the activities at the firm.
Peters repeated the number and signed off.
I had no real hopes of them finding her, but at least there would be a police presence at Southwold and they may be able to find out something.

Treddick spoke again and completely changed the direction of my thinking.

"You know the only prints on that box were; yours, the family at Southwold, and my officers, the one who had picked it out of your bus. Strange that!
It had been wiped thoroughly clean. It was as though it had been left by the roadside deliberately. Perhaps whoever did it believed that if it was handed in, that somehow young Terry Berrysford would be finally identified, and that he would be incriminated in some way in something dark and shady that was going on. We didn't let any of the other dealers touch it, not even old man Berrysford.

Whatever it is that you are involved in, Michael, it has to be worth a great deal to someone. One young man dead already, a young woman a possible kidnap victim, and the further possibility of a major theft taking place in a few days time."

Said as matter of factly as that, it made me feel even more despairing of any hopeful outcome. I tried to work out in my head, how long it would take the police to get to Southwold.
If they had started just before four o'clock, then maybe...

"My crew should be there well before six," Treddick stated. Interrupting and answering my unspoken thought. "They'll have a bit of time before it gets dark, Who knows? They may hit on something fairly quickly."

His optimism, I'm sure, was well intentioned, but it did not allay my increasing fears at all.
At precisely five o'clock Michael arrived.

"You're earlier than I thought you'd be, how come?"

"Flexitime!" his voice was sharp. "Who's this?" He had noticed Treddick.

" Michael there are other things you don't know about, that make our situation even more complicated and, I am afraid, even more dangerous. Michael, I thought it right that we should get some help.
This is John Treddick from Chelmsford he's with the CID.
Let me tell you the rest of the story."

I could see that he was uncomfortable with the stranger being present, and it took a good deal of persuasion to get him to accept that we needed police help. But eventually after he had listened to the new facts, he saw that it was the only thing that could be done, and that perhaps it was a good thing that police would soon be on Sam's trail at Southwold.

The mention of Terry Berrysford's death and the Felixstowe connection quickly brought him to his senses.
I told him that I had also told my pal Harry, 'the one who had phoned whilst we were in McDonalds on Sunday afternoon,' and that was all, nobody else was aware of what was going on.

"I have left a message on the answerphone at Southwold for your Mum and Dad to phone me as soon as they are in. It is going to be tough for them,
I know, but they must be put in the picture. If they phone whilst you are still here you must talk to them as well. Do you agree? Now, what is the update from the firm? And have you managed to get the manifest papers that will tell us what will be in the containers at Felixstowe?"

All this time Treddick had been quietly listening, but as Michael's mood began to change from one of suspicion, to one of tentative trust, Treddick spoke his mind, and forcefully at that.

"I know that this is no time to be high handed, but you do realise, the pair of you, that by your desire to keep control of things, you may have caused problems for everyone concerned, and especially for Sam.
We may have lost valuable time."

Michael began to protest that there had been nothing else that we could have done. We did not know what we were up against.

There was nothing definite up until now! Sam's message had changed everything. His voice was cracking as he was speaking. Tears were not far away.

"I've said that once," Treddick carried on, "I won't say it again. We must be positive from now on. We must work together on this. We must all know what each of us is doing at any given time. So, what is the status of things at work? And where are those manifests?"

"I'm seeing the Overseas Manager to morrow morning at ten. My work on the new programme is complete. I will tell him that I will need to see whoever it is who is going to operate the programme so that the specialist information and formulae can be exchanged.
I am hoping that I will find out who is behind all this.
I know I've told you this before Uncle Michael, but I still don't think that it is the Overseas man at all, he just doesn't have the computer skills to handle it.

I've not sidestepped the need for our Company's basic security code procedures to be employed. That would have made things far too obvious.
The Company code and the Department code will still have to be used before a re-route of goods can be achieved. I am sure that I shall be able to convince whoever it is about that.
That means that I will still be able to have some limited control over things right up till the moment that the 'black hole' is closed.
Whilst all the new information is being inputted I have 'arranged' for a shadow copy of all the instructions to be transferred to a special file I have created on my personal computer.
The very moment that the 'black hole' is opened, my secret shadow file will be opened, and I will receive all the information.

Up until lunchtime today I thought I had been so clever, and that because of my cleverness, it would be easy to get the police to catch the crooks red handed at the new destinations. But now with Sam involved, as she is, my bit of cleverness wont do us any good at all."

"Don't be so sure," Treddick said. "Your cleverness, as you call it, which I confess is way beyond me, will give us time. And time is what we need in order to find Sam.
Right now we do not know if she has been kidnapped.

And whoever it is behind this wont know that we have any information about Sam at all. They must think that it will be tomorrow at the earliest that that news will come through. The fact that we know that something is up should give us just a little leverage in the situation.

If by tomorrow at ten, when you have your meeting, we have been informed by your parents that Sam hasn't turned up, you can ask the Overseas Manager for assurances concerning her well being. It might come as a real surprise to him to hear that you already know. You will have to be very careful though. Do you think that you can manage that?"

"With Sam's life in danger, of course I will manage it. I'll tell him that I must hear her voice and that she must tell me that she is unharmed, or else I wont cooperate with them any more."

I was amazed at Michael's sudden composure and clear thinking.
Treddick thought differently and made us painfully aware of what we may be dealing with.
"If Terry Berrysford's death is part of this," he stated coldly. "We must recognise that we are dealing with someone who is prepared to kill in order to get what he wants. You, Michael, have got to be very careful indeed. None of this 'cops and robbers' mentality. This is deadly serious.
We must think carefully of what you should say.

Now you two can start going through those manifests.
See if you can build up a picture of what may be about to disappear.
I must go now to Scotland Yard, I have a friend there who will be waiting for me to turn up, I phoned him before I left Chelmsford.
We do have our procedures as well. The Yard must be informed."

Michael emptied his briefcase, producing page after page of manifests.
The lists were endless. We settled to the task of discovering just what was up for grabs. Michael started on the Sotheby's containers. And I took the lists that referred to Bantock Berrysford and Brownsmoor. We were quiet to our task, reading, without comment.

"It's nothing out of the ordinary, as far as I can see." Michael was the first to break the silence. "Smetton's are doing this all year round. The shipping of antiques and fine art all around the world. It's just what we do!
Why has someone taken a particular interest in this lot?

One thing that is unusual is the fact that there is such a large build up of goods coming through Sotheby's. Ten containers waiting, yes, that is unusual. We don't usually have such a huge amount as this at any one time. Maybe that's a clue. Could it be a disgruntled employee? It would have to be someone very high up in their organisation, Director level, I should say, someone who had access to all the routing and holding procedures."

I had been quietly going through the Bantock's lists. Two things of interest came to light! Michael must have seen the changed look on my face.

"What have you found, Uncle Michael?"

"Two crates in particular! The first containing a load of ornamental boxes. The second containing a selection of fine art including two Titians.
They are a couple of pictures that I know quite well.

And the boxes... they are 'enigma boxes.'
You remember I told you about the box I had picked up... It was an 'enigma box' one of a collection that Terry Berrysford was building up for an overseas client. It has to be a clue. If only we could check that crate of boxes!"

"And what's so interesting about the Titians, Uncle Michael?"

"Well it goes right back to my student days. As soon as my fine art tutor found out that my middle name was Titian, she encouraged me to do an in depth study of his life and works. I was very often in the National Gallery, here in London, studying his paintings. One of the paintings mentioned in this manifest was the subject of a paper I wrote.

I can even remember the title of the paper. 'The eyes have it!' I thought it was very clever at the time. The painting is huge, the largest group portrait that Titian painted. If I remember rightly it is over ten feet long. It is a portrait of the Vendramin family, or at least the men in the Vendramin family.
One of the things that is so powerful about it is the treatment of the eyes. When you look at the painting you can really believe that the eyes are seeing things. I wrote pages and pages about every aspect of the picture.
I've probably still got the paper somewhere.

I wonder why the painting is part of this shipment?
I guess it must be on loan to another gallery somewhere in Europe."

"Did Dad share your interest in Titian?" Michael asked.

"No, not really, he had other interests, mainly chasing after your mother!"

Mention of Stella made us both pause. I wondered how soon it would be before the phone would ring.
What would I say to them? What would Michael say to them?

As though not wanting to think too long on that subject, Michael broke the silence.

"So the only unusual item appears to be the crate load of boxes. Out of all this stuff the only clue is in the boxes."

I agreed with him. We must see the boxes. Perhaps Treddick could arrange it. Without the necessary papers and proof of ownership it would have to be a Customs job, but they would be able to search without questions being asked.
The phone rang. It was Harry, asking whether there were any developments.
I told him as much as I thought advisable. I told him of Sam's predicament as well as the fact that the Chelmsford police were now involved. And then I asked him what he was doing for the next couple of days. To his reply of 'nothing much only one or two local deliveries,' I replied, asking him to stick around, that I may need his help.

The phone rang again. It was Peters, Treddick's man. They had arrived in Southwold. Treddick had actually contacted them from The Yard some time ago telling them to contact me only when they had something to report. This they were doing now, saying that they had located a green Mini Cooper that was parked up in a quiet road, and did I know the registration. I turned to Michael and asked him if he knew Sam's car details.

"SGT 121," he replied without hesitation, "Dad bought her personalised plates last year for her birthday."

I relayed the information to Peters who immediately confirmed that that was the car they had found. There was, unfortunately no sign of Sam. But they would carry on the search and would be in touch later.

The phone rang yet again, a third time, it was Stella.

"Your message was very terse Michael. What's up?"

"Stella is John there with you? Can you get him to the phone as well?" I only wanted to say what I had to say once.
She took a moment to get John, he had been putting the car away. But now they were together, waiting for what I had to tell them.

"Is Sam there with you?"

As I asked them the question my mouth went dry. Both Michael and I were waiting for their unsuspecting answer.

"No. She's obviously out walking the dog somewhere. Why do you ask?"

"Stella, John, I've got Michael here with me, there have been some serious developments. We think Sam may be in some danger."

Stella gasped! John spoke.

"What on earth do you mean Michael, Sam may be in some danger? She's out with the dog. Her car isn't in the garage and Canny is not about.
Michael she is out with the dog. There's nothing unusual about that. She often walks him during the evening."

"I think you had better listen to your son, he has a very difficult story to tell the pair of you. Just listen to him, he will tell you everything."

I handed the phone over to Michael, who reluctantly began, first with profuse apologies, and then with increasing animation and emotion, to tell all that had gone on in his life over recent weeks. I could only listen as he poured out his story. I could feel his pain and his desperation as he pleaded for them to forgive him for getting Sam into danger.

He spoke without interruption, and as he finished he broke down with childlike, inconsolable sobs. I took the phone from him, my own emotions very poorly in check. Although twenty two he looked but a child as he slumped into a chair beside me.

"John, Stella, the police are already active in Southwold." I tried to sound positive as I spoke to them. "They have found Sam's car.
The next time they contact me I will let them know that you are back home. They will come and see you and update you on their plans.
Don't do anything until they have been in touch.

It is important that you keep out of the way. Do you understand me?"

They reluctantly agreed and asked to speak to Michael again.
There followed a rare moment of parent child communication that was filled with expressions of personal feelings so deep and moving.
Relationships so recently hurt were being repaired slowly yet surely.
I felt I was an intruder. I made to leave the room so that it could be a more private moment for the three of them.
But Michael grabbed my arm encouraging me to stay.

It was a while before the conversation concluded. I took the phone again.
And as I did so, the front door bell rang. Michael answered.
It was Treddick returning from his visit to The Yard.
With John and Stella on hold, I explained to Treddick what had transpired.
He took the phone from me, and with a strong reassuring voice spoke to them at length. He persuaded them that there was nothing that they could do for the moment and that they must sit tight as though nothing had happened. We did not want to alert whoever was involved. He told them that in his experience Sam would be alright as long as we didn't provoke a hostile reaction.
It would be difficult for them but that they must try and be calm. His plans, he said would be to be with them some time tomorrow to discuss further details.

As I listened I couldn't help but think how alone, and utterly helpless they would be feeling in the coming hours.
Finishing the conversation with them was difficult, we spoke of very fragile human feelings and our sense of total inadequacy and our ineptness to perceive in others their deep needs. Would I make sure that

Michael was alright. Tell him to take care. And tell him just how much we love him.

We said our goodbyes and I heard myself saying not 'good luck!' but 'God bless you!' and I wondered where from within my distant past that particular sentiment had sprung from. Those words were echoes of very distant bells, but I felt strangely reassured.

"Now. What have you found?" Treddick took command of the situation once again. "Is there any clue at all from all this paperwork?"
He looked at the pair of us with a sort of hopefulness, eager for our response.

"Nothing much at all I'm afraid. Michael cannot detect anything out of the ordinary in any of the documentation that he has looked through. And as for me the only thing that is of interest is this."

I showed him the manifest that contained the information about the boxes. "Terry Berrysford's boxes. His enigma boxes are all apparently included in this shipment. Apart, of course, from the one in your possession.
And that, if you remember what his father told us, was the one that wasn't worth as much because the instructions for opening were not with it when it was purchased by Terry.
Is there some way that we could go to Felixstowe and look into this container and examine the contents. The coincidence surrounding the boxes is surely too great for us to ignore."

Treddick readily agreed, and said that we would go tomorrow.
We can go to Felixstowe on our way to Southwold.

"What about Michael? Aren't we forgetting that he has a crucial role to play here. He does after all have this meeting tomorrow."

"Yes I know, I have not forgotten Michael's meeting. I have made arrangements for the 'Met' boys to wire him up. That was the reason for my trip to 'The Yard' to make sure that that facility would be available to us.
Can he stay the night here?"

I nodded my approval. He carried on, this time addressing Michael directly.

"They will be here early in the morning. Is that OK with you Michael? It will enable us to be sure of hearing everything that is said to you. The wire will be very discreet. No one will know. It will be for your protection and for our forward detection procedures to be put on a better footing. The 'Met' boys will be in an unmarked vehicle close by. Now it's Smetton's in the City, yes? You must give me the full address."

"Yes." Michael replied. He proceeded to write out the address, and whilst doing so casually asked. "And what am I supposed to say to the Overseas Manager when I meet him at ten o'clock tomorrow morning?"

I thought it wise at this point to try and calm him down.
He was, after all, taking an enormous responsibility upon himself.
Sam's safety, and his own depended on him being extremely cool in his approach to whoever it was who was behind all this.

"Michael, you have already made very good plans. We just need to rehearse them and do a bit of fine tuning here and there. You want to find out who is going to operate your programme, so, as you have already decided, you must insist when you speak to the Overseas man that he fetch the person concerned. You can speak to the subject of your programme in such a way as to convince the Overseas man that he would not be able to run it.
You can do that can't you."

"Yes, of course, that will be quite a simple procedure."

"We will know early tomorrow morning whether Sam has turned up or not.
Sad to say, but we already feel that she has been taken.
We can only imagine that it is so that pressure can be put on you to complete the task. It will be their, whoever they are, insurance on the job. You must assess the delicacy of the matter, and, only if needed, ask for telephone confirmation of her safety and well being. To be able to speak together would be a good thing for both of you. Sam, after all, knows nothing of the story.

Now you remember that she took the dog with her. If you are allowed to speak to her, is there a question you can ask that might allow her to tell you if Canny is with her or not. It might help us to know that. The police have only found her car, there was no mention of the dog."

"I'll have to think on that one." Michael replied. "You mean to try and use some sort of code to find the answer. To ask about 'Canute' would be a bit of a give away, any one listening to the conversation would want to know what that was about, but to use the word 'mystery' or 'Canny' or 'the third,' or 'Mr Brown' there are numerous possibilities."

Treddick interrupted the proceedings once again and reminded us of his insistence about not playing 'cops and robbers' but was only half hearted in it this time. He was aware of the need to discover all that we could about Sam's situation, and he reluctantly agreed that Michael should take every opportunity to find out.

So the emphasis would be on meeting the 'main man.'
Then if possible to find out about Sam and Canny.
Then to deliver the programme details.
All the while remembering to speak clearly and directly to the people concerned so that the 'Met' boys could pick up everything.

Treddick told Michael that the police would be on hand at all times, and that he should have confidence in the unseen presence of the law.
We went over the plan again and again until Michael was sure of every possible twist and turn.

Treddick left at nine thirty, to return to 'The Yard' and Michael and I settled to the task of trying to be calm about things.

Harry phoned at ten o'clock asking if we needed his help, telling us that he had cleared his diary of the couple of jobs that had been there, and was available now for the next few days, coming up to the weekend.
And to my question 'fancy a trip to Felixstowe tomorrow?' his ready answer was a very definite affirmative.

"What about May?" I asked him. "Won't she mind?"

"You know my May." he replied. "Always keen for me to help you. What time shall I come round?"

"Can you make it by six thirty?"

"That's OK by me! I don't mind a late start once in a while."

His cheerful voice was welcome. His attempt at a joke broke the atmosphere. He laughed, and with his 'later then' said he would see us in the morning.

Michael and I spent the rest of the evening getting more and more despondent, particularly about Sam's welfare.
Michael phoned home to see if there was any further news, and found out that Peters and the other two officers had made their base at John and Stella's, but were still out in Southwold looking around the place.
With nothing new to report, he said his goodbye to them, and I overheard his final remark of 'Mum I am so scared.'
I had to confess that he wasn't the only one.

We slept fitfully.

Harry, true to his word, was with us at six thirty, eager for anything.

Treddick and the 'Met' boys followed soon after in two vehicles.

Peters phoned from Southwold at six forty five.
There was no news of Sam.
The police woman was doing her best with John and Stella.
Their state of mind was reasonable.

Michael was 'wired' by seven fifteen, and with everything working in a satisfactory manner was on his way to work by seven thirty.
He went by train up to the City.
His 'ears' made their own way, by unmarked van, to get themselves in place ready to be on hand at ten o'clock.
Treddick was calm.
Harry was calm.
I was not.
Treddick argued with me about Harry coming with us to Felixstowe, but finally agreed that his 'docker' experience might be useful.

If there were a large scale theft about to take place, who would know whether or not there were people at the Felixstowe container depot who were also in on it. Harry's independent view might prove to be very useful.
That was my side of the argument.

Thankfully Treddick began to see the wisdom of it.
The three of us were on the road to Felixstowe by seven forty five.

Treddick was a very good driver. Traffic was reasonable. We were out of London and on the A12 passing Brentwood by nine o'clock.

"Should be there by ten thirty!" Treddick said.

Harry had sprawled himself on the back seat and was asleep, 'So much for the early bird' I thought to myself.
Treddick and I chatted quietly, and in an off guarded moment I found myself replying to a question he put to me quite deliberately about Jaguar cars, 'why was it that I had been so sure that it was a 4.2 Sovereign that had raced away from me?' He was a sensitive man. He listened without comment as I told him of Lara's death. I realised that I had not spoken in such detail for all of the five barren years since the accident.

There was an intense anger as I spoke.
My remembered sense of guilt and unrelieved pain were still there.
I had no will, ever to forgive the young lad who had careered out of control and smashed into Lara's car.
My feelings of injustice surfaced and my tone of voice took on a cold edge.
I needed retribution for all that the lad had caused me.
But the lad was dead.
Both cars were in the same garage when I went to get Lara's things.
I examined them both at the time with the insurance company's engineer who described in detail what he thought had happened.
He clinically described the terrible impact details and how Lara had had no chance at all.

"I am so sorry." Treddick said. "Forgive me for asking."
"You had no reason to understand. But maybe you do now.
I will never ever forget the shape of a Jaguar Sovereign 4.2. It robbed me of all that was precious."

We continued the journey in silence. I found myself thinking of Sam, and then of Michael. I looked at my watch. It was coming up to ten o'clock.
What would he be doing? How would he be feeling? Were the 'Met' boys in position? Would everything go to plan?
As if sensing my thoughts, and understanding my need of knowing, Treddick switched on his radio. He was in touch immediately with Michael's 'ears.' The line was brilliantly clear, the London voice was loud, and eager to relay what was going on.

"We've got him, Sir, reception is excellent. We can patch him through to you if you would like to hear what's going on."

Treddick looked in my direction. He could see that I was eager to hear as much as possible. He told the listeners to put us in touch as well.
The car became alive with the sound of Smetton's office chatter. You could hear Michael thanking someone for asking him if he wanted a cup of coffee. His reply was no, because he would be going through to Overseas in a couple of minutes time.
It was so off putting to hear him so perfectly, right in this vehicle that was steadily driving away from him. We were now just beyond Colchester and he was there in the City of London.

"Well here I go, lads. I hope you're hearing me loud and clear." It was Michael. "I'm on my way."


What Michael was feeling like, who might know?
What the three of us in this speeding car were experiencing... who knows... the atmosphere was electric. All of us were alert to catch every word of what would transpire from now on in.

You could hear the opening of doors... the shutting of doors... footsteps along a corridor... a bell sound summoning a lift, presumably... lift arriving... doors opening... shutting... the swish of the lift in travel... bell sound alerting lift stopping... doors opening... footsteps along a corridor... a knock on a door... a very faint 'come in'... door opening... door closing.

"Good morning, Michael." An unknown and somewhat distant voice sounded out from across a room. "You're right on time. Excellent. Now what have you got for me. I do hope that it is all that I need."

"Good morning Mr Flatton."
This time it was Michael's clear reply. "Yes, I have the programming details. Are you going to be dealing with it yourself? You do know that it needs code input from your Department Senior as well as the Company."

Who was Flatton? The Overseas Manager? Must be!
Michael was sort of talking down to him. There was a definite superior tone to Michael's voice. Michael was for the moment dictating terms.

He sounded quietly confident, which was good. Flatton spoke again.

"Mr Chartham, Trevough is here in my office. He has what you need. Would it be possible for you to come? You remember I did inform you that you would be needed. I left a reminder with your secretary early this morning."

There followed a brief pause and silence. The technology, although brilliant, was certainly not able to hear what was being said in reply.

"Mr Chartham will be with us in a moment," Flatton said.

"Is that Andrew Chartham, the Outside Director?"
Michael spoke the name slowly and deliberately.
He wanted his 'ears' to understand who was involved.

"Yes! Who else." Flatton sounded a little irritated.

"O, it's just interesting to know who I have done this work for, that's all. I knew it couldn't be for you, you don't understand what I'm talking about half the time."

"You watch who you're talking to, young Trevough! And just remember who it is you're working for, and who pays your salary."

"I thought I was working for Smetton's. It's their name on my cheque every month. Maybe they don't know anything about this programme I've been working on."

Michael was certainly pushing his luck. He was sounding more and more audacious with every statement he was making.

Treddick glanced at me, a worried look on his face.
Harry said 'watch it, youngster' out loud.
And I sat back in my seat wondering how things would change when Chartham arrived on the scene.
Change they did, and dramatically. There was no knock on any door.
Just the sound of one opening and shutting.

"Well, Trevough, we meet at last."

Andrew Chartham's voice was City polished and refined.

An air of immediate command was established.

"Now , you're not going to cause me any problems, are you?" there was a menacing cut to his question. "Show me the programme and tell me what I have to do. And why the blazes did you programme in the need for two codings before it would operate?"

"Well, Sir, if I hadn't done that, alarm bells would have been ringing all over the place. After all, I have been employed to keep security tight in the place. It has taken all my skills and patience to produce this system for you, it is very difficult to build such a set up. What do you want it for anyway?" Michael asked.

"Never you mind! Bring the paper work over here. And make sure you tell me exactly what it is that has to be done."

There was the unmistakable sound of keyboard activity, and nothing more for a while, no conversation. We presumed that the basics of Michael's system was being inputted.  Then there was silence... no keyboard sounds at all.

"Why have you stopped,Trevough?" The voice was Chartham's.

After a few minutes of non communication Michael spoke.

"What have you done with my sister?"

The atmosphere in the office, and in the car changed completely.
"What on earth do you mean, Trevough." It was Flatton's voice.
"We don't know what you are talking about."

"Be quiet, Flatton, you fool. Of course we know what he's talking about."

"So, what have you done with my sister?"
Michael's voice was calm thankfully.

"Your sister is well. Insurance... shall we say!
We'll let her go when you've finished."

Chartham's reply was cold and calculating. His City voice did not show any emotion at all. He was a man who meant business. He was in control.

"I'm not going to do anything more until I hear that my sister is alright!"

Michael had staked his claim to the next move. What would Chartham's response be now. He was quick to reply to Michael's demand.

"Get them on the phone Flatton! Here, use my mobile. And be careful what you say. We don't want young Trevough to find out where she is, do we?"

What followed was a distant conversation from somewhere in the office.
Although all three of us in the car were straining our ears to hear, it was impossible to understand anything that was being said.
After what appeared to be an interminable length of time, Flatton's voice became perfectly clear. He had obviously crossed the office floor, and was now talking directly to Michael.

"Here! Take this. And watch what you say.
Our people at the other end of this line have very strict instructions as to what to do if you step out of line."

Treddick rapidly stopped the car, and switched off the engine, and turned up the volume on his radio, giving us all the best chance to catch even the slightest clue in the conversation that would follow.

"Sam! Is that you? Are you OK? They haven't hurt you, have they?"

"O Michael, what's going on?"
Sam's voice was so clear. It was as though she was in the car with us.
We seemed so close, but yet so far from knowing where she was.

"Sam! Where... this mystery.... is going to end I don't know. Are you sure you are all right? Are you all alone? For... the third... time of asking are you your usual... canny self?"

There had been a slight pause as he had said... where... and mystery... He had emphasised... the third... and very subtly made his voice suggest a question when he said the word... canny.
Would she realise what he was trying to do?
Would that brother sister relationship do the trick?

"Yes, Michael I'm all alone, and feeling very... browned off... I thought I was going to meet you yesterday lunch time. Instead of that I'm sitting here in a room without windows, and I haven't a clue where I am. Are you OK?"

'All alone and browned off,' she had said. She had realised. Clever girl! The dog was not with her. So where was the dog?

"Yes I'm fine. I have to complete something here at work. They say that they will let you go when I finish what they want me to do. So just hold tight and don't do anything silly. Do you understand me?"

"Yes, Michael. I understand. Can you tell Mum and Dad that I'm OK."

On the surface it seemed an innocent enough conversation, or at least that's what I hoped. But it had told us one essential thing. The dog was definitely not with her.

"That's enough! You know she is alright." It was Chartham's voice.
"Now get on with your job here, we haven't got all day."

All we could hear from then on was the sound of a keyboard being attacked very vigorously, and Michael's voice giving instructions to Chartham.
The technical language that he was using meant nothing to the three of us.

Treddick started the car.
We were back on our way to Felixstowe.
Treddick spoke to his London 'ears' and asked them when they had opportunity to study the replay of the part of the conversation when Sam was on the line to see if they could detect any background noises that might give us a clue to her whereabouts.
We had been at the roadside for about ten minutes.
We had not added much to our scheduled arrival time.

We turned eastwards on to the A14, bypassing Ipswich on its southern side.
Soon passing the A12 to Woodbridge on our left.
Felixstowe seven miles.
The road to the docks turned right missing the town centre completely.

Traffic now was very much of the heavy goods container carrier variety. Straight on at the Lower Street roundabout.
And then on towards the container depot.
Treddick stopped, phoned ahead to Customs.
At Dock Gate No2 we were met, and were taken directly to the main Customs Office. The presence of Harry and myself was not questioned.

Treddick had cleared the way.
We were for the moment seen as art experts 'assisting Treddick with his inquiries.' Customs made contact with the depot's office, and through the computerised cargo processing located the whereabouts of the containers we were interested in.
We were soon on our way through the forest of stacked containers.
Smetton's containers were easily identified. They had a distinctive livery.
The two containers that had been there for a few days were at the end of one row, and just as Harry had described, they were nose to tail, doors on the inside. The SSSD was bold enough and the seven figure numbers tallied with what we had on the manifest.
A huge RTG (Rubber Tyred Gantry) container crane lumbered up and spent no time at all in lifting the containers on to a road train that then took them to the Custom's sheds.
There under Customs jurisdiction the containers seals were cut off, and the huge doors opened.

Treddick explained that our immediate interest was in one particular crate load of antique boxes. The container had to be discharged. A fork lift man took over for a while. With real expertise the pallets were being unloaded.
I could see Harry looking with interest as the driver completed his work without fault. The system was very clear. Crates were numbered.
These numbers were checked against the manifest.
Contents were identified. The huge crate containing the Titians was unloaded before the one containing the boxes. I was intrigued by the fact that I was so close to a picture that I had known so well in years gone by, it would be so good to have a look at it again.
The crate containing the enigma boxes was lifted out. Number checked against manifest. Everything correct. Customs started opening the crate.
A Customs officer took a call on his radio. It was the Container Depots main office stating 'did we know that this would be the second time that this container had been opened up in the last couple of weeks? The first

time had not involved Customs at all, it had been the owners who had requested that they add some more items to the manifest.

The young man had had all the right identification, and so had the other visitors who had come to meet him, so the container had been opened then by the depot staff, no queries.'

Treddick looked at me, nodded, and smiled a 'that's interesting' smile.

The lid of the crate was soon off. The fibre insulation board removed.
The contents were being carefully placed on inspection tables.
But the trouble that soon became clear even to the most unpracticed eye was that the boxes were nothing very special at all. Possibly antique but certainly not with the condition and craftsmanship expected of the enigma boxes.

They were a sorry collection of work boxes, many having damaged veneer. Hinges were broken, escutcheon plates missing. Inlay work damaged. They were the sort of boxes that filled the dark recesses of antique shops. Boxes that would never ever be sold for any price at all. For the most part worthless.
There had been a switch! All the priceless enigma boxes had disappeared. And in their place was a load of worthless rubbish.

Who had come, a couple of weeks ago? Was it Terry Berrysford?
If it was, who had he met up with? What had happened that had eventually caused his death? I spoke with Treddick.

"If a switch has taken place here with the enigma boxes, what about the other crates, should we look to see if anything else is suspect?"

Treddick agreed. And we were soon at the task of opening other crates.
In one that was manifested as containing silver candelabra we discovered only bent and broken examples that could only ever have a scrap silver value.
Why had someone bothered to substitute worthless equivalents?

"What about the Titians?" I explained to Treddick my interest.

They were listed as being on loan from the National Gallery, to a private collector who was putting on a show of sixteenth century Italian art. They were to be picked up in Hamburg.

Treddick agreed to have the crate opened up.
Customs set about their task with great care, removing all of the insulation board that surrounded the picture.
I told them that they were dealing with a priceless national treasure.
The painting that I remembered was over ten feet wide. The painting that emerged was over ten feet wide. The painting that I remembered was the family portrait of the Vendramin menfolk. The painting that emerged contained the self same men, and the family dog. The painting I remembered had the once lost reliquary placed high on the altar. The painting that emerged had the self same holy relic in place. The painting I remembered had such marvellous eyes.

This was not the Titian!

The 'eyes' certainly did not have it.
It was a very passable fake.
I looked at it even closer.
The candle flames were not being troubled by the blowing breeze.
Every remembered detail that had so impressed me those many years ago came flooding back into my mind.

This was not the Titian.
What was it that Delacroix had said about Titian's work?
I thought for a moment, and then slowly repeated that great quote.
'... in his work... pictorial qualities are brought to their highest point... what he paints is painted... eyes look and are animated by the fire of life... life and reason are apparent everywhere.'

Harry applauded me.

"Are you sure it's not right?" Treddick asked.
"I'm certain it is a fake. Presumably the other is as well.
But again, who would go to such trouble in getting someone to reproduce a picture to such a degree of accuracy. If you were going to steal it, why bother to fake it?"

"And why has all this been the cause of young Berrysford's death?" Treddick said.

On inquiry we found out that two of the Sotheby's containers were on site already, the others, as we knew, were expected in the next few days. All three of the Christie's containers were there as well. Checking them all, which took a fair amount of time, proved to be a bit of a waste of effort. Against the manifest details everything appeared to be correct. What was on the manifests was in the containers, as far as we could tell.

Treddick told the Customs men to put everything back in order.
He convinced them that it was a police matter and not an issue for Customs control. He thanked them for their cooperation, and said that he may need them again to check the rest of the Sotheby's containers when they arrived.

I wondered if any of them were involved in any way. I took Harry to one side and asked if he had any thoughts on that particular question. 'He didn't think so,' he said, 'they appeared to be as surprised as we were.'
We would have to trust that that was true. If news of our visit to Felixstowe got back to Chartham, both Sam and Michael would be in trouble.

"We must go to the depot office before we leave," Treddick stated. "We must ask what they know about the visitors of a couple of weeks ago."

The office personnel were very helpful. They had their procedures which were very tight. Everyone coming on site had to sign in. We had only escaped that procedure because we had had Customs clearance, they told us.

They found the records of visitors.
There sure enough was Terry Berrysford's signature. He had been there on Tuesday, two weeks ago, the day before his unidentified body had been found in the burnt out car at the side of the road on the diversion in Chelmsford.
The day before I had found the enigma box by the side of the same road.

But it was a signature that was further down the page that caught my eye.
It read 'A. Marsters.'

"Are you sure that spelling is correct," I asked the clerk, pointing to the name in the book. "We need to be absolutely sure."

"O yes, Sir," she replied. "Our security demands that we write out the names in a duplicate book. I remember the man quite well, he said to me 'that's Marsters with two 'Rs.' I'm sure of it, Sir.
Then I put down in my book, the Company name, and the reason for the visit. Would you like to see that?"

Sure enough against A. Marsters was, Company name, Bantock Berrysford and Brownsmoor. Reason for visit. Checking manifest detail.

It was all accompanied by the correct numbers and detail.
Against Terry Berrysford's name were similar details regards Company name, but when it came to, Reason for visit, it stated.
'To add goods to manifest.'
Treddick asked the young lady whether there was anything else that she could recall about that occasion.

"Well yes, there was. You can see that our office here overlooks the visitors car park. I remember that the young man had a big argument with Mr Marsters. The young man had parked his car right there." she pointed out of the window. "He ended up by going with Mr Marsters and he gave his car keys to the other man who was with Mr Marsters, and the other man got into the young man's car and drove away."

Treddick asked who it was who had been signed in with Mr Marsters.
The young clerk looked once again at the visitors book and pointed at the name that was below the 'Marsters' signature.

"It was a Mr R. Charles. And it just says 'with the above,' there's no Company name, or Reason for visit."

"Mr R. Charles. Thank you, young lady, you have been very helpful." Treddick shook her hand. "We can be on our way now. I think we have seen all we need to see here."

He turned to me as soon as we left the office.
"That's a turn up for the books. Eh! Michael. Alan Marsters meets Terry Berrysford here two weeks ago. They give different reasons for being here. They are seen to have an argument. Terry Berrysford leaves with Marsters. And this other guy, Charles, drives off in Terry Berrysford's car, which is later found burnt out on waste ground here in Felixstowe.
The plot definitely thickens. But I don't yet see the connection with what is happening in London."

We were quickly on our way to Southwold.
In the car I explained to Harry, who Alan Marsters was, that Treddick and I had met him at the Berrysford's place, that he was one of the directors of the firm on the finance side.
But what he was up to now, who might know?

Treddick checked in again with regard to Michael's situation at Smetton's and was told that Michael's meeting with Chartham had gone on for a further thirty minutes. They had a full recording of everything said. They had listened in particular to that part when Sam had been on the line, and with a bit of sound enhancement had thought that they could hear sea birds in the background. But nothing more positive. Michael had been warned by Chartham to say nothing and to do nothing out of the ordinary.
If he did, Sam would be in trouble. Michael was back in his own office.

They were still listening in.

## IV

We arrived at John and Stella's in time for a late lunch. Even though they were at their wits end about Michael and doubly stressed out about Sam's disappearance they were still able to provide for us. They dearly wanted to know what the news was. Peters and his team had kept them informed as much as possible.
As far as Sam was concerned there was no further news.
Treddick, as sensitive as ever, put them in the picture fully, trying to convince them that Sam would be alright. Michael was sure to do nothing to put her life in further danger. Treddick told them that we had heard Sam on the phone, in conversation with Michael. Both Harry and I agreed that she sounded alright.
We discussed where we thought she might be, and came to the possible view that she was still somewhere local.
The police listeners had said that they detected the sound of sea birds.

Looking at John and Stella I could see that the strain of things was beginning to show. How long they could keep up this brave face, I didn't know.

John was eager to do something. The inactivity was causing him great anxiety. Treddick's suggestion that we went down to Southwold, was readily accepted. Harry and I would go with John.
Treddick said that he would meet up with his crew and get an up to date briefing from them, and then see us later, back at John and Stella's about seven o'clock.
Treddick's firm instruction was to search in an innocent fashion, and to be very careful. If we saw anything of interest, we were to note it and return with the information. He underlined the fact that we must not get involved in any situation. Nor create one by being foolish. He asked where we thought we might go.
John and I, after a little thought, agreed that a search along the beach, passing the beach huts and going on towards the river Blyth, might be a route that was as effective as any other.

We had three hours.
John made speedy progress to Southwold. He parked, and we were very quickly into our stride heading for the beach.
But what were we looking for? Whoever had taken Sam would not put up a notice that said 'here she is.'
'Look casual,' that was the final piece of advice that Treddick had given us.

How on earth do you look casual, when you are searching for someone who has been forcibly taken, whose situation and safety you know nothing about?
How on earth do you remain casual, when someone you care about is in danger? First of all, we decided that we must slow down.
Although there was an urgency to know. We had to be careful.
We must be casual in our approach so that we did not alert anyone.
We took to throwing stones into the sea.
Harry was by far the best.
We passed the beach huts with their crazy personalised names...
Happy Days.. Sandpiper... All Mine... Here's Hoping... Linga Longa...
We went up top along Gunhill cliff and on towards the Marshes.

Could she be in one of those? Not very likely.
Most were occupied and even this early in the season there were plenty of folk still enjoying the late afternoon sunshine.
Harry proved very good at getting into conversation. He asked innocent questions about the sea and the weather and visitors.
All the while we were looking and listening for any clue that might suggest a less than easy answer.
Were any of the people we saw, attempting to hide anything, anyone?
Surely there was no reason to suspect any of the mixed group of happy go lucky folks we saw here?
Anyway the walls of the huts were far too thin. And they were so close together. The place was far too crowded and busy, at all times of the day.

We progressed on towards the camping and caravan site.
Now that, we all thought, was a possibility.
But still there were plenty of people about, the noise wasn't simply of sea birds. There was the sound of human activity, babies crying, excited children shouting, laughing, dogs barking, all the regular holiday campsite stuff.
We did not venture in. We agreed that three strangers wandering around the tents and caravans might provoke more interest than we wanted.

The River Blyth has on its northern bank a great deal of light industry, most of which is connected to boats, be they fishing or pleasure. I knew that this spot that we were approaching would give rare opportunity for concealment. Such a mixture, in some places there were tumbledown boats, decaying old wrecks and discarded sea going paraphernalia, and

in others, most expensive cruisers and yachts and fishing boats of all different classes.
Sheds old and new, in varying states of dilapidation.
But as we walked its length we saw nothing that was out of the ordinary.

Although it was good to be active in the search for Sam, it was getting more and more obvious to Harry and myself that John was not coping too well.
What had started out with a sense of purpose, was rapidly becoming a source of increasing distress. He became more and more disconsolate and depressed.
We walked on quickly, and were soon on the road that would take us back down to Southwold, passing the golf course and the water towers and then inevitably the spot where Sam's car was still parked.
We couldn't see Peters and his crew who were well concealed in their surveillance task. We dared not stop as we came to the car, just in case we might attract attention from any others who might be watching.
In all the time that Sam had now been missing no one had approached her car. Peters confirmed that every time he reported in.
John had become silent, his thoughts were his own.
We concluded our walk through the town and were quick to retrace our steps to where John's car was parked. He got in and opened the doors for Harry and myself, he said nothing, but his face betrayed the deep anxiety that was breaking his heart. We had gained nothing from our hopeless search.

He drove home at speed.
We were back well before our stated time of seven o'clock. Treddick was there. He had spent most of his time with Stella, probably far more profitably than we had spent ours, she seemed a lot calmer. She was quick to comfort John, urging him still to be hopeful of the outcome of things.

Treddick informed Harry and myself that we must be on our way back. He still had things to check out at the London end.
We said our goodbyes to John and Stella and were on our way directly.
The journey back was uneventful and fast, and for the most part we travelled in silence.


Treddick dropped us off at a little after ten thirty, saying that he would check in with me sometime Friday morning. Harry left straight away without coming into the house, he too confirming that he would still be available to help in any way he could, should he be needed. I asked him to apologise to May for me keeping him away for such a long time.

"Good night Harry, and thanks."
"Any time. Cheers. See you later."

There was a message from Michael on the answerphone.
It simply asked that I should ring him whatever time I got back in.
He was quick to answer my return call.

Each of us had much to tell the other. Our days had been totally different.
Michael was surprised to hear that we had listened in to all his conversation with Chartham. And he found it difficult to imagine that we had shared the intimacy of his call to Sam. He asked me how I thought she sounded, and in all honesty I confirmed what both Harry and I had told his parents, that she appeared to be OK and not in too much distress. I told him of the outcome of the Felixstowe visit, amazing him with the apparent audacity of those involved with that part of the crime, the fake Titian, the scrap silverware and the substitute boxes. I told him of the visit of Terry Berrysford and Alan Marsters and the argument. He asked how things were at home in Southwold.

My retelling of the story of our ineffective search and of his father's deepening mood of despondency caused him to express his own sense of increasing anxiety. He told me of his awareness of the powerful manipulation that was evident in Chartham's control of things at Smettons.
He confirmed that he must now be watchful of events to an even greater degree, because there was something quite cold and calculating in Chartham's approach to him.

To my question concerning his proposed movements up to and over the weekend he replied that Friday would be a regular day at work and that Saturday and Sunday would be spent watching events. He wouldn't explain what he meant by that but reminded me of his many skills and how that Smettons had after all employed him to facilitate all manner of secure systems. I reminded him once again to be careful, and asked whether he was still 'wired' to which the answer was 'yes, but that he could switch things on if he were in a situation that demanded that others should hear what was going on.' We spoke more of our concern for Sam.

My attempt at reassurance did not sound too convincing.

We closed our conversation, telling each other to be careful.

I slept and dreamt of haunting themes that kept me on the edge of fear.
I could hear the clinical ice cold tones of Chartham and see the menace of an arguing Marsters.
John was there, but disappeared all too often into a black and distant place and Stella reached for him with long white fingers.

Michael and Harry threw stones far into the sea.
And Sam... Sam was but a little child of eight or nine... on a remembered beach in Cornwall... she was dancing bare foot on shimmering golden sand.
She danced, oblivious to the fact that others watched her... she was sylph like... wraith like... her long blond hair flowing free... her arms entwining would reach for clouds and sunshine... she moved herself with young seductive grace to nature's windblown music... skies darkened into night and still she danced, inviting stars... and moon... and Lara... and me... to join her in her dance of... death!

I woke at once in panic, afraid to move, lest everything were true.

B e     s a f e     S a m !     P l e a s e     b e  safe.

Treddick phoned early on Friday morning informing me that 'forensic' had released Terry Berrysford's body to the family, and that the funeral would be on Monday at eleven. Old man Berrysford had particularly asked if I could be there. Treddick would be going and would be pleased to take me if I could be up in Chelmsford by ten o'clock.

I agreed, for two quite opposing and complicated reasons.
The first, a simple statement of respect.
The second, an opportunity to see Marsters, he must surely attend.
What did I know of this man? I had met him just the one time at Berrysford's place. His only worry then was that news of the manner of Terry's death would be 'bad publicity' for the firm.
He had not shown grief, or shock, it was the financial repercussions that he was worried about.
He had visited the container depot at Felixstowe with another associate.
He was seen having an argument with Terry Berrysford.
Terry left Felixstowe with Marsters.
And the associate had taken Terry's car, which was later found gutted by fire on wasteland in Felixstowe.

There was no other conclusion to reach save that Marsters was heavily involved in the whole thing, including Terry's death.
Apart from the regular contact with Smettons, was there a deeper connection with the sinister Chartham?
How did this whole thing come together?

Harry phoned, '... would I like a game or two to take my mind off things for a while? May was baking and I would be welcome to go back to their place to enjoy the delights of her home cooking.'
It sounded good to me.

Treddick phoned again on Saturday.
Customs from Felixstowe had been in touch, the rest of the containers had arrived and had been grouped with all of the others.
Everyone in authority had been alerted to look out for anything out of the ordinary. Staff in the Quay office, from their commanding view point which was almost like an airport control tower, were watching for unusual visitors.
They would be in constant touch with the Felixstowe Dock and Railway Company Police Department, which was a twenty four hour policing operation. The police on the gate were also in the picture, every security tag would be checked and double checked with their usual polite precision.
The Felixstowe Cargo Processing Office had received information from someone at Smettons that a small container ship would be docking and would they please process the onward transit of the containers in question as soon as possible, Monday was the preferred date as there was a deadline to be met.

Events were being very tightly scrutinised at Felixstowe.
Treddick would be informed of any slight deviation from usual procedures.
Customs had told Treddick that no actual offence had yet been committed upon which they could act. They suggested that the crime, if there was one, was still in preparation, and that further onward surveillance would be advised. Treddick told me that he had already set things in motion with regard policing of any off loading on the continent, and also any onward transmission further afield.

We would all have to wait.
That was the agonising part of the whole affair.
The waiting.
And all the time we waited, Sam was held somewhere as insurance.

Saturday turned out to be a very long day.

I kept in touch with John and Stella throughout the day but there was no more news of Sam.
And nothing to report from Peters.
And no, they had not heard any more from Michael.
I had actually phoned him a couple of times at his home, but there had been no reply. Whatever he was up to, he was keeping very quiet about it.

My night's sleep was interrupted by the insistent ringing of my phone.

It took a while to realise that that was what it was. It was John. He first of all apologised for the fact that the time was only four o'clock in the morning but he was sure that I would want to know.

Canny had come back home.
Exhausted, soaking wet, hungry and hurt.
The dog's whimpering outside the back door had woken the pair of them just a half hour before. Stella had dried Canny off and cleaned up some wounds on his paws and the dog was now eating as though he hadn't eaten for days.

Should they ring Treddick and let him know?
I told them that I didn't think that was necessary at this hour but that they should tell him at a more respectable hour later in the morning.
Canny coming back home was a good bit of news.
If only he could tell us what had happened.
We talked for a while, then wished each other well.

But what can you do when you are woken unexpectedly at four o'clock in the morning? Your body tells you that it is still time for sleep, but your mind wont let you. My thoughts raced through all the many developing situations, finally settling on this most recent piece of news.
Maybe Canny could help.
The bond between the dog and Sam was so obvious. This I had seen when first meeting up with them.
When we had walked together I remembered that Canny always brought the interesting things that he had found back to Sam.
A bit of old plastic rope dropped at her feet, enticing her to play tug of war.

A stick inviting first a throw and then a chase to retrieve.
I convinced myself that Canny did know where Sam was.
Canny could lead us to her.

At five o'clock I cooked myself a huge breakfast. I ate it with real eagerness. At this unheard of time on a Sunday morning I was alert to the possibility that something good had actually come our way.
Something positive.
For the first time in a long while I was feeling cautiously optimistic.
Canny would, not could, lead us to Sam.

I determined to travel on to Southwold after Terry Berrysford's funeral on Monday. Together with John and Stella and Brown Mystery the Third, we would discover where Sam was.

For some unaccountable reason my mind was gripped by the thought of the funeral I would be attending on Monday. I had not been to one for five years.
The last had been Lara's. I did not know how I would react.
There was to be a service at the cemetery chapel, and then the committal.
Echoes from the past would be sounded.
Terry's death had been a violent one, his young life snuffed out by someone's evil design. Was that someone Marsters? If it was Marsters, how would he react at the funeral? Would he hold on to his composure, or would he betray the fact that he had been involved?

Around lunchtime I tried to get Michael on the phone.
There was still no reply. What was he up to?

After lunch, I called Harry. I put him in the picture. 'What about a trip to the club, just social, with May?' Harry and May both thought that it would be a great idea.
Sunday ended with a degree or two less stress, for which I was thankful.

On my return I discovered an intriguing message from Michael on the answerphone.
'Uncle Michael, I've been at work over the weekend, preparing one or two little surprises for you know who.
I've also phoned Mum and Dad, they told me that Canny came home.
But there's still no news of Sam.
Leave me a message in the usual way if you want to get in touch.'

I did as he suggested, telling him of my intention to go up to Southwold on Monday after the funeral. I told him also of my hopes concerning the possibility of using Canny to find Sam.
I asked him whether he was aware of the fact that the remaining containers were now at Felixstowe, and did he know that someone from Smetton's had told Felixstowe that a small container ship would be docking over the weekend for their rapid onward transit, and that there was a good chance that everything was ready for the green light.
And, as always, that he should be careful.
And for reasons completely unknown to me at the time, I gave him Harry's phone number as well.

Thinking to myself that tomorrow would be a very full day, I decided on an early night, and, unusually for me, was in bed by ten thirty.

The trip up to Chelmsford on Monday morning was uneventful. I was beginning to know the route very well indeed. I was at the police station in good time and was met by Treddick.
We made our way to the cemetery and were there well ahead of the family and other mourners.
We did what people always do in cemeteries. We walked and looked.

Cemeteries are strange places. In some parts there is a trim correctness of lawns cut by clinicians in the art of tidiness, and in other parts there is the very obvious sign of a lack of attention. Broken gravestones, decaying flowers. Memorials that you read give stark attention to family history.

Some offer classic poetry and others unintentional humour.
Added names of those who followed after. 'Here lies the body of...' and then further down the marble slab 'and now his beloved wife. At last on top!'

We both stopped at a headstone that read.
>    'God my redeemer lives, and ever from the skies,
>    Looks down and watches all my dust.
>    Till He shall bid it rise.'

My view of God was typical of my upbringing and experience. I didn't bother Him much and He didn't bother me. I had expressed deep bitterness and sometimes a very explosive anger when Lara died. I had found then that I was directing my anger at a God 'who was supposed to care.'

Treddick, who was by my side, broke the silence.

"Do you believe in God, Michael? Do you think that He looks upon us now? Can you believe that He is concerned for our welfare and our future?"

It took me quite unawares. I stumbled over an answer. I'd not been forced to think in such a way for these last five years.

Before I had time to reply, and perhaps fortunately for me, others started arriving. Most of the mourners had parked where we had parked, way out of view of the chapel, and were walking together towards us.
It was just the hearse and the one family limousine that pulled up at the sheltered entrance to the chapel.
The only people whose faces I knew were the ones Treddick and I had met at Berrysford's place. Jack and Joanna Berrysford were helped carefully out of the limousine by a very gracious attendant. They were followed by Faye Berrysford, Terry's wife, and then Bertie Bantock.
Alan Marsters and Moira Brownsmoor were in the walking party and came together, arm in arm, heavy in conversation.

Treddick met my glance. We were both wondering if we were in the presence of a murderer. Marsters appeared totally calm. His conversation ceased as he joined the family. Moira Brownsmoor, looking far younger than I had at first thought, was attentive to the obvious change of mood presented by his silence. Flowers were off loaded from the hearse. Floral tributes of all sorts described affection, love, and that eternal promise of remembrance.

I had not noticed all these things when last I was involved in such an event.
It had all been so personal. Lara's death had occurred in winter.
I remembered most of all the cold freezing wind. It had matched my frozen feelings. But now, there was a warmth in the early spring sun, and though there was the obvious signs of bitter grief, people all around were watching for opportunity for real consolation. Several who passed by the Berrysfords on their way into the chapel reached out a hand to touch them, others offered looks of deep concern. Even Marsters

managed a sort of smile of acknowledgement as he went on in to the chapel.

It was, for the most part, the younger people who showed the greatest grief. Terry after all was only in his late twenties, and Faye perhaps a year or two younger. She bravely kept tears at bay, showing a maturity and composure far greater than her years.
The organ music was of gentle sound, thankfully not strident in any way. Treddick and I moved on in, and as we came to pass Jack Berrysford, he moved towards us, and with a graciousness that was so genuine, thanked us both for being there.
We stood together, with all who had gone before, maybe a hundred or so people of varying ages, awaiting the entrance of the simple coffin.
A young cleric led the procession in. The coffin, carried a little hesitantly by four young men, who must surely be Terry's friends, then the family, just the three of them, Jack Berrysford flanked on the one side by his wife and on the other side by his daughter in law.

What can you say about funerals? They are sombre affairs.
But here there was real dignity and truthfulness being expressed. I found myself actually listening to what the young cleric was saying. There was no false intoning or deliberate manipulation of feelings, just a simple honesty that required us all to reach for something more beyond the brutality of the circumstances of Terry's death. This young cleric dared us all to reach out for consolation and a compassion that might be discovered through the love of the Almighty God. It was obvious that he knew Terry very well indeed, he spoke of his friendship with both Terry and Faye. There were real sentiments of lasting worth spoken of with intensity and passion. Hymns were sung, and sung well. The music reached warm crescendos, inviting all present to seek for nobler things.
I'd come out of duty and curiosity, and with a firm intention to watch the reactions of at least one of the mourners present. I found myself reliving sad moments of my past and actually receiving comfort, albeit five years too late.
Of all the voices raised in the singing of the hymns, Treddick's was one of the strongest. He stood beside me showing a stature that was quite challenging. There was more to this man than I had at first realised.
Where did he find his inner strength? And why had he responded so willingly to my demands upon his time?

The service concluded and we processed in silence to a nearby open grave.

It was obviously a family plot.
There was a headstone that had been removed, lying by itself.
The inscriptions bore the Berrysford name already.
The committal was a straightforward affair, more prayers, especially for the family, followed by a time of quiet reflection and remembrance.
We moved to where the many flowers were on show.
I couldn't help but notice the note that was attached to one of the most beautiful displays. It read. 'To my darling Terry Berry. All my love, Faye. Thanks for all the good times.'

So much of what had been said had the ring of truth. This young man was no criminal. He was a cruel victim of someone else's greed.
I determined there and then to add the justice of his cause to my endeavours.

"You will come back to the house, won't you?"

It was Joanna Berrysford who spoke.

"Why yes, of course." I replied.

People were gradually moving away from the grave side. There was gentle conversation and at times hesitant laughter. Treddick and I followed on towards the car park, agreeing together that going to the house for a while would be a good opportunity to complete any further watch on Marsters.
We carried on in silence.

Treddick roughly interrupted my quiet moment, gripping me forcibly with a strong restraining hand, forcing me to stop.
We both stood stark still and watched as Alan Marsters and Moira Brownsmoor climbed into a silver grey 4.2 Jaguar Sovereign.

There it was, this vehicle that told all the world how luxurious it was, how refined, and with such great quality, such comfort, and grace.
Over the last five years I had built up a complete reference picture of this particular model.
Impressed forever in my memory was the impact of its near 4000lbs weight on the drivers door of Lara's little red Polo.
The sleek Jaguar shape, why, I even knew why Sir William Lyons had chosen that name for his new car, way back in 1935. He had rung his advertising department and asked them to supply him with a list of names of insects animals and birds and fish. He was given within the

hour a list a some five hundred creatures. Lyons made his choice. 'I like the sound of Jaguar... it has everything we want... power... speed and grace.'

And the ability to kill!
Lyons never added that to his list of virtues for his precious Jaguar.

Marsters drew away, with Moira Brownsmoor in the back seat.
As the car passed us by she turned to look in our direction. Everything became so clear to me. It was the self same car that had driven away at speed the day that I had found the box, the day that Terry Berrysford had been murdered. It was Moira Brownsmoor's face that had looked at me then as it was her face now that stared me out. And yes, radio aerial on the right hand side, though not extended, and telephone aerial on the left.

"Is that the car?" Treddick asked.

"Without a doubt!" I replied. "They are both involved up to their necks in this whole affair. What are we going to do now?"
"First we must be calm. We must do as we have planned to do. Joanna Berrysford has invited us back to her home. We must be sensitive to the needs of the family. And we must be eyes open to every move that Marsters and Moira Brownsmoor might make. Michael, this is going to demand real caution on our part, remember that Marsters may be involved in murder."

It seemed bizarre to think that someone who had just attended the funeral of a young man murdered in cold blood, whose body had been cruelly set on fire, could just possibly be the actual murderer.

As Treddick drove us the few miles to the Berrysfords' elegant home, I couldn't help but wonder what I was letting myself into.
This sort of situation may well have been within the regular pattern of things for Treddick, but for me... my mind failed to grasp the enormity of it all.
What on earth were the two unlikely partners in crime up to, and what had happened that had demanded that Terry Berrysford lose his life? And what was the link with Michael and Chartham?

We reached the home and drew into the palatial driveway.
There ahead of us, neatly parked, was the Jaguar.

Treddick parked some distance from it.
As I got out of Treddick's car, and walked passed that sleek lined Series Three, towards the house, I shuddered to think of all that a similar car to this had done to my life. I moved my hand across its polished chrome grille, to its low, streamlined bonnet, beneath which were the six in line cylinders, twin overhead camshaft engine developing 200 BHP at 5000 revs.
I could see inside.There they were, the luxurious leather seats and headrests, and the polished walnut dash board. I experienced an evil sensuousness as my hand felt the warmth of the recently moving engine. Its beauty, I knew, could seduce me into some form of forgiveness.
But I took my hand away, and as I did, the loathing of this cat like creature of death returned.
It was all that I could do to stop myself from inflicting damage.

Treddick, I could see, was understanding a little of what was going on, and with a discerning glance, and a hand on mine, he lead me away towards the house. I could not say a word.

"Bad memories! Eh!" He spoke quietly. "Perhaps one day, Michael, you will break the hold it has on you."

The doors were open. A member of the staff led us through to where a lavish luncheon was spread out.

On a glorious Jacobean oak refectory table there were cold meats. And next to it an oak and mahogany, cross banded dresser base that held a great variety of salads. All the priceless surfaces in this unbelievably beautiful room were in use as serving areas, holding wine, and cutlery, and glasses and plates.
The very best was being used in a generous outpouring of affection for the newly buried son of this household.
The place was already crowded with people eager to offer shared memories of Terry, in conversations that would be remembered long in the more subdued moments that would inevitably follow.

The Berrysfords were talking quietly with a small group of elderly folk who were seated in one corner of the room. Jack Berrysford noticed our arrival and immediately excused himself from the seated group and made his way towards us.

"Joanna and I are so pleased that you could come," he said, "it means so much to us to know that you are trying so hard to get to the bottom of this dreadful affair. Terry was a good son. He never did anything to make us feel ashamed. He was so full of life. Can you tell us anything more? Is there any progress at all?"

"Well yes." Treddick replied, "there are a number of useful leads that we are following. I'm sure that we will discover the truth, in time. We will keep you in touch with our progress."

Little did Jack Berrysford know that the subject of one of those useful leads was right here in the room. At the exact moment in time that Treddick was speaking I could see Alan Marsters out of the corner of my eye, in the far corner by the open window, he was speaking on his mobile phone.
The conversation appeared to be quite animated.
Moira Brownsmoor was in close attendance.

"You will excuse me won't you," Berrysford said, "there are so many people I must speak to. And do help yourselves to the food."

"Thank you. We will."

We did. It was a splendid spread. No expense had been spared.
We found space at a beautiful Sheraton table that was occupied by Bertie Bantock, one of the partners in the firm.
He was alone and obviously deep in thought.

"May we join you?"

He readily agreed, inviting us to sit in the two remaining, beautifully carved Sheraton style bergere chairs that were beside him.
He looked a lonely figure, half empty glass in hand, half empty bottle of a very good claret on the table.

"Will you join me?" he put down his glass and took up the bottle.

"No! No thanks!" we both chorused almost in unison.
"We wont be staying long."

"You know we did all this eight years ago...
Right here in this same room...
The furniture is different of course.

But the sense of real occasion is just the same...
It was when Freddie died... Fred Brownsmoor, you know, our partner.
Jack and I said that we must give him a good send off... He had only been married for just over a year... That was his second marriage.
Moira didn't know what to do, she was such a flighty thing.
Jack and I took control. It was just like this.
Look at her over there with Marsters. I never know what they are up to."

It was obvious to both Treddick and me that the very good claret that Bertie Bantock was downing was making him very talkative.
He needed someone to share his thoughts. We needed someone to tell us more. Treddick obviously favoured the direct approach.

"How long has Alan Marsters been with the firm?"

"Two and a half years." Bantock replied. "Friend of Moira's. Came in with all his computer stuff, talking about modernising our procedures. Profit sharing, cost effectiveness, loss adjustments and all that... It's beyond me."

Bantock filled his glass again, and drank slowly.

"Is he a partner in the firm?' Treddick inquired.

"O no! He's just finance... There's just the three of us... Jack, myself, and of course Moira. She inherited Fred's shares... She doesn't do much in the business of things... She doesn't know a thing about antiques... Her only interest is the value. The higher the better... Terry was going to become a partner... If only all this hadn't happened."

"Did Terry get on alright with Alan Marsters?" Treddick asked, getting very direct.

"He didn't see too much of him," Bantock replied. "You see, Terry was always out and about on the road, buying the stuff. He had a real nose for the business. Jack had taught him all he knew... Jack was so proud of him."

That thought caused Bantock to heave a great sigh. Tears came to his eyes.

"I loved him like a son as well. I never married, you know.

Never had the time, so I told myself in the early days...
Too late now...
Who would have me? Who would marry old Bertie Bantock?
Worth a small fortune... but all alone!
Who am I going to leave it all to now? Now that Terry is dead..."

"Did they get on? No not very well.
You see Jack had taught Terry all the old time respectful ways.
Buyers and sellers were always treated with respect.
Alan Marsters and Moira were against Terry becoming a partner, said he was far too young."

Faye Berrysford approached us, tired eyed and still a little tearful. She put her arm around Bantock's shoulders and gently kissed his cheek.

"How are you doing Uncle Bertie?" She spoke with real affection in her voice. "Wasn't it a lovely service?"
That put an end to our conversation.
She turned to Treddick and said in a most determined voice.

"You will find out who killed my Terry, won't you?"

"We are doing our very best Mrs Berrysford."

Treddick sounded confident and reassuring. I could only hope that progress was being made. What we had understood from our conversation with Bertie Bantock was that things had not been all that good between Terry and Alan Marsters. With all the rest of the information that we had there seemed to be a case to be put against Marsters. But did that case include murder?
My thinking was interrupted as I saw Alan Marsters and Moira speaking with Jack and Joanna Berrysford.
It looked as though they were saying their goodbyes. They were departing together. I wondered what they might be up to, leaving so soon.
They paused at our table, saying goodbye to both Faye and Bantock.
With hardly a glance at Treddick or myself they left. Left to go where?
Jack Berrysford came over and explained to Faye.

"They said that something had cropped up, some unfinished business they must attend to. They have to journey up to somewhere in Suffolk.

They were sorry to leave."

Treddick moved uneasily in his chair.
I froze.
Jack Berrysford took Faye by the arm and led her over to join Joanna.
As they left our company he was asking her to stay with them overnight, suggesting that it would be a help to Joanna as well, if she would.
Bertie Bantock poured himself the last of the claret.
A decision had been made for Treddick and myself.
It was time for our departure as well.
We had more than fulfilled the respectful role.
And more than acquainted ourselves with the information that we required.
We said our goodbyes to the almost sleeping Bantock.
Then we promised our ongoing help to the Berrysfords.
We exited with both haste and decorum, not wanting to cause any suspicion as to why we had thought it time for us to go.
We were at least ten minutes behind Marsters and Moira Brownsmoor.
We could not, of course, be sure that they were on their way to Southwold.
But Treddick thought it wise to telephone Peters to look out for the 4.2 Jaguar. Treddick drove at speed back to the police station where my vehicle was parked. He told me on the way that there were things that he must organise. He knew also that nothing would prevent me from going to Southwold. He simply told me to be cautious, and that he would contact me at John and Stella's, and that he would come as quickly as he could.
The firmness of his handshake, as I climbed into my Transit, confirmed my growing awareness of this man's friendship.
I knew that he would do all that he could for Sam's welfare.
Surely we were not going to be too late.
I drove out of the police yard, praying that the road would be clear.
Praying that we would be in time.

Praying...

The road was reasonably clear. I made good time. Given a long stretch of road the Transit can sit nicely nudging eighty. The A12 provided such stretches. There was plenty of water at Blythburgh, the tide was obviously in, how amazing the change it makes, all those acres of mud transformed into a glistening, rippling mirror of light.

Throughout the whole journey I had seen no sign of the Jaguar. Were our suspicions correct? Had they come to this same spot?

I drew in to John and Stella's at just about five.
Canny did hear my arrival.
He wasn't so fast on his toes but he was there to meet me as I got out.
So too was John.
He saw the look of urgency on my face.

"What's up? Michael. Tell me what has happened."
"Is Stella in?" John nodded.
I continued, "then let me tell the pair of you together."

We went through to the kitchen, Canny fussing for attention, even from me.
The kettle was already on the stove.
Stella gave me a hug. Her eyes told a story that already had anxiety as its main theme. I was about to add considerably to the weight of that.

"I've just come from Terry Berrysford's funeral." I said. "I was there with John Treddick. It was a deeply moving occasion. So many people were there in support of the family. But both Treddick and I believe that because of what we saw and heard when we were at the Berrysfords' house afterwards, that we know for certain who is involved in Sam's disappearance. We think that people who work with and for Terry's father are involved. The trouble is, we think that they are on their way here, right now."

My bluntness did nothing to improve the anxiety levels in the household.
Stella, ashen white, collapsed. John caught her just in time, guiding her to a chair, where she sat in a forlorn pose, her world in despair.

"The police have been told by Treddick to be on the lookout.
Peters and his crew know all about the new turn of events. They should be watching for the car right now. If, as we believe, Sam is being held somewhere very near the coast here in Southwold, then there is only the one road in. We must think positively about this. This car will lead us to her. I'm sure of it."

John and Stella were not so sure. They were unable to speak.

The phone ringing broke the anguished silence that had descended on us all. It was Treddick. John answered. 'Police patrols, including a surveillance helicopter, had been set up. They had watched the progress of the Jaguar all the way up the A12. It had turned off and was now parked at The Maltings in Snape. The couple had got out of the car and were deep in conversation with an unknown third party, a male, who had just arrived.
The situation was being monitored very carefully. Treddick was in the helicopter and would reach Southwold very soon.' He rang off.

I could sense a slight rise in the confidence level. Not much, but Stella got to her feet and busied herself with making some coffee.
I told John of my plan to use Canny, and would he please let me go right now to see if the dog knew where Sam was. He hesitated at first but then reluctantly agreed, urging me first to drink the coffee that Stella had made.
He got Canny's lead.
The dog realised what was on offer and was quick to respond.
John held Canny tightly, lifted his head and began speaking softly.

"Find Sam! Canny! Find Sam!' He began to sob, 'Canny! Find Sam!"

The dog was alert and licking John's face. With every mention of Sam's name Canny responded with an eager grunt.
John and Stella agreed with me that they must stay to coordinate things with Treddick when he arrived. Would I please, please be careful.

Canny came with me.

We both jumped into the Transit.
We were off.
The short journey was completed, and with little time lost I was quickly parked, not too far from where I could see Sam's car.
I looked about but could not see Peters or the others. Presumably they were on watch somewhere on the road leading into the town.
I got out, shut and locked the doors, and put the lead on Canny.
The dog began pulling straight away.
He headed directly to Sam's car.
He was whining and barking in a muffled sort of way.
He jumped up and pawed the windows of the car.
I hoped fervently that no one was watching what was going on right now.

"Canny! Find Sam! Find Sam! Where is she? Canny! Find Sam!"

The dog gave me a questioning sort of look.
His head cocked to one side as if he was working out whether or not I was to be trusted. He barked right in my face.

The big dog stood still, a violent shudder shook his body.
He started whining again, he turned in the direction of the water towers and made off purposefully, at a steady pace.    He nosed around the padlocked gate that secured entry to the old tower. I looked through the fence and could see that it would have been an effective hiding place, but there was no other apparent interest shown by the dog. And it really was too far away from the sea. Canny relieved himself and made off once again, passing the adjacent new tower with no interest whatsoever. His nose first tight on the ground then up high sniffing the air.
He pulled me from side to side of the road that ran down towards the sea.
On either side of the road there were the drainage dikes that controlled the water levels in the the Town Marshes, these were occasionally crossed by rickety wooden bridges. He was sniffing them all out.
Taking me this way and that.
I couldn't tell whether he was following the route taken by Sam and her captors or whether he was following his own wanderings of the previous days. I began to wonder if my plan was going to work. He turned back on himself. And for a while he took me right across the Marshes to the path that led from the Town to the Harbour Inn. He followed that for a while but then darted to his right, along a track that led back to the road, close once again to the clubhouse. I decided that I would choose the direction at that point.
I pulled him quite roughly in the the direction of the golf club.
But he showed no interest whatsoever.
I let him have his head again, and he was off once more, this time taking me further down the road towards the river Blyth.
The roadway ends at the river, with car parking and a rough track turning left and right. A few houses to the right and buildings more to do with the boat building and fishing activities to the left.
Canny took me first down behind the Harbour Inn. There were tables and children's play things. He nosed around there for a while.
The path across the Marshes met the road at this point.
We came to the harbour side of the Inn.
I noticed the sign on the wall that showed the level that the flood water reached in 1953. It was impossible to imagine what the picture would

have been like then. You would have seen no river at all. Only a new coastline stretching deep inland.

Canny was definitely interested in all sorts of things at this point. He was keen to be off the lead, but I thought better of it. To lose sight of him now would be disastrous.
What kept crossing my mind was that only just over two weeks previously, John Stella, Sam and myself, plus the dog, had walked here with a sense of real joy in prospect, having made the decision to get in touch with Michael.
We had walked on up river to the bridge and gone on to Walberswick.
What a difference now.
And only four days ago I was at this very spot with John and Harry.
We had failed to find Sam then, why should I succeed now.
But I did have Canny.
And he was eager for something. He had started that whimpering again.
Looking at the river I could see that the tide was not quite full.
It was still on the way in.
I always got a feeling of awe when I watched the sea and everything to do with it. That feeling engulfed me right at this moment.
The different craft, some ready for seaward journeys, others on shore awaiting paint and refit. Some up for sale.
Lifting cranes that could launch boats with ease.
There were still people about.
Some on board their expensive yachts and cruisers, others going about their seabourne trade, fishermen and boat builders.

Could Sam be here?
Canny was definitely up to something, he was straining hard against my hand.
I walked him forward. First to one building then the next.
There was the strong smell of the sea.
How could Canny detect that rare human odour amongst all of this?
Still he led me on.
We passed the Harbour Master's Office close to the water's edge.
Then we came to some boat building units.
Canny began to bark. Loudly, insistently. I tried to quieten him.
He was dragging me with his massive animal strength towards one building in particular.

"Damn dog was here last week, making a nuisance of himself."

A soft spoken Suffolk voice surprised me from behind.

"I'm glad you've got hold of him now... The Harbour Master very nearly called the police... but we couldn't catch him.... We thought he'd come from the caravan park... Kept running away... Looked pretty vicious when we got him cornered once, but he made off back there over the wire, boy did he yelp. Now you keep hold of him. He looks pretty skittish even now."

I turned to discover a man of middle age high above me on the decking of a fishing boat, there he was in paint spattered faded blue denim, brush still in hand. He carried on with his job, taking no further notice of Canny or myself.
I tried to quieten Canny down, but it was not much use.

I called out to the man.

"Do you know who owns this unit? It looks deserted, not much activity. If its not in use, I might be interested in renting it."

I tried to sound convincing in my lie.

"O! That's Old Eric's place..." he replied without even turning his head.
"He had a stroke a couple of months ago... his missus wants to sell it... but I think you're too late. There were a couple of fellas around last week going in and out... They brought a young lady with them once... laughing and joking they were. Didn't see the going of any of them... It's all locked up now.
One of the fellas came yesterday, but he left pretty quick...
Harbour Master might know..."

"Thanks!" I said.

The huge double doors on the front of the building were securely locked with a hasp and padlock that looked very new.
No entry there except without making a lot of noise.
Around the side there was another door, this too was firmly shut.

Canny was sniffing about at the base of the door and trying very hard to dig his way in. I was sure that if I'd let him get on with it he would have been inside in no time at all. He was seriously interested.
And so was I.

The windows were covered over on the inside with what looked like tarpaulins. There was no way of seeing into the building.

But what I couldn't do in the daylight with all the bustle that was going on,
I knew I could do a little later on.
I would need a little assistance.
I felt sure that Stella could supply all I needed.
I pulled Canny away with some difficulty. And marched him off back the way we had come. He was turning his head and complaining bitterly.
It was all that I could do to lead him away.
I hurried as best I could back to the bus, and was quickly heading back to John and Stella's wondering if Treddick would be there. I knew that if he was there with them he would be sure to refuse me leave to do what I was already planning. Fortunately he had not arrived.
Both John and Stella were anxious to hear what I had found out.

Had I been successful?
Well not really.
But!

"Stella, have you got a tin of treacle?" I asked. "A full one preferably. And also an old tea towel that you don't want?"

"Yes. I have both," an astonished Stella replied. "But what on earth for?"

"I'm going back later to do a little breaking and entering, and I don't want to make too much noise. I think I may be on to something. Canny was certainly interested in one of the locked up units down at the Harbour. And a guy painting his boat said that he had seen a couple of fellows and a young woman going into the same unit some time last week.
I know it's just a hunch I have, but I must satisfy my curiosity.
Has Treddick been in touch any more?
I don't want to be around when he turns up. He will only say no to my plan."

"Michael, you're not thinking of doing anything silly are you?" It was John, in the sternest of voices.

"No! You know me. I just want to see inside that unit. What about Treddick?"

"Yes he has called us. He's been delayed. But he will be here this evening. The car has not moved from The Maltings. The three people concerned are having a meal. They will be watched at all times, he's reassured us.
Talking of a meal, you must eat something."

That was a good idea. Whilst Stella busied herself with fast food preparation I busied myself with John finding one or two other items I might need.

Hammer and screwdriver were quickly found. Torch, pliers, pocket knife, an old towel, the tin of treacle, all were deposited in an old canvas bag. I thought that would be enough. It was just the things necessary to make an effective entry, look around, and get out. I wanted to know why Canny had been so keen to get in.
If Sam had been taken in to the place there might be some evidence of her stay that could be useful to the police. And why wait for them to come?

I ate the meal provided by Stella. And just as it was getting dusk made my planned exit and was quickly on my way back to Southwold.
I decided this time to drive right through the town and along the coast road. I passed the caravan site entrance, turned right and parked at the spot right on the harbour wall where, close by, as a child on holiday, I had spent hours with a cheap line and hook catching crabs.
The noise from the caravans filtered across the still, early evening air.
It was mid April, and there was a distinct chill to be felt. There was not a cloud in the sky and the rising moon was three quarters full.
The tide was ebbing.

My adrenalin levels leapt somewhat as I got out and locked up the Transit.
I slung the canvas bag over my shoulder and set off for the short walk towards the spot where I would intentionally become a lawbreaker making a forced entrance into property not my own.
I hoped that Treddick would eventually understand why I had decided to go through with things before he arrived. I trusted that our growing relationship would survive my step on to the wrong side of the law.
There were still lights on a number of the boats moored at the jetties.

One or two couples walked along the harbour side presumably making their way to the Harbour Inn at the other end of the harbour. There was light enough from the moon's glow to be sure of my step. Had it not been for the reason for my nocturnal jaunt I would have quite enjoyed the easy feelings that were engendered by the sight and sounds of nightfall beside the sea.
I passed by the fishermen's huts, some still showing on chalkboards what they had had to sell that day. A number, it seemed, still eked out a reasonable living. It surprised me to see that the business appeared to be surviving quite well. I reached the spot where earlier I had been speaking to the gently spoken Suffolk man who had been painting his boat. The smell of new paint still hung in the air.
I looked around to see if I had company of any sort.
I was alone.
I stepped back into the shadows and allowed my eyes to get accustomed to the lower level of light, and there viewed the scene of my proposed crime.
The window, to the left of the rear door, was easily accessible.
First mistake! I had forgotten to bring an implement that I could use to spread the treacle with. So much for careful planning!
I had to hunt around to find something suitable for the task. Fortunately for me there were plenty of bits and pieces of broken boxes around the back of the unit. I laid out the towel on the ground, began to pour the treacle, and spread it as best I could with the stick of wood that I had found.
When well enough spread, I picked the towel up, trying desperately to avoid getting the treacle all over me. I stuck the towel on to the glass, making sure that I covered as much of the window as possible. Inevitably I had to lick my fingers before proceeding with the next step. I enjoyed the sweetness of that moment knowing that what I was about to do might have bitter consequences for me. But I was committed to my plan. Now for the breaking of the glass!
I checked to see if anybody was around. There was no one. I was alone.
My first blow with the handle end of the hammer was totally ineffective.
It surprised me that I had failed. I struck again a little harder. Still no success! The third blow, this time with the business end of the hammer, achieved the desired result. The glass cracked in several places and bowed inwards.
Holding on to the towelling with one hand and applying gentle pressure on the glass with the other, allowed me to carefully remove a large expanse of the broken fragments all at once.

The putty was old, cracked and unpainted, the glazing bars were not in good condition, so the removal of the rest of the window pane was easily done.
Fortunately I could feel that the tarpaulin that was covering the inside of the window, was hanging loose. I tried pushing it in as far as I could reach.
There were no obstructions in the way. There was nothing left to do but to get through and find out what was within.
I searched around again and found an old milk crate which I placed up against the wall beneath the now open window.

I climbed up and squeezed through. The inside of the building had that unused dank smell. The tarpaulin fell back against the window and I was in complete darkness. Lighting the torch and sweeping its arc around me enabled me to see the rough lay out of the place.
There were work benches on two sides and along the back wall. All manner of boating equipment strewn about. Ropes, nets, trestles, paint tins, tools, oil cans, everything looked in a dilapidated condition as far as I could see.
There were some chairs, a couple of portable flood lights on stands, with trailing leads snaking over the floor to sockets above one of the benches.
In the far corner was a portable toilet cabinet.

The chemical smell made me feel extremely nauseous.
Whoever Eric was, he hadn't much cared for what was in this place.
On a table set towards the back I could see the remains of a meal.
Two dirty mugs and a number of equally dirty plates, and some cutlery. But it was difficult to detect how recently they had been in use.
Above me, anchored to cross timbers in the roof I could see engine lifting tackle, chains and pulleys and suchlike.
I walked towards the front of the building.
Situated there was another shed like structure, which on closer inspection turned out to be a small metal container.
However much I searched the place, there was no sign of Sam, and apart from the plates and things, no sign of recent human habitation at all.
Despondency at my failed efforts was setting in. How would I explain my actions to Treddick. But Canny had been so keen to get in the place. I had trusted the dog's instinct. Was there anywhere else? A cellar maybe?
I searched the area of the floor all around the container. Nothing, just piles of old rags, and rubbish of every description.

Under one of the benches I could see what looked like off cuts of very thick polystyrene. Now this I could see was very newly cut. I'd used a great deal of this stuff in the past on design jobs, and I knew that cut polystyrene very quickly takes up the dirt if left about. On the bench above it there was a hand saw, and yes, the unmistakable traces of the white foam particles still clinging to the blade. Plenty of evidence of very recent industry, but for what? I could see by the light of the torch that the tell tale white flecks were all about the place, but especially so in front of the small container.

On inspection, the container wasn't so small, perhaps fifteen feet in length and six or seven feet wide.
The double doors at the back were bolted shut but were not locked in any way. The bolts, I could see, had been recently oiled.
I turned the bolts easily, without sound.
I opened first one door, then the other.
I was confronted by a white wall of polystyrene covering the whole of the back of the container. It wasn't in one piece though.
There were three sections, the middle of which had black linen sticky tape handles attached to it.

My mind was racing, my heart pumping
I put the torch down on the floor, and by its light, eased the middle section of foam out of its place. Having stood the section of foam against the side of the container, I returned to the now open space, picked up the torch and peered deep into the inner darkness of the cavity that had been exposed.
Was it going to be drugs or drink?
Hell No!
I could see the slumped form of Sam. Her hands and feet tied, and her mouth covered with some of the black tape. There she was cringing in what I could now see was a perfectly kitted out padded cell.

"Sam! It's me, Michael!"

My voice was deadened by the total insulation effect of the foam, it sounded so weird. I clambered along inside the cave like cavity, little realising that Sam could have no real clue as to who it was who was apparently advancing upon her.
Her eyes showed a cat like fear.
She was turning her head away from the light of my searching torch.

I stopped for a moment, and turned the now weakening beam of light on to my own face, hoping that she would be able to recognise me.

"Sam! It is me. Look it's me, Michael! I've found you at last."

After a few moments more of what must have been a frantic search for truth, and reality, she did recognise me. There was the muffled sound of someone trying to speak, someone who had become very excited indeed in a desperate sort of way.

I moved towards her once again. 'Please let the torch hold out,' I thought to myself. I eased the tape slowly away from her mouth. She gasped!

"O! Uncle Michael!" She was near hysterics.

I proceeded to undo the tape that was securing her legs, then the rest of it that was wound round her hands. At last she was free.
She stood up, but immediately collapsed again on to the floor of the container. I bent to lift her up once more, and very unsteadily, she gained her feet. She held me so tight. There was an animal closeness about the contact between us. I couldn't tell who was the stronger in the holding.

"Come on, old girl. We must get out of here straight away."

We struggled together to get her out of the container. She hardly had any strength in her legs. She was both crying and laughing at her inability.
Her nervous state was obviously one of near exhaustion and she was finding it very difficult to cope with her new found freedom.

As we got out of the container, fear gripped me once more, I couldn't help but notice, from high on the wall of the building, the flashing red light of some alarm system. I must have triggered it somehow in opening the container doors. It was pulsing a red glow at regular intervals, a glow that intermittently lit up the scene.
It would be signalling to someone, somewhere.
How soon would they be alerted?

"Come on Sam! We must move quickly. We have got to get out of here. Can you make it to the door?"

As I was speaking to her and trying to hold her up at the same time, and holding the torch, I was endeavouring to get the hammer and screwdriver out of the canvas bag. I knew that I would have to break the lock on the door in order for us to get out. Sam was definitely in no shape to clamber out of the window through which I had made my entry.

Too late!

There were sounds outside. Men's voices.
A key turning in the lock. We both froze.
The door opened slowly. A torch light pierced the darkness.

"O! Samantha. My dear Samantha. Where do you think you are going?" the voice was cynical in tone. "And who the hell are you? How exceedingly clever of you to find her. But I am afraid you were not quick enough.
Now sit down on those chairs, the pair of you."

I did not recognise the cold and cynical voice of the person who was speaking to us. Nor could I clearly see who it was who had come through the doors. There were two of them. One, I could see, was holding some sort of weapon in his hand. The other was motioning us to sit at the table, waving the light about, and roughly pushing us along. Sam, fortunately, was regaining a little strength and was able to walk now under her own steam.
We both sat down. I could feel Sam's fear. She was trembling. I held her hand. My own state of mind was reaching critical overload, I was desperate to know what we might do.
"Fetch one of the lights. Let's see what we can do with the pair of them."

There was no longer a cynical edge to the voice. It was becoming far more angry with every new word spoken.

One of the portable flood lights was wheeled over to where we sat.
It was put right in front of my face. This I knew would be the beginnings of some form of interrogation, it had all the hall marks of a second rate movie scene. But this was no movie, and it was very much my life and Sam's life that were in danger.

"Switch on... let's see the pair of...."

The high intensity halogen light hit my face full on.... my head began its involuntary response... I realised that Sam and I would have a split second to make some sort of move for the door... We must make the most of it....

"Aaaaatishooreshoo."

The reaction was spectacular. I plunged forward as the eruption took place, knocking the flood light and the table to the ground in one fell swoop.
The lamp burst. The plates and mugs crashed in pieces.

The surprise element was mine, I had known what was coming. And trusting in natural reactions that seek to catch things that are falling, we had a moment or two of real advantage. The other two were caught completely off their guard. Each stumbled into the other as they tried to prevent the crash taking place. The torch was dropped, but didn't break.
The light from its beam went spinning round and round making crazy circular illuminations all round the floor.

The gun was fired.

I still had hold of Sam's hand.
My grip on her became vice-like.
I dragged her up from her chair and raced for the door.
She followed without hesitation fully realising the need for haste.
The new life threatening situation that we both found ourselves in, had given her tired and frightened body an adrenalin kick start that immediately gave her renewed energy.
I knew in which direction the door was, but my now aching and out of focus eyes were useless for a moment.
I crashed on. And crashed in to the door.
I searched for the handle.
I found it and wrenched it open.
The cold night air hit me full in the face.
I almost threw Sam out of the door, slamming it shut as we hurled through, and out into the moonlit night.
There was a second shot and a great deal of cursing and swearing as the two inside got themselves to their feet.
Splinters of wood burst all over us. The panel of the door was shot to pieces.

"Come on Sam! You must lead the way I can't see for the moment."

Now the strength was hers, the direction was hers. I felt my arm being pulled to the limit. I knew she must be heading up towards the Harbour Inn. Would there still be people about? What was the time? I had lost all track of things and had no clue as to the duration of the events through which I had come.
I fell. She dragged me to my feet.
My eyes began to clear.
The jumping horizon came into clearer focus.
The Harbour Inn was all in darkness.
There was no one to help.
We dare not try the road back to town, it was far too long and straight.
We dare not try the track across the fields. There were the dikes to be crossed.

"Make for the bridge! Sam! The bridge!"

Another shot rang out.

We were both now at full stretch, and both fortunately fleet of foot. We knew where we were going. Hopefully our pursuers did not. We dodged first down by the boats then up on the pathway, scrambling through foliage, jumping over staging. Tripping over mooring lines. Running for our lives, each occasionally touching the others hand. We made good progress to the bridge and clattered our way over it.

Yet another shot.
Sparks flew as the bullet ricocheted off one of the girders.
Were they closing on us? I didn't know.
Left at the end. Down to the river bank again.
A large catamaran had settled its twin hulls down on to the mud. It provided a little cover from those who were charging after us.
We could hear them across the river. They were not yet on the bridge.
Their progress was not as good as ours. It appeared obvious to me that they did not know where they were going. The advantage was still with us.

On the Walberswick side of the river we could run right down by the water's edge for quite some way. Occasionally we made tracks for the higher pathway which was far easier. But up on the high path we were in full silhouette against the bright moonlit sky.

As I ran, my mind was trying to make sense of a distant memory. That day when we had all been together on this very path. We had had our coffee at the Parish Lantern, then returned to the river.
Canny had tried to jump out of the ferryman's boat as we had been rowed across. That's it... the ferryman had got out of the boat after we had paid him and had gone to his vehicle that was parked on the Southwold Harbour side.
I remembered it was a Transit, the van equivalent of my own bus.

I had seen that van earlier this evening.
On the Southwold side of the river.
I had parked right by it before starting on my search for Sam.
Unusual that...

The ferryman obviously had some business in Walberswick...
Was he still in Walberswick...?
Please God! Let him still be in Walberswick!

We ran on, ever increasing the lead we had on our pursuers.
The probing light from their torch tracked after us, but we were succeeding in getting away from them.

If the ferryman's boat was there, on this side of the river, we would be in luck. If the ferryman's boat was there...

We reached the line of fishermen's huts, the last of which belonged to the ferry man. As a young boy, on holiday, I had spoken for hours to the old man who had made this river his life's work.
His was the leather brown face I had remembered
with so much affection. His were the stories I had entwined with my own fantasies about the place. I had sat on the steps of his hut and watched him for what seemed like hours pulling into the strong run of the river, making aim far ahead of him and letting the tide take him to the right spot for his passengers to disembark.

The floating jetty, now, was a new affair, much safer than the old one. Much wider planking had been used. I ran its length. And looked to the left to where I knew the rowing boat should be if our luck was in.

Our luck was in! I ran back to Sam.

"Trust me Sam! Come and get into the boat."

Sam quickly obeyed and stepped down into the boat.
I had never done this before, not even in the daylight.
But I had seen it done many, many times.
In my mind I had pulled every stroke with that wonderful old ferryman.

The night was moonlit and still without a cloud.
I unshipped the oars. And released the mooring rope.
I pushed away from the jetty and out into the ebbing river.
The lapping of the water against the bottom of the clinker built boat was a wonderfully reassuring sound. I settled to the task. Aiming, as I knew I should, not for the jetty on the opposite side of the river, but at an imaginary spot up river. To let the ebbing tide take us to where we wanted to go. The long oars felt good in my hands and with each stroke we left the shore behind.
We were not, however, out of gun shot range.
Our two pursuers arrived at the jetty, and ran its full length.
The tide was fortunately low, and we were beneath the horizon.

The torch light tracked left and right, and caught us in its beam. Shots rang out and fizzed into the water by our side.
I pulled harder on the oars.
We finally reached the relative safety of the other bank.
If only we could avoid being shot.
I had aimed a little too high up river and had to wait a disturbingly long time for the boat to settle against the side of the jetty.
I looped the mooring rope over one of the tall standing timbers that had been driven into the river's bed, and shipped the oars.
Sam had become far too quiet.
She was slumped down in the back of the boat.

"Uncle Michael," it was a sort of gasping sound. "I think I have been hit."

"O God! No. Sam!"

I scrambled towards her, missed my footing and fell awkwardly at her feet.
The boat pitched about all over the place and the pair of us nearly ended up in the dark, uninviting water. I reached her now still and silent form and cradled her in my arms, kissing her gently on the cheek.
The only good thing at that moment in time was the fact that the shooting had stopped. I raised my head to see what might be happening

on the far bank from which we had just come. I could see the torch lit pair making their way back along the bank the way they had come.
They were travelling fast.
How long would it take for them to retrace their steps and find us now so totally vulnerable?
I was losing control of rational thought altogether. My mind was unable to find a next step to take. Sam could be dying right here in my arms.

Though the moonlit sky was still so clear, there was insufficient light for me to see where she was hit, or the extent of the trouble she might be in.
My own torch had failed.
I had failed.
I had failed Sam. I had failed John and Stella.
I had failed Michael and Treddick.

Sam moved slowly in my arms.
At least she was still alive. I rocked her gently.

Into my numbed brain came a different set of sounds.
Not just that of the water lapping at the sides of the boat. Not just that of the gentle wind disturbing the rigging of nearby moored boats. Not just that of Sam's changing breathing pattern.
I could discern the sound of crunching feet on gravel and whispered voices.
'O no!' I thought, 'there are more of them.'

Whoever they were, they were getting closer by the minute.
I heard the sound of feet on the jetty.
The mooring began to rock with the weight of a steady advance towards us.
I let go my hold on Sam. She winced with the pain.
I took hold of the oar that was at my side.
I paused, waiting for the right moment. Then swung the oar with all my might in an arc above my head, sweeping the air in vain hope.
I made rough contact with at least one of the dark advancing shapes.
There was a muted cry of pain. The whole jetty rocked as whoever it was fell into the water. A second silhouetted figure stooped towards me and roughly grabbed my arm.

"Good God! Stop it . Michael it's us."

It was the unbelievable sound of Treddick's voice.

"You've just knocked Harry into the water."

Harry came up spluttering. A third person took his outstretched hand and heaved him up on to the now madly rocking jetty.

"Well, thanks a million, mate." he gasped. "You just wait, I'll get you back for this one day. Thanks Michael."

When thanking 'Michael', he wasn't speaking to me. It was to the one who had hauled him out of the water.

"Uncle Michael, it's me, Michael! We've come to help."

His voice sounded so matter of fact.
As though it might be the most usual thing in the world to be doing what he was doing, at whatever time it was, in the still dark, early morning hour, by a river bank, with gunshots flying everywhere.

"Sam's hurt." I said. "You must get her out of here. She needs help.
She's taken a shot and I don't know where.
And where on earth did you three spring from?
I thought it was more of them come to finish us off."

There was a growing sense of relief pouring into my whole body. But things were not over yet. We needed to act fast if Sam was to be attended to.
Michael had got down into the boat and was speaking softly to his sister.
She, fortunately, had roused sufficiently to recognise who it was.
It was touching to see such brotherly love and concern being shown.
Where there had been unnatural distance between them because of all that had happened, there was now an intimacy of tender reunion.

Treddick took control.

"Harry, you and young Michael here, stay with Sam. Keep her as warm as possible. I'll contact the helicopter pilot and get him to meet up with you here. There's just about enough room for him to land. As he is parked up in a field behind the Trevoughs' I'll get him to bring Stella and my WPC with him. Then you can all get Sam to hospital. That is your job. Whatever you may hear going on where we are right now I want you to disregard it all. Your job is to stay with Sam and get her to hospital. Do you hear me?"

Harry and Michael were quick to agree.
Whilst Treddick was making his call, I got out of the ferry boat, and Harry, still squelching, took my place. I gave him my jacket, which he took with some gratitude. As he clambered by me, he gave me a more than gentle dig in the ribs, with a friendly 'you just wait.' I hoped there was a smile on his face.

"Michael." Treddick was now addressing me. "We have a job to do here. Peters and my other chap are with John. We've been observing and tailing the Jaguar ever since it turned off the A12. I got them to pick John up from the house. He knows the area far better than they do.
They are currently following the Jag down the road passed the golf course. They tell me that the Jag has no lights on and is travelling very slowly.

The car can only be coming here. Marsters, hopefully, does not know what has happened in these last few minutes, so we have a slight edge, thanks to you. Remind me to have a word with you some time about meddling in police procedures. We will take your Transit and block the exit from this direction. Peters will follow the Jag up and block the way back. We must get into position quickly. We don't want to lose what small advantage we have.

The helicopter will be on its way any minute now.
So! do we all know what we are doing?"
There was a general murmur of agreement.
I looked back to the boat and saw the huddled forms of the three of them.
The two men were cradling Sam in their arms.
I did not know what I would do if anything more happened to her now.
She was quiet but still awake to what was going on.
I found that I was murmuring some sort of prayer for help for Sam, to a God who may be there and watching us.
I reached the Transit with Treddick. We climbed on board.
I started the engine.
We moved forward slowly, the light of the moon providing sufficient view of the way ahead. I had been this way on foot only a couple or so hours before.

I wondered where our two attackers had got to. They had slipped my mind for the moment. I told Treddick that we were getting close to the boat shed where Sam had been held captive.

"Right stop here." His voice was calm.
"Switch off, we will wait for them to arrive."

Whilst we waited he asked me how many attackers there were? I answered, 'two.' How many guns? I answered, 'only one,' or so I thought.
There was a noise ahead of us. The sound of wheels on gravel. The car stopped. Then the sound of voices. Animated, angry voices. I recognised the one belonging to the guy who had spoken my name, and the other quite possibly Alan Marsters. The car started once more and came further forward towards us. It stopped again at the doors of the boat shed. Two people got out. Two others who had walked behind joined them. All four disappeared into the darkness down the side of the shed, presumably to go inside.
Treddick was in contact with Peters, they were parked on the roadway blocking the exit. John was in the car and would remain in the car. Peters and his partner were on their way, on foot. Treddick informed them of the whereabouts of Marsters and informed them also that there were four involved, one of whom was a woman. At least one was armed.

Treddick, gun in hand, slipped quietly out of the Transit, urging me on his departure, to remain where I was and definitely to keep out of the way of any of the action that might follow. I could see him moving cautiously ahead towards where the Jag was now parked. He too disappeared into the darkness. The waiting was unbearable. But the waiting was not for long. There were shouts, there were shots. All hell appeared to be breaking loose. The noise went on for a good length of time. The early dawn light was beginning to show, someone ran into view. It was Marsters. He raced for his car. He too had a gun and as he got into the Jag he turned and fired yet again at another figure who was after him.
Whoever it was dived for cover, so allowing Marsters time to make his get away. Or so he thought.

I had started my engine. I knew exactly what I was going to do.
I slowly advanced towards him.
I could see that he was fumbling for his keys.

As I closed on him I slammed my foot to the floor. My wheels were spinning on the gravel but then I finally took off and hit him just before he had time to try that nought to sixty stuff. He had parked at a slight angle to the pathway. So when I hit him, I turned him. The weight of the blow smashed him into a mobile boat launcher. I reversed and spun my wheels back the way I had come. He was attempting to disentangle himself. I drove hard forwards again. This time I hit him, crumpling the doors, and pinning the car yet again against the boat carrier. He just had time to throw his body out of the way, and on the passenger seat. The look on his face was of purple anger.
He was shouting all manner of filth at me.
I drew back again.
I didn't care that the front end of the Transit was looking the worse for wear.
Steam was rising from a split radiator.

I surveyed my handiwork.
The front wing of the Jag was crumpled in... those lovely smooth lines were no longer so smooth. The front twin headlights were smashed. The wing mirror ripped off. The flush fitting door handle not so flush fitting now.
There was electric blue where there should have been just silver grey. That body shell made at the pressed steel Fisher Plant in West Bromwich didn't look so great now.
I wondered what Sir William Lyons might think of his beautiful baby now if he could see it in this condition.
I unnervingly found a liking for what I was now intending.
The Jag had been parked near the top of a slipway into the river.
My third blow took it towards the waters edge.
Marsters, with murderous intention, gun in hand, was trying, in vain, to wind down the windows. I must have broken the circuits on the electric windows.
I saw him pointing the gun directly at me.
The screen of the Jag shattered as he fired.
He missed me.
I reversed again and lined up my next blow.
The slipway was wet and greasy. His screaming Pirelli P5 205s were spinning away, but he wasn't going anywhere.
This time I made a nasty mess of the precious chrome grill and the shapely front end. Sixteen feet and two and three quarters of an inch long, nose to tail.
Well damn it! It wasn't now!

Marsters smashed his fist through his windscreen.
I could see the blood begin to flow over his knuckles.
We were facing each other.
He pointed his gun straight at me.
I sat motionless.

"Lara!" I was shouting her name at the top of my voice.

A manic laughter started in my throat.
His gun had jammed.
He flung it at me.

"Got you! You God forsaken piece of filth." I was still in charge.

Slowly, so slowly, I inched him backwards down the slipway.
Steam was pouring from my radiator. I could hardly see.
There was blue smoke from his spinning tyres.

Marsters was tearing at the broken glass in the shattered screen with his bare hands. He was frantic to get out.
He understood full well my intention.
Little did he know that a destroyer was at work.
For all that he had done.
Was he Terry's murderer? Was he the master mind of this whole affair? Was he the one who had planned Sam's kidnap? Was it his cronies who had wounded her? Was he the one who had tried to destroy my friends? If yes was the answer to all my questions then Treddick, with his due process, would deliver a verdict on all of that.
For the moment I was my own private judge, jury and executioner.

"Die! Damn you! Die!"

I screamed it at the top of my voice.
I drew back once more. Still unsatisfied.
Then crashed at him one more time, with an awful sound of metal devouring metal. Forcing him deeper into the water.
Marsters was shrieking all sorts of blasphemies at me.
I hit him again. My thirst for destruction was insatiable.
Again I hit him.
A                  n                  d
again.

Just one more time.

I drew back.
My vision was now crystal clear,
I could clearly see the young lad's eyes gripped in the fear of death.

My only thought was of Lara. My Lara!

Selector in forward
Foot to the floor.
'To hell with you!'

Only just in time I saw Treddick.
He had stepped directly into my path.
He just stood there.
There was a pleading look on his face.
I stopped the Transit with just inches to spare.
But I failed to stop the convulsive shaking that swept my body.
My hands were locked in a vice like grip on the steering wheel.

He came to my side and, with difficulty, opened the door. He lent in and began purposefully to uncurl my stiffened fingers from the wheel.

He spoke, gently, persuasively, lovingly.

"Michael! Stop now... You've killed the beast...
The dragon is dead... Lara is safe."

I began at last to weep. Great sobbing, childish tears poured down my face.
I could feel their stinging warmth. He placed his arm around my neck, and held me to him in a powerful embrace.

I struggled to understand what he had said. 'Lara is safe!'
Surely he must have meant Sam!
I felt so weary of everything. My mind was beginning to fail in its attempt to think more rationally. There was a fearful drumming noise in my head.
The early morning light took on a brilliance all around me.
I looked to the sky and was enfolded in its glorious brightness.

"Aaaaatishooreshoo."

The high powered search light of the low hovering helicopter had us all in its powerful beam. By its light, through out of focus eyes, I could just

make out the now desperate Marsters who was still in the Jaguar, but up to his waist in the cold waters of the Blyth. I could hear his even colder invective as he hurled his abuse in my direction.
The 4.2 was a total wreck.
The Transit too was dying visibly before my tired eyes.

"I've made a bit of a mess of things," I said to Treddick. "I'm sorry."

"Never mind, Michael. We've got a result, here at least! But there is still a lot to do."

He waved the helicopter away towards where he knew Harry and Michael were waiting with Sam. We were no longer in the bright pool of light.
The morning took on a sombre greyish tone.
Treddick and Peters began to sort things out. They left Marsters to his own devices for a while. He wasn't going anywhere.
John appeared, walking cautiously towards us. Seeing me, he ran the last few steps. I climbed down from my shattered bus, and took him by the hand, leading him to where the ferryman's boat was moored. Harry and Michael still had Sam in their arms. They looked a picture of compassion.

Father took the place of son. Sam spoke, her pain had eased somewhat.
John held her close.
The pilot landed in the car park a short distance away and was soon racing towards us, along with Stella.
The morning light of dawn increased, allowing a mother's searching eyes and careful probing fingers to find the site of Sam's wound.
It was not actually so bad as first we had all thought.
Her upper left arm was the only part that was injured. The bleeding, at first so profuse, had finally stopped.
The pilot had brought the first aid kit from the helicopter and he took over very efficiently, rapidly cleaning and securing Sam's arm.
Treddick arrived on the scene and asked the pilot what the situation was.
Decisions were made.
The pilot would fly Sam, Stella and the WPC to the Accident unit at Norwich.
John, Michael, Harry and myself would go back in Harry's van to John's place, where we were to stay until Treddick arrived.

Peters and his partner would stay at the harbour awaiting police transport for the prisoners. Not all of whom were alive.
Whilst Treddick would also wait and arrange with the Harbour Master, when he arrived, for the removal and storage of the two damaged vehicles.
Treddick would see us all later.

"What the hell's going on?"

It was a most irate ferryman calling from the other side of the river.

"What are you doing with my boat?"

"Police business." Treddick answered.
"Thank you very much for the use of it. Shall one of us row it back? Or would you prefer to walk round and get it yourself."

Fearing the worst if some inexperienced person dare to make the trip, the ferryman replied that he would pick it up, but would someone please give him an explanation of what had gone on.
Treddick informed him that he would be pleased to do so, knowing that he would be at the scene for some time.
The ferryman began his walk.
The helicopter roared into life, whisking Sam away to hospital.
John, Michael, Harry and myself walked back with Treddick to see how Peters was coping at the scene of crime.
What we hadn't noticed before, was a growing crowd of onlookers, all eager to discover what had happened to disturb their early morning quiet.
The Harbour Master had arrived, having been summoned from his bed by Treddick. Peters and the Harbour Master were organising temporary barriers to protect the evidence for forensic investigators.
But where was Marsters?
I asked.

"Containerised with all the others." Peters informed me, with a grin on his face. "Except of course the one who's dead. He's lying where he fell inside."

I tried to imagine Moira Brownsmoor and Marsters and whoever else it was, inside that darkened sound proofed coffin. I felt little compassion for them. They had done too much harm. To too many people.

Would I ever know the full story?

Treddick, calm as ever, waved us on our way.

"You don't need to stay. Go back and get yourselves cleaned up. I'll see you as soon as I have finished here."

It was then that I did look at myself.
Blood all down my chest and arm from where I had held Sam.
Mud all over my shoes and trousers. Torn trousers at that.
I explored a pain that had its origin somewhere on my shin.
A graze of quite spectacular proportion, or so I thought.
Harry, who was peering at me, said it wasn't worth the trouble of too much sympathy, and any way I didn't deserve any for what I had done to him.
Standing together, we made a right pair.
He raised his shirt to show the nicely developing bruise that I had inflicted.
And he was still drying out after his unexpected soaking.
Between us there was a developing odour of all things to do with the river.
John and Michael said that they would prefer not to travel with such disreputable down and outs.
There was a sort of 'ladish' humour being thrown around.
A humour that surely owed much of its origins to the incredible release of tension that we were all experiencing.
Sam was on her way to hospital and was safe at last. Thank God.
Marsters was no longer free to do her any harm.
At least part of the story was nearing an ending.
The events of the last two and a half weeks must, I thought, be reaching some conclusion. But what the whole story was, who could tell us that?
And what about Chartham?
What had happened at Smettons?
And why had Michael come to Southwold with Harry?

I climbed into the back of Harry's van. Very sensibly he had asked John to drive. Harry clambered in beside me. Michael travelled alongside his father.

"Who's for the early bath?" I said.

# V

On the brief journey back, Michael began to tell his story. The previous weekend had been a busy one for him. He could not answer my calls to him, because he had spent most of the time at Smettons'.

He had orchestrated, for his own advantage, a controlled virus breakdown in the Company computer system. This had 'conveniently' occurred late on Friday afternoon, after Chartham had left.

Michael, much to the Chairman's delight, had volunteered to go in over the weekend to fix it all.

His actual purpose was far different. The virus would be quickly eliminated. The whole system was easily 'saved' by the running of a 'suitable' programme that he had already devised.

No! His purpose for wanting to be in the office for an extended period on his own, was to 'arrange' something special for Chartham, something that required more than just a couple of hours work.

When Michael was first employed by Smettons, he told us, he had been given the job of installing a video conferencing facility that would link all of the offices together if needed. He had designed the system himself and provided plenty of surplus capability. His first objective at the weekend, was to rewire the camera that was attached to Chartham's computer so that Michael could view and hear what was going on in the office, without Chartham knowing that anything was going out 'live.' This he achieved reasonably quickly. He was able to test his handiwork by calling the security guard on the front desk, asking him to help him check the internal phone system in Chartham's office.

The security guard was totally unaware that Michael could see his every move as soon as he had entered, what, for the security guard, was usually forbidden territory. The guard answered the phone at Chartham's desk when Michael called, but interestingly failed to leave immediately when the test was over. It helped Michael a great deal to be able to watch what the guard was interested in.

Unlocked drawers were opened. Contents viewed.

Filing cabinets were searched.

The executive toys were played with for a while.

The guard was obviously making the most of his opportunity.

Michael brought it all to a hasty conclusion by ringing Chartham's line once again. The guard, realising that he should have been long gone, beat a hasty retreat without picking the phone up.

Michael had been satisfied that his set up would enable him to keep an 'eye' on any developing situation.

His second objective was to work on a further addition to the 'black hole' programme that he had installed for Chartham. A little 'surprise'

if ever Michael got the opportunity to use it, he said. He wouldn't reveal what that surprise was all about.
The third, and most sophisticated objective, was to bring 'on line' a dormant system of security that he had been working on. A system that only the Chairman knew was on the point of being operational.

"When you went to Felixstowe with Harry the other day.
You saw the Smetton's containers in their smart livery colours.
You remember? Uncle Michael!"

"Yes," I replied. "Very smart indeed."

"You saw the picture of the world at the centre of the logo. Well that world is made up of light sensors and solar panels and a unique ultra thin battery, and a very neat transmitter that enables us to have satellite contact with the containers wherever they are in the world. I've been working on putting the 'smart' into Smartway Security for some time now. Well it is all up and running as from this last weekend. That's what I was doing. We will be able to track the whereabouts of the containers wherever they go."

John had been driving in silence all this time. But from where I was in the back of Harry's van I could see the look of pride on his face.

We arrived at the house and stopped on the gravel drive. Canny had heard us arrive and was desperate to greet us. He was barking loud and clear.

"That's what you were doing over the weekend," I said.
"But It doesn't tell me why you are here in Southwold with Harry."

"Let him tell you later," interrupted John. "You and Harry have a shower or bath or whatever you like. You can use the spa in our bathroom if you want something special.
Michael and I will contact Norwich hospital and find out how Sam is doing then we will make the biggest breakfast you have ever seen."

Harry and I 'tossed' for the spa. Harry won. I made do with the en suite facilities in the visitors bedroom, if 'making do' was the right phrase to use.

I was called for breakfast a good half hour later.

I woke, somewhat startled, to find myself still immersed in the now cooling water. Some of John's clothes were laid out for me on the bed. We were of similar size, but our tastes were not quite the same.
I came downstairs to find Harry already at the table, dressed similarly to myself. The kitchen was warm with the heat from the cooker.
My mind was slowly calming down.
Breakfast, I knew, would be so good.
It was.
Hot steaming coffee.
Toast, eggs and bacon, fried potato, baked beans.
It was breakfast, 'by the boys' and 'for the boys.'
Canny fussed around, but was told to lie down.
I couldn't help but fondle the dog every time he disobeyed and joined us at the table. Canny had led me to where Sam was. And Sam was safe, now.

The helicopter had arrived at the hospital and Sam was being attended to. John had found that out when he phoned. The WPC would let him know more as soon as she could.

"So why are you and Harry here in Southwold?" I continued with the spreading of my toast. "Something drastic must have happened.
Tell me more."

Michael continued with his story. Before going into work on Monday morning he had wired himself up, for the sake of the Met's boys 'ears' who would be listening for him, he had checked that that link was operational by contacting them by phone. He arrived at Smettons to great congratulations from everyone. He had 'saved' the situation by his 'brilliance.'
Little did they know!
Everything had gone through normally up till lunch time.

On occasions he had switched on the 'seeing eye' in Chartham's office enabling him to check on what was happening there. His system was working perfectly. Chartham was busying himself with routine stuff. It was quite by chance that Michael was watching the scene at exactly the time that Chartham received a phone call which, Michael could see, made Chartham very excited indeed. Michael could only hear Chartham's end of the conversation and that, at times, not very clearly for Chartham kept turning away from where the camera link was.
But Michael was able to get the drift of the one sided conversation.

The small container ship had been loaded at Felixstowe and was now on its way to Hamburg.
Chartham had paused for a moment after putting his phone down. He had moved to his computer, and stood before it rubbing his hands together.
Michael could see a twisted smile appearing on Chartham's face.
Chartham sat down at the keyboard and started methodically on Michael's 'black hole' programme. At exactly the same time Michael's own 'shadow programme' sprang to life on his own PC.

The 'black hole' was open.
Michael could see on his own screen the progress of the programme as Chartham worked at it.
The numbers of the Sotheby's containers were typed in at the relevant places.
It interested Michael to see that the Smetton's ones were not included.
Apparently it was only the Sotheby's stuff that would ultimately disappear.
Chartham started the 'holding programme' and sat back in his chair. The look on his face had turned to one of real malevolence. Michael could then see that Chartham had taken from a locked draw in his desk, a lap top. Michael sensed what Chartham was about to do. Michael was correct down to every detail. Chartham was transferring the requirement for the final 'black hole' closure to his portable. Michael now knew that Chartham would be able to execute the completion of the programme from anywhere he liked.
It was what happened next that had caused Michael's immediate change of plans. Chartham had made a phone call. Michael could not see what he had dialled. He only heard Chartham's voice in conversation. Chartham was ordering whoever it was at the other end of the line 'to put the final part of the Suffolk operation into place. There should be no loose ends.' He repeated. 'No loose ends. Do you understand Marsters.' He finished the call by saying that they would meet up at the pre-arranged place.

"Uncle Michael," he spoke directly to me. "I remembered when you spoke to me about what had happened at Felixstowe. A man by the name of Marsters was involved with Terry Berrysford. Well I couldn't take a chance could I.
I didn't know what to do. I phoned to leave a message on your answerphone, just in case you checked if I had called. I listened to your message and took a note of Harry's phone number. I decided there and then to ask him if he would take me up to Southwold. I phoned him and

he agreed straight away, saying that he would pick me up from Smettons.

Whilst I was waiting for Harry to arrive I transferred all my stuff on to my lap top. What Chartham was planning to do I could do as well, and probably better. I could at least carry on monitoring from my 'shadow programme' all that he was doing computer wise. I wasn't going to let him beat me.
I had no idea of where he was going, but it sounded too close to home for my liking. I let the 'Met' boys know what I was intending and where I was going.
And I told Smettons that I wasn't feeling too good and that I had asked a friend to pick me up. They were happy with that, believing that it may have been due to all my extra weekend work."

"What time did Chartham make the phone call to Marsters?" I asked.

"It was about one to one thirty. I'm not too sure."

It was unbelievable to realise that that was the phone call I had seen Marsters take there at the Berrysford's home. I was in the very same room as him. We had all just returned from the cemetery where the burial of the murdered Terry Berrysford had taken place.
Marsters, more than likely, was the poor boy's murderer. There he was as large as life, in the process of offering his condolences to the boy's tearful wife and parents. He was as cold and clinical as the first time I had met him. But as I had watched him take that phone call, with Moira Brownsmoor at his side, I had seen the strange, haunting look on his face.
How could I have imagined then that the man I was looking at had just been told to apply the final solution to Sam. This man had been told to kill Sam. I'd seen him leave. He'd passed by me as I sat with Treddick, without so much as a glance. A killer off to complete his task as though his day's work was incomplete.

"Harry and I," Michael continued, "arrived here some time after you had set out on your search for Sam. There was a message from Mr. Treddick telling us to do nothing until he arrived.
So we had to wait, not knowing what you were really up to.
The rest you know.
As soon as Mr Treddick arrived we formed up our plan. Dad went with Peters and his partner, and Harry and I went with Mr Treddick.

I tell you this, Uncle Michael, when we got close to the car park we heard the first shot ring out. I've never been so scared.
We didn't know what on earth was going on.
Dad had told us that your plan was to break into one of the boat sheds at the harbour. But he didn't know which one.
There was a second shot soon after the first and then after a space of time there were others.
Mr Treddick told us that we must keep our heads cool, we needed to assess the situation and not just rush into something we knew nothing about.
When we finally arrived we could see your pursuers using a powerful torchlight to search the other bank of the river.
We caught sight of the pair of you just once, of course we couldn't really know it was you and Sam. You were running like mad things.
We saw you make for the ferryman's boat.
We were willing you to make it.
Well... that's it...
You did brilliantly Uncle Michael.
You saved Sam's life."

"O, I don't know so much. I actually got her shot.
Its lucky for me that it wasn't as bad as I had thought.
You say that you were scared.

I tell you I was frantic with fear.
When we were there in the boat, and she was so quiet, I began to think that she was going to die.
There was nothing I could do.
Then you lot turned up. Thank God for that!"

"And you! You blighter! Knocked me into the river!"

Harry's voice was reassuringly strong. I took his mild rebuke as a real encouragement. We were discovering that there was a deepening sense of trust developing between us.

"If you can't knock a friend into a river once in a while," I laughingly replied.
"What can you do?"

The laugh turned into a stifled yawn. I hadn't slept at all, apart from the few minutes in the bath. My body was demanding sleep. I excused

myself from the breakfast table, admitting to all of them that I was a bit of a bore, but that I must shut my eyes for a time before Treddick turned up. Harry whispered 'wimp' in my ear, but to no effect.
I left them all drinking even more coffee. John got up from the table and walked with me to the foot of the stairs.

"Michael, I know we haven't had a moment to ourselves, but can I just say thank you for finding Sam..." His voice faltered for a brief second.

He took my hand in his.

"You are truly a good friend... I'll call you when Treddick arrives."

John woke me at eleven thirty. I had been dead to the world for three solid hours. Treddick had arrived and had straight way set about organising phase two of the operation. I was surprised to find that he needed me to help. I thought I was going to get a tough dressing down for going ahead without waiting for his advice, but no.
Moira Brownsmoor had been 'singing' like a bird. She had been trying to convince him that she had no real part in it at all.

A man by the name of Chartham had organised it, she said. Marsters and she had met up with him at some 'do' organised by Smettons at Christmas last year. It was a customer relations event. Chartham and Marsters had hit it off and had become interested in forming some private arrangement where their separate business skills could be used to their mutual advantage. It had all got out of hand.
It was Chartham who had met them at Snape.
He should be still there because he was organising the travel arrangements for the 'real' picture and the 'real' boxes and the 'real' silverware. It was as though, Treddick said, that that was all that was involved.
Moira Brownsmoor made no mention of the Sotheby's containers.
She had only spoken of the picture, the boxes and the silverware.
It was some insurance fraud, or so she thought. The picture was covered in its travels by some Government Indemnity because it was a National treasure.
The other stuff had been highly insured in the usual manner. The real items were going to be sold on to some rich collector who had no qualms about handling gear that was 'hot.'
Moira was 'singing' like the proverbial nightingale.
Treddick had left Peters to listen and take note.

"I need you to come with me," said Treddick, talking to me, "to see if we can check out the picture before Chartham moves it on. We can be down in Snape in a half hour. Harry, you can come with us. Young Michael you must stay here with your father to monitor Sam's condition and the computer side of things. The computer evidence is absolutely crucial, for at the moment we don't have all that much to link Chartham with the murder of Terry Berrysford and the kidnapping of Sam.
I still have men watching at The Maltings, the man we now know to be Chartham. Right let's be on our way. You two OK here?"

His calm efficiency had its affect upon all four of us.
We agreed with his plan.

The journey down to Snape was without event.
The A12 was clear.
We travelled in silence, apart from those occasions when Treddick was in touch with his team who had already been at The Maltings on watch for some little time. He was constantly monitoring the situation.

So much had happened in the last day or two.
The half hour was spent with my own unvoiced thoughts

Every year of childhood's holidays that I had spent with my parents in this part of the Suffolk countryside had seen us make a musical pilgrimage to the Aldeburgh Music Festival.

My parents always pulled me out of school for a week during the Festival time in June. I had loved every minute of it.
I grew up with the music of Benjamin Britten and the singing of Peter Pears, and, as a young lad, had never understood the questioning of their lifelong friendship. I was still a 'live and let live' person.

For me it was the music. The music was everything.

It was in 1967 that I spent my last holiday with my parents at Southwold.
We were there the week after the Queen had opened the brand new Concert Hall and Opera House at The Maltings just beyond the little village of Snape.
The whole project had been Britten's pride and joy.
Who would ever have guessed that only two years later almost to the day that that beautiful building was going to be burnt down. I

remembered that Britten's Steinway piano had been destroyed in the fire, along with other priceless instruments and costumes.
Britten's energies for rebuilding had seen a second new building rise from the ashes only a year later.

We drove through Saxmundham and turned left off the A12 at Bigsby's Corner and went straight through Sternfield on the little road that led to Snape. It had been there, in the village of Snape, that on June 7th 1969, a son of one of the local farmers was coming out of the Crown pub, and had first seen the fiery glow that announced the destruction of Britten's dream at The Maltings. We crossed over the bridge where, because of the sluice, you could always see water upstream, whatever the state of the tide.
Below the bridge it was different.
There were a number of boats of all sorts moored by the side of the river.
Beyond the bridge and before us, on our left, the mellow red brick of The Maltings, now much more than just a collection of fine, tall, imposing agricultural buildings.
My parents had told me its history. Brewers malt had been made there by the same family, the Garrett family, for over a hundred years, right up until 1965, but no more. The business had been closed down then and bought by the developers, Gooderhams, who rented out the buildings for all sorts of new, alternative use.

Alongside the magnificence of the Concert Hall there were art galleries supporting the talent of both local and well known artists.
Antiques and crafts, fabric designers, kitchen ware, a great music shop, plus industrial units of all sorts.
And of course now a very different use.
Chartham was there.
What use was he making of the place?
Treddick told us that his men had seen Chartham enter what appeared to be a wood machining shop, a place that seemed to be in the fabrication business of some sort.
Treddick parked up in what was a reasonably full car park for this time in the year. The place was alive with tourists eager in their endeavour to savour the culture of the place. The Maltings had real charm and character.

Treddick first checked whether anything new had occurred. 'No, the man was still inside the building. His car was still parked in front. Two men had left on foot, about ten minutes ago, and that was it.'

Treddick settled on the direct approach.
He marched straight up to the huge double doors, the rest of us in convoy behind him. He rang the bell that was on the doorpost, but with no success. No one came. He tried the handle.The doors were not locked. He pushed at the door, it opened easily. There was no noise. He called out. There was no reply. He went straight in.
We followed, without hesitation, shutting the door behind us.

There were packing boxes and crates of every size stacked all round the place. We split up to do a thorough search. None of the packing cases was large enough to house the Titians. But several were of the size to accommodate the enigma boxes and the silver ware.
Two nearest the door were addressed for delivery.
Harry set to work, with some tools he found, to open up the two crates.
He was immediately successful in finding the silver, and equally after a further few minutes, the boxes.
Treddick was searching through a small office at the back of the building, where he found, neatly folded on a table, a pile of clothes. He realised straight away what it meant. He mildly reproached the officers who had been watching the place, for failing to recognise Chartham, who must have changed his appearance in some way. He had left the place undetected. Maybe he was one of the 'two' who had been seen leaving just ten minutes before we had arrived.
There were a couple of obvious ways to leave Snape. By road or by river.
The tide had been high enough for escape either up or down stream.
And the road was busy enough with the cars of holiday sightseers to make a get away by road just as easy. Chartham had eluded us.

Treddick was none too pleased. For the very first time I saw in him a developing anger that he was finding difficult to control. His orders to watch for Chartham had been handled in a sloppy fashion.
He certainly made his displeasure known. Politely, but firmly.
One of Treddick's officers called us to a corner of the building where he had discovered something that suggested a further plot was in hand. The officer was pointing to a timing device that could be easily seen in the middle of a pile of stacked timber and mineral fibre board, its red pulsing LEDs were relentlessly counting down their seconds.
Two hours thirty five minutes were still to go.

Was it Chartham who had set a course for the destruction of the place? Had he hastily tried to devise a way to set fire to all the evidence of his involvement in this whole affair.
With the amount of flammable material in the place it would have been more than a 'fiery glow' that would have announced this particular fire to the neighbourhood of Snape.
The Maltings were set to have another major conflagration.
Treddick was quickly on the phone, organising the necessary visit of the specialists who would deal with this new turn of events.

The main door opened.
A cheery voice called out.

"Where are the crates you want delivered then? The phone call said there would be no one here, that the door was going to be left open, and that I was just to pick them up and make sure they were delivered.
Two of them the caller said. Near the door. The money agreed would be stuck on the side in an envelope"

The young man who was speaking was getting a little more unnerved.
All he could see was that we were advancing on him.

Treddick showed his identification. The young man stopped in his tracks.

"I don't want any trouble. I only came to pick up a couple of crates to be delivered. Honest, that's all I've come for. The guy on the phone said the place would be empty. 'Just go in,' he said."

He was busy telling his story for the second time.
Treddick got him to calm down.
During this time, Harry had removed the envelope that was stuck to the side of one of the crates. The contents were revealed to be two hundred pounds worth of ten pound notes.

"Is two hundred pounds the going rate for this sort of delivery then?" Treddick asked the lad.

"The guy on the phone said I'd be doing him a favour, if I could come right away. Said he'd make it worth my while. I've done business with him before. And everything has been alright."

Treddick ushered him outside and calmed him down well enough to begin to get his details. One of the local officers took over and completed the task efficiently, wanting, presumably, to present a better picture of professionalism than had previously been the case.

Harry, meanwhile had been searching the office, finding, to his satisfaction, a set of keys with which he proceeded to start up a fork lift truck that was parked at the rear of the building. He started to move the crates out of the building with an expertise obviously learnt in his previous employ.

Treddick busied himself with the organising of safety at The Maltings. There were people and cars to be moved. The Managment were quick to respond.

An explosives expert was on site within the hour, and the device, which turned out to be incendiary rather than explosive, was deactivated and rendered harmless half an hour later.

The expert told Treddick that in his estimation the device had been produced in a bit of a hurry with very little sophistication.

A timing arrangement that set off a switch that in turn activated a battery connection that produced sufficient power to light some highly flammable material in which it was wrapped. It was basic, but it would have done its job very effectively.

The expert had examined the proposed site of the fire and discovered that the fibre board that was stacked around the device had been impregnated with highly flammable liquid of some sort.

It was then that something clicked with me.
Another of my 'grabbed' memories.
I had seen that sort of fibre board before. I recalled the colour of it.
Yes! it was at Felixstowe.
When the crates containing the fakes had been opened.
The crates had been lined with the same style of board. Customs there had not been able to re-pack the crates with the same efficiency as those who had done it originally, some of the fibre insulation had been left out.

Treddick was more than interested when I told him.

"If that is the case," said Treddick, "then we may have a direct lead between Chartham and the death of Terry Berrysford.
There's been a lot of fire involved with all of this. The cars at Chelmsford. Terry's abandoned car at Felixstowe. The proposed fire

here. And maybe a consignment of fakes and worthless substitutes that are about to burn themselves out of recognition somewhere on their journey."

"Now we know where they are going," Harry said. "It was only the Sotheby's containers that Chartham consigned to the 'black hole' so we should be able to locate the others as soon as they are discharged at Hamburg."

The operation at The Maltings was speedily concluded and provided us just before we left with an incredible moment of sheer luck. Treddick had been clearing things with the Gooderham's Management team. He was concerned to make sure that the story given to the press was simply about the place being saved from a disastrous fire. He needed Chartham's activities to be held under wraps for a while.

It was as he mentioned Chartham's name that one of the staff recalled a recent event.

Chartham had only rented the place a couple of weeks previously and one of the very first things that he had asked was whether there was any storage facility on site at The Maltings that had excellent fire prevention equipment installed. He was naturally informed of the set up at the Concert Hall. Since the fire there in 1969 the whole fire precaution thing had been improved tremendously. The new building when it was opened in 1970 had the finest of sprinkler systems installed.

A visit to the Admin office at the Concert Hall enabled us to discover why Chartham had made that inquiry. He had asked them, and they had agreed at a suitable price, to store for him in their scenery store, a somewhat large packing crate.

The crate, Chartham had told them, would be stored there for a maximum of one month. He had paid the storage charge in advance.

The crate was still there.
Hopefully we had found the Titians!
It did not take too long for our hopes to be proved correct.
The crates were located and opened. Both Titians were there.

For all too few moments I was able to feast my eyes on that wonderful portrait once more. The Vendramins were there in all their glory.
The intensity of the look in the eyes of the adult men involved, had been captured by Titian, with such tenderness. The looks in the eyes of the boys in the family were painted with equal care.

The 'eyes certainly did have it!'

Michael did not wait for Chartham's final move.
He attacked his keyboard with ferocity.
'Execute Chartham.'
'Enter.'
He hit the 'Enter' key with equal ferocity.
"Now just watch!" he said with glee. And he sat back in his chair.

A picture of a man appeared on screen.

"That's Chartham. I got his photograph from personnel.
The 'surprise' I told you about, Uncle Michael!"

Chartham's eyes began to weep huge tears. The tears fell all around the figure and began to fill up the screen. Chartham's image on screen began to flail around in the watery flood. It was a simple animation but very effective in portraying his downfall. He was drowning in his own tears.
When the figure was finally submerged beneath the water, a single word exploded on to the screen.

'Gotcha!'

"With a bit of luck, and if I was quick enough," said Michael, "Chartham will have seen all that before he switched off.
I hope it puts the fear of God into him."

My thoughts were very different.

If Chartham had seen it and realised what it might mean, then Michael may have made him into a very serious enemy.
I was more fearful of the outcome but I kept my thoughts to myself.

The mood in the house, what with all the laughter that Harry had provoked, was buoyant. I did not want to dampen the feeling of confidence.
Everyone was busy congratulating Michael and asking him how he had managed it. Michael was enjoying his moment of success.
John made the wisest comment suggesting that we ought to communicate with Treddick straight away to let him know what had happened.
I had his mobile number so it was down to me.
Michael chipped in asking me if I wanted my mobile back.

It had served its purpose well whilst in his possession.
He took it out of his pocket and threw it across the room to me adding the comment, 'Don't lose it... it's a very special phone!'
I left the room to make the call, wanting to inform Treddick privately of my fears about Michael's little 'surprise.'
Treddick, though pleased with the knowledge of Chartham's actions, shared my worries concerning Michael's. He reassured me of his every intention to alert the Port Police in Hamburg.
I asked him whether he knew of Michael's further brilliance in setting up the satellite watch on the Smetton's containers.
He was aware of it, he said, because Michael had informed the Met before he had left London with Harry.
The fact that Chartham had closed down the computer side of his operation must have meant that the containers had arrived in Hamburg and been unloaded. They were now sitting somewhere in the port area of Hamburg.
The container ship on which they had been carried had been quite small, meaning that there was a possibility of them being off loaded at any number of smaller quays in that vast port.
We would have to rely on Michael's technology to find them.

I rang off, not before Treddick had confirmed the time of our meeting with the Berrysfords, it would be at eleven o'clock and would we please be on time as we then had to get down to London to take Michael to Smettons.

I sat by myself for a while before rejoining the rest of them.
My thoughts turned to the City of Hamburg.
Each time that place had been mentioned, throughout this whole experience,
I had recalled a vivid mental picture.
I had visited Hamburg just the once.
Many years ago.
My father, who had served in the RAF during the war, had taken part in the fire raids on that City in 1943.
He had helped to reduce the dock area to burning rubble.

He had thought it right to take us, I was fifteen at the time, to the very place where the destruction had been so devastating. So we had seen the reconstructed port area that then looked so modern. He had shown us the church of St. Nicholas - the bombed ruins had been left as a timely reminder of the war time horrors. I remembered that the thin tall spire

stood out as a lonely monument. My father had impressed me with his sensitivity - the journey for him had been more than one of mere nostalgia.
Both mother and I had seen in him a real sense of questing for something.

These days the idea of reconciliation has at times been overworked on the themes of personal guilt that has simply to be confessed.
But for my father it had been so different. We saw a need in him to reach out to the people. Whilst we were there we had talked for hours with many of the folk we had met in cafes and bars, in churches and museums. He helped us to do that as well. Making sure that we got in touch with people.
Many we had met spoke in very good English.

He told us when we returned home, that he had found the people to be far less like the ones he had been taught to hate. The journey had had a deep emotional impact on him.

My father was a quiet man. Towards the end of his life the hard edge of ruthlessness that personified much of twentieth century living caused him to become very inward in his thinking. His reactions to the sordid and profane side of modern life caused him great hurt.
I had seen him in the years before he died, withdrawing to a safer place, a place of solitude, that few of us could enter.

I know that I too had caused him grief.
So eager to succeed, and yes, at times, at the expense of others.
John and Stella had been a part of my life in those early aggressive days.
And up until five years ago had shared every good thing in my life.
Lara's death had finished all of that, and I had fought to find a way of dealing with it, but had only distanced myself from them.
But now... Within the space of a few brief weeks of hectic activity...
Our lives had changed once more...
The feelings that I was experiencing within me, were feelings of renewal.
Treddick had caused me to think of things in different ways...
Harry had added an unquestioning friendship...
I could still hear his laughter...
He was right there, now, as large as life, sharing profound simplicities with John, Stella, Michael and Sam.

Throughout the evening we had moved from kitchen to lounge.
And now here I was sitting at the foot of the stairs probing the mysteries of my life, with an increasing sense of inner well being that I was feeling sure I did not deserve. It had cost so much of everyone.

It was Sam who broke my train of thought. She came in search of me. I had been far too long away from the others. She took me by the hand and led me back into the room where the others were still apparently engaged in the re-run of all that had gone on, or so I thought.
It was John who spoke. There was a facetious grin on his face.
The others were all smiling. I felt unsure of what might happen.

"Michael. What was the picture you had to look at?" His grin broadened.

"It was a Titian!"

"Bless you. But what was the picture I said?"

"A Titian!" This time I spoke in a more resigned fashion, aware of what would follow.

"Bless you. But what about the picture?"

John and I had not done that silly routine for at least twenty six years. It had been one of our regular student stupidities. Every time I returned from the National Gallery after my study of the portrait of the Vendramins, I would have to go through the same old stuff.

"There! I told you he would remember."

The evening ended with generous laughter.

Tomorrow it would be a journey for three of us, Michael, Harry and myself.
The continuation of the recuperation process for Sam.
Putting life back together again for John and Stella.
They did after all have a business to run.

Sam was not awake when we left the following morning.
She had advisedly taken something to help her sleep.
Thankfully, whatever it was was working.

She needed the rest.
She had only spoken briefly of her ordeal.
What had started out with so much hope for her, the possibility of meeting up with Michael, had ended so dramatically with her being taken as hostage in Chartham's plan.

She had been hoodwinked into believing that Michael was going to meet her.
The story became even more believable, she had told us, when instead of
Michael near the golf course it was someone she remembered she had met at Smetton's pre-Christmas party. This young man had simply told her that Michael had been preparing a great surprise for his parents and that she should go with him and his friend to one of the boat builders just down the road at Southwold Harbour. Michael was there, he had said, adding the final touches to the surprise. She had naturally thought that her brother was at last fulfilling a childish promise that he had made about 'one day building a boat for them all.' She had gone with the two men so eagerly. They had laughed together about Michael's secret. They were very convincing. There had been no sense of apprehension at all.

It was only as they went through the door into the boat shed that they had grabbed her, smothered her and tied her up and then taped her mouth so that she could not speak.
She had been put into the soundproofed container and was left there alone. She had suffered the indignity of being taken out of it on occasions when the two had allowed her to use the stinking portable loo.
When Michael had phoned from Chartham's office she had been allowed to speak to him but was under gun threat at the time. She had been advised not to shout out or do anything silly as the people at Smettons were ruthless, and Michael would be harmed if she did.

I had wondered whether it was that young man who was now dead.
How many were involved in the intrigue at Smettons?
We knew of Chartham, Flatton and now this young man... who else?
We would have to be cautious when we got there.
Treddick had not yet had opportunity to speak with Sam.
He did not know of that further connection.
We met up with Treddick and were quickly on our way to talk to the Berrysfords. All three were there, plus Bertie Bantock.

As our story unfolded their shock level rose considerably. When they heard that Alan Marsters was involved up to his neck in all of it... and Moira.
They found it all too much to believe.
Faye was the most alert of them, she it was who began to relate instances concerning disputes between Terry and Alan Marsters. They had often been at loggerheads about policy in both the buying and selling.
Treddick advised her to begin to collect together and to write down her memories of the occasions when Terry and Marsters had argued. It would help, he said, when the court case was brought against him.
Jack and Joanna Berrysford took small consolation in the affirmation of their absolute trust in their son's innocence of any involvement. Their sorrow was increasingly evident... Terry had paid for his honesty with his life.

"When will the court case be heard?" Jack asked.

"O not for some time," replied Treddick. "There are still many loose ends.
The person we believe who has master minded it all is still on the run somewhere. We are still trying to prevent him from achieving what he set out to do. He is a very clever man. He has escaped us so far."

"What will happen to Moira?" Faye asked.

"It all depends on how much she knew of the whole set up. At the moment she is helping us with our inquiries."
Treddick was non-committal in his answer.

"Mr Grantsman." It was Jack Berrysford who spoke directly to me.
"Mr Grantsman, we want to thank you so much for bringing us this peace of mind about Terry. We are going to miss him so much... Mr Grantsman... the police have given us back the box you found... we want to give it to you... just as a thank you."

He left the room for a while, returning moments later with the enigma box in his hands. He held it out towards me. I took it from him.

"I think I should let you know that I found out its secret." I could be nothing but absolutely honest in the company of this fine man. "Would you like me to show you how to open it."

"Please do," he said.

"The tails of the dragons," I didn't think it necessary to correct myself to use the proper name of Wyvern. "The tails can be depressed, each is connected in some way with a release mechanism that allows you to open the box.
Here let me show you properly. I need three other pairs of hands."

Faye volunteered together with Michael and Harry. I told them of how we had discovered it quite by chance. They were as surprised as I had been the very first time the box was opened.
The command 'press' produced the same result.
The satisfying 'click' and the box was opened.

There was a genuine gasp of amazement from all the onlookers, including Treddick. They each viewed the wonderful workmanship of the interior of the box with keen interest. I showed them the tracery lettering. Jack Berrysford moved his finger over the lettering and spoke aloud the words.

"ARTIS EST CELARE ARTEM"

He needed no one to translate for him. He paused for just a while, then spoke.

"The perfection of art is to conceal art...
How beautiful...
Terry would have been so pleased to have found that out...
He was a bit of a perfectionist himself wasn't he Faye... wasn't he Mother? Wasn't he Bertie?"

He looked around at his womenfolk.
His wife so stately and serene.
Her composure was so strong.
His daughter in law so young and vital looking, but now with tears beginning to fall down her face.
Her weeping caused Bertie Bantock great inner grief as well.
It was obvious that he too had had a great affection for the boy.

"O Faye," Berrysford said gently. "I never meant to upset you again."

He put his arm around her and kissed her lightly on her cheek. "We all loved him so much Mr Grantsman. It hurts so much to know that he is gone.

No! well done Mr Grantsman. You thoroughly deserve to keep the box. You found out its secret. Please take it with our grateful thanks."

Why I do not know, but my thoughts had turned to Chartham.
He had almost succeeded in a perfect plan for concealment. There certainly had been artistry in his work, but Michael's had proved the better.

Hopefully Michael's 'smart eyes' would lead us to him, and we would save the stolen treasures.

We had spent a little over an hour with the Berrysfords.

They did not want to let us go.

But we at last excused ourselves and were soon on track for London and the City and there in the City, Smettons.
I travelled with Harry in his van, and Michael went with Treddick. Treddick had already communicated with Smettons.

We were to meet all the Directors at three o'clock.

## VI

Smetton's offices were typical of much of the new building in the City. A lot of glass and stainless steel. Stark against the skyline. They had reserved us space in their limited basement parking zone. Treddick and Michael were already there when Harry and I arrived. We met up in the spacious foyer. Our security was checked. We were issued with visitor's badges. And in the company of a very efficient secretary we were escorted up in a lift to the third floor, to the Board Room.
Michael was deep in conversation with the secretary obviously trying to gauge the delicate political temperature, perhaps a little unsure of what was going to transpire when he met up with the full force of the Smetton hierarchy. My thoughts were somewhat different.
How many other such buildings had secrets?
How many hid dubious dealings from the public?
In how many others had murderous plans been put into operation?
In how many of these worthy institutions had greed been the downfall of the men of power who walked their corridors?
What would the reaction be from these men as they listened to our story?

The Chairman took the lead.

"Well young Trevough, what have you been up to?
Mr Treddick, when he phoned told us to expect to hear things that were very disturbing and perhaps damaging to the Company."

Treddick spoke before Michael had a chance to say anything at all.

"Perhaps I should make introductions."

He proceeded to do this, outlining, for each person introduced, their part in what he described as a most significant case of high risk criminality that had involved kidnap and murder. The visitors present in this Board Room, he said, had lived on the edge of that situation for some time, but were now in a position to reveal the whole story so far. A story, he knew, that would shock the board members of Smettons to the very core of their belief in their abilities to provide top level security procedures. Smettons were currently the victims of a very sophisticated plan to divert into private hands a considerable amount of extremely valuable articles entrusted to them by very important customers. There were at the highest level within Smettons, individuals who were prepared to instigate these things with no thought of compassion for those they were using to bring about their evil plans. Outside associates of high ranking Smettons individuals had already committed the crime of murder. And people within Smettons had coerced actions of one individual in particular, using kidnap and fear of reprisals as the tool for accomplishing their plan.

The Smettons Board members sat with ashen faces.
The Chairman spoke once more.

"Mr Treddick, you shock us all beyond belief. What can we do? Is there no measure we can take to change things?"

"You must be thankful," replied Treddick, "that young Michael Trevough has the brains and the wisdom to enable some course of action to be put into place. His family has been the unwitting victims in all of this.
His friends have been in danger as well, through no real fault of their own.
But we must move quickly to enable the best possible result to be achieved.
Even now we may be a little too late."

"Who, within Smettons, are you talking about?" The Chairman asked.

"The master mind, we believe is one of your Senior Directors, Chartham. His understudy, your Overseas Manager, Flatton. Plus at least one or two others of very much lower ranking. One of whom we believe has been killed as a result of his involvement. We are talking very serious business.
We need your absolute cooperation in order to complete our inquiries."

The Chairman gestured to his secretary, "Get Personnel on the phone, ask them the whereabouts of Chartham and Flatton."

"Chartham, we believe," said Treddick interrupting the Chairman, "should be well out of the country by now.
We have been watching his activities for the last few days.
We have no knowledge of Flatton."

The reply to the secretary's call confirmed that Chartham had taken a few days holiday, and would not be back until at least the end of the month, and Flatton had called in sick.

"We will need the home addresses of both Chartham and Flatton, and all the information you can supply us on their family circumstances."

Treddick was at his most authoritative, and was definitely commanding respect from all the Smettons people present.

He took good advantage of their immediate realisation that the name of the Company was in danger. The whole reason for them being in business was to provide secure passage of goods worldwide.
They were all quick to see the need for damage limitation, and were aghast at the knowledge concerning allegations of kidnap and murder.
For highly respected and very professional men they were all visibly crumpled by the information they had received.
The Chairman was only just managing to remain calm. He could not avoid asking what he saw to be the crunch question for them as a Company.

"Do you have any idea of the value of the goods at risk?"

"There seems to have been two quite distinct operations that have been started. The major one, in my view," said Treddick, "because it has already involved a very nasty murder, was the stealing and the faking of the Titians, and the substitution of the enigma boxes and the silverware. Had we lost the Titians they would have been under Government indemnity, being national treasures.
The boxes and silverware seem to be a straightforward insurance job.
Now they may have been a greedy sideline for Berrysford's man Marsters.
We have yet to question him fully.
The second operation, and Chartham's major acquisition appears to be the goods in transit from Sotheby's.
The value there may be twenty million pounds or more."

Shock followed shock for the Smettons men.

Had it not been for what we had all been through I may have begun to feel sorry for them. Even now, Michael may be in a position to redeem the situation for them.
Treddick advised the Chairman to listen to what Michael had to say.

- 187 -

The Chairman voiced his deep gratitude to Michael.

"On behalf of the Board may I say how indebted we are to you, Michael.
Tell us now of your family. How are they all?"

Michael responded by informing them of Sam's condition, in particular. And also, much to my embarrassment, of my involvement in the whole affair.
He told of the incredible pressure that had been exerted on his whole family.

"Mr Grantsman you must be a very good friend indeed," the Chairman said, turning to me. "Thank you very much."

But I could sense that he was interested in other things.

"Now, Michael, Mr Treddick informs us that you may have a plan that can help us?"

Michael's opportunity had come at last to reveal the fact that he had completed the final detailed programming of the highest level of security he had ever devised for Smettons. The container satellite search system was now activated. He would need to take them to his office to show them his handiwork. If everything was working properly then we should be able to track the containers. His very obvious enthusiasm was the spur they all needed. They were keen to see what Michael was talking about.

We were all invited to go to Michael's office. Treddick needed he said, to make a few calls regarding the possible whereabouts of Flatton, to check on his home address. The same with Chartham, although he feared that they would draw a blank there.
By the time Treddick joined us, Michael had his system up and running, much to the absolute astonishment of the Board members. They had known that he was working on a very special system that was in the development stage, but were totally unaware that he had completed his work. He was busy explaining that because the sensors contained in the Smetton logo on the sides of the containers had now been activated and the batteries were drawing and storing power that he could in fact plot the journey of the individual containers using a link to one of the many satellite systems that covered the globe. He typed in a container identification number and then, at the push of a key the screen changed

to show map coordinates, revealing exactly where that container was in the world. He struck another key and the screen changed once again to show the map of the world. A pulsing green light was evident in the European sector. He enlarged it once, twice, three times.
There was the coastline of Northern Germany.
He enlarged it even further, the River Elbe was clearly marked. Hamburg, the docks. The pulsing green light was clear indication of the whereabouts of that particular container.
He typed in the numbers of the other nine, and they too could be clearly identified as being still there at the dockside in Hamburg.

"Michael, does this mean to say that we have been lucky." The Chairman was visibly excited.

"Who knows, Sir? My programme can only tell the location of the containers. They may have been unloaded by now. My personal view is that they are still full and are waiting for collection. We may see them move at any time."

"Michael!" It was Treddick. "Give me those map coordinates, I will phone them through to the Port Police in Hamburg.
It would be good to get some human eyes looking at the scene.
They will be able to confirm or not whether the goods are there.
Although we need a lead on Chartham we don't want to lose sight of the valuables in the process.
These ten containers were the only ones dumped in the 'black hole?'
The container with the Titians and the boxes and the silverware or rather the fakes and the substitutes was not affected. We must presume that it will be discharged normally and the items collected for delivery to the required destination. I am intrigued at what may be in store for them.
Michael can you locate that container, and can you find out the address for the delivery of the Titians and the other goods?"

Michael was quick to oblige.
The container was there with the rest.
And the address of the gallery that was to show the Titians, that too was quickly on screen. Somewhere in Denmark was the final destination.
Michael said that it would take a little while to print out a map that would give the exact location, but he would do it if it were needed.

Treddick was in decisive action mode.

"Michael you must stay here to be in control of the computer side of things.
And, yes, will you print out the map? But you two…" and he pointed directly at Harry and myself, "what do you say to a trip to Hamburg?"
As if my life had not been filled with so much excitement.
I heard myself eagerly agreeing.
Harry too was game.

But then Harry was game for anything, any time, he needed just a minute to let May know his whereabouts.
My immediate inquiry concerned passports.
Treddick told us we would be travelling under police authority and that would be sufficient. We weren't going on holiday.
There would be no time for seeing the sights and definitely no time to visit the Reeperbahn if that was in our thoughts.
Harry protested his innocence, and with a twinkle in his eye, told us all that it was not as good as it was 'cracked up' to be!
His attempt at humour provided a moment of relief for all of us.
But no one thought to ask him how he knew that to be true.

Treddick was immediately on the phone attempting to organise our flights to Hamburg. Speed was of the essence, he told us we could not afford to waste any time. London City Airport was the most direct if there was a flight available. The required information was quite straightforward..
A 16.30 flight on KLM would get us there but it was not direct.
There would be an unfortunate stopover of an hour at Amsterdam.

The Smettons Chairman suggested the use of the Company jet.
It too was at London City. He would count it a privilege if Treddick would let the Company help in this respect. Treddick accepted the Chairman's generosity agreeing that it would be the quickest way by far.
I wondered how long it would take for the flight to be organised, but was truly amazed to discover that it took just a single phone call.
By the time it took for us to get to London City Airport the pilot would have filed his flight plans, and with the police clearance that Treddick put in place, we would have immediate OK for take off.

I had often used the London City Airport for my European business trips and was always impressed by the approach to it.
You could speed along the new roadways for the developing docklands, passing the overhead Docklands Light Railway, which always reminded

me of a children's train set as it chuntered along its computerised track, and then turning towards the airport, you would view the great expanse of water in the Royal Docks.
Royal Victoria on the right and Royal Albert on the left with King George the Fifth lying beyond. All of the waterways now appeared to be in use for sporting activities. Long gone was the time when a huge tonnage of worldwide merchant shipping was discharged by the expert hands of an East End workforce. Apart from the airport this area of the new docklands still had that 'waiting for tomorrow' feel about it.
There were still vast spaces waiting for development.

Treddick parked up in the long stay area and was soon deliberating with airport officials asking the whereabouts of the Smettons pilot.

To our surprise a very smart young woman introduced herself, explaining, as she led us through all the formalities, that she was often flying on lease to other companies when Smettons had nothing on hand that required her flying skills. We would be in Hamburg before we knew it.
Fuhlsbuttel Airport was about six miles north of the City Centre, would we need a decent place to stay, or a car? She could arrange that for us.
How long would we be needing her services?
Was she to stay in Hamburg to await our return?
Smettons had told her to be available.
To meet our every need.
She dressed Calvin Klein, had the homely allure of up market Body Shop, and smacked of self assured efficiency, in the nicest way possible.

Treddick got us through all the officialese.
Gaynor Morris, for that was her name, led us the rest of the way to the Smettons jet. Just off the runway there was a very smart Cessna 525 CitationJet with its distinctive high 'T' tail and its two Williams/Rolls Royce FJ44 Turbofans.
On that distinctive tail was the equally distinctive Smettons logo.
I wondered if that logo had been 'smartened' by Michael,
as the logo was exactly the same as the others I had remembered seeing at the dockside at Felixstowe, I presumed that Michael could now track the whereabouts of the Company jet with equal ease. I hoped that it would not be necessary.

On boarding we discovered that the interior was laid out with a touch of executive splendour. Computer facilities, well stocked bar, daily papers, all that those on a 'short haul' would require.
Gaynor went through the flight checks. When these were finished and the OK given for take off, she settled into, what for us appeared to be, a very dedicated and professional routine that saw us into the air and away over a quickly disappearing London.
It would be Hamburg next stop.
When all the air traffic requirements had been completed she spoke to us, telling with obvious pride, that Smettons had been one of the first to buy into this particular area of high security delivery. Any package that was of a highly sensitive nature could be delivered very discretely by using the Company jet. Smettons had invested in the 525 way back in 1994 just a year after its completion.
The Company was very pleased with its performance.
And she Gaynor Morris, had been employed by them three years later in the early part of 1997.
Harry asked her how far it would go.
Her reply was direct and textbook in nature. Range, she told him, with one crew and maybe four passengers (there were six seats) would be in the region of some seventeen hundred miles.
She added without being asked that we would be flying at just over three hundred miles an hour.

When asked, we all settled for coffee, rather than alcohol.
Harry obliged by making it, venturing forward, moments later, to take a mug full of the steaming brew to Gaynor.
She made his day by asking him to take control whilst she drank her coffee. Just keep her on a steady course, she told him.
She came back to Treddick and myself.
Both of us were just a little wary that we were now in Harry's hands, but we were told not to worry, there was a glint in her eye.
The plane was safely on 'auto.'

She finished her drink and returned to the controls. Harry returned to us, boyishly excited by his experience.

In what appeared to be no time at all, we could hear Hamburg air traffic giving Gaynor details and clearance for landing.
We touched down safely in a fairly heavy drizzle.
What the locals describe as 'Schmuddelwetter' Gaynor told us.
A very descriptive phrase.
'Dirty weather.'

In this 'dirty weather' dirty things were afoot in Hamburg.

After touch down we were met by two men from the Hamburg police who spoke privately with Treddick for a while.
Meanwhile, Gaynor gave me the phone number of where she would be, telling me that she would be available at any time for the return journey.
The Cessna would be checked and refuelled and would be ready for take off at any time. Treddick informed us that the return journey could be as soon as the following morning as the Hamburg Port Police were certain that the containers had not been discharged.

Michael's satellite location set up had pinpointed the exact position of the Smettons containers, which was a very good thing.
There were over forty miles of dockside and quays in the Hamburg Port. To have had to have searched without any help whatsoever would have been a nigh on impossible task. The small size of the ship on which the containers had come had enabled them to be off loaded at an extremely private location.
The police had had some difficulty in setting up surveillance but that had been achieved with positive success.
All ten Sotheby's containers were there.

Our next task was simply to identify, and check the contents to see if they matched the original manifests.
All three of us had been present at Felixstowe when Customs had checked the containers the first time round, so it would be fairly easy for us to sort them out now. Treddick suggested that we look through them all straight away and then devise some waiting plan to see if Chartham would turn up at all to redirect the contents to his own destination.

The container with the fakes on board had been discharged and the crates were awaiting collection for their onward transit to the Gallery in Denmark.

With the assistance of Customs officials and Hamburg Port police the task of examination of contents of the containers was accomplished with ease.
As each was discharged and the contents checked against manifest each was discovered to be OK.

There was just one shock, or rather two!

Although the security seals were all intact, the last two of the containers were found to be completely empty!
Stuck to the inside of each of the empty containers was a crudely scrawled notice. The first stated. 'One day I'll make you cry Trevough!' The you was heavily underlined.
And the second. 'You'll need better eyes to find me!'

The three of us who knew what that meant, fell silent.
My heart went cold. Harry came to my side and gripped my shoulder.
Treddick swore.
It was not over. Chartham had succeeded in emptying just two containers and transferring their contents, whilst they were on the high sea.
We would never know where they were going now.

After his inquiry, Treddick was told by the Port police that the small container ship had already sailed, its stated destination Rotterdam.
Not one of us believed that to be true.
All three of us believed that trouble was still in store.
But when? And for whom?

"We won't see Chartham here." It was Treddick who broke the silence. "He's well on his way with his ill-gotten gains. We might as well go home."

It was late in the evening. The 'Schmuddelwetter' had really set in.
Along with the weather we were all dismal and despondent. We had had only partial success. There were still dangers ahead. Chartham had proved to be a very cunning man. He had outwitted us. And had now declared his hand.

Treddick concluded his business with the Port police. The police in Hamburg, he informed Harry and myself, would track the delivery of the fakes and would let him know what transpired. Smettons would complete delivery of the Sotheby's stuff.
We could find somewhere to stay the night.

We found that lodging in a small inn just off the historic Grossneumarkt.
The early spring had made this lovely seventeenth century tree lined square into a place of beauty and even late in the evening the lights of the many bars and theatres made it all so pleasant.

There were people spilling out of drinking houses and cafes, milling around the pedestrianised walkway.
The chatter was international and friendly.
This place too, brought back memories.
On that one occasion the many years before, when my father had brought us to Hamburg, we had spent an evening of great excitement at the Cotton Club.
It was some of the best jazz I had ever heard.
It was so difficult to realise that my current trip to Hamburg was of such a drastically different nature.
Treddick, Harry and myself enjoyed the late night Hamburg scene, finally finding sleep a little after three in the morning.

We breakfasted early and when we had finished, I phoned the number that Gaynor Morris had given me, only to be told that she had already left for the airport. Breakfast over, we paid our bill and left.
The taxi journey to Fuhlsbuttel was without incident.

On arrival, we put a message over the tannoy for Gaynor. She was quick to respond. Everything was ready, we could be on our way straight away.

We took off, a little after eight o'clock in the morning, the now cloud free skies giving us splendid views of a rapidly disappearing Hamburg.
The Elbe stretched lazily beneath us, we were over the sea in no time at all.
We were bound for home where we would find Michael.
I did not want to be the one who would tell him of Chartham's cruel promise.

Gaynor had been busy with the take off and had been quietly efficient in everything she had done.
Half an hour into the flight and well over the sea she called back to us that she would enjoy a coffee, 'would some person oblige!'

I took the cue and busied myself for a few brief moments.
Water into the kettle.
Mugs on to the counter.

"Where's the coffee?" was my shout to Gaynor.

"Under the counter," was her reply.

Sure enough she was right.
The coffee jar was obscured from my view by a large package.

I couldn't help noticing that it was addressed to Smettons.
My inquiring and somewhat suspicious mind forced me to ask what I saw to be the obvious question.

"Where did the package come from, Gaynor?"

"Mr Chartham gave it to me this morning. The airport phoned me early saying that he had arrived and would I meet up with him as he had something I should deliver back to Head Office. He was breaking his holiday plans especially so would I please come straight away. He couldn't stay around too long. Why do you ask? I do it all the time."

We had all heard every word that she had spoken.
Harry, no longer had his head buried in the paper.
Treddick had got up from his seat and had joined me at the bar.
I had frozen stock still.
In the process of moving it, my hand was on the packet.
There was not one innocent thought in my head.
I knew; Treddick knew; and Harry, who had now joined us at the bar, knew as well. The cunning fox Chartham had put us all in peril.
This could not be a simple delivery job.
There was something far more sinister about this little sequence of events.
How did he know that the company jet had flown in?
Was there someone still at Smettons who was informing on us?
If the package was innocent in character, to open it in order to find out its contents, would cause no damage.
If it was of a malicious nature, we were doubtless in danger already.
The nodded conclusion to our spoken thoughts brought a unanimous decision from all three of us. We must discover its contents.
Gaynor, oblivious of the new situation, inquired as to the state of the coffee, that 'she would appreciate it before touch down.'
My somewhat cavalier answer was that 'it would be with her in a moment.'
My voiced thought to my companions was a simple acknowledgement that all of us may well have not only coffee in a moment, but our chips as well, and way before touch down.

This was no time for stupid attempts at humour.
A cool head and steady hands were required.
Our joint decision was not to tell Gaynor of our plight for the moment. Far better that she fly on unaware of the predicament. If our number was up, better that she didn't know.
With great care, I eased the package off the shelf and placed it on the counter.
Typical of Harry, he took hold of the coffee jar that was now in view, and said that we may as well have a cup, especially as it may be our last!
He would make it for all four of us. It would be the best cup of coffee we had ever tasted! I was sure that the look of wry humour that spread over his face hid other emotions.

Both Treddick and I examined the package with great care.
Brown paper, string, neatly tied, obviously covering a box, about twice the size of a cereal packet.

Treddick undid the neat bow in the string.
The brown paper was easily loosened to reveal, as we had imagined, a cardboard box, the lid of which was stuck down with sticky tape. Treddick cut the tape with his pocket knife. I lifted the lid of the box. The first confirming horror was to see some of the flammable insulation board that we had all seen at both Felixstowe and at The Maltings. The top layer of board appeared to be loosely covering the real contents.
Treddick removed the covering.

Harry, who had finished making the coffee, let out a low whistle of surprise.
Blinking away at us was a device, similar to the one we had seen before. But this time it wasn't a matter of hours ticking away. There were just eighteen minutes left on the display. It was obvious to the three of us that the incendiary part of the device was quite small. Much more sophisticated than the crude device at The Maltings. The package was as large as it was, because of the extra flammable board that surrounded it. On closer examination you could see that a fine glass pressure switch had broken obviously under the change in pressure on board as we had reached cruising altitude. This breakage had caused the timer to start.
We now had seventeen and a half minutes to do something about it.

"What if we got Gaynor to fly real low over the water, and as slow as possible. Would it be possible to open the door and simply hurl the whole package into the sea?"

Although it sounded very much like super hero stuff, Harry's suggestion had a ring of possibility about it.

We needed to inform Gaynor quickly.
There was no other way of putting it.

"Gaynor," I said, as calmly as possible. "We have a serious situation back here. The package that Chartham gave you is actually an incendiary device that is timed to go off in sixteen minutes."

To her absolute credit her hands did not shift from the controls, it was simply in her eyes that you could see an immediate response. Her jaw tightened and she spoke with difficulty.

"Did I hear you correctly? An incendiary device? How do you know?"

"Gaynor." This time it was Treddick who spoke. "The story is far too long to tell right now. Believe us. It is an incendiary device that we need to deal with as soon as possible. The seconds are ticking away. Harry has come up with a possible plan. Can you reduce height and speed and fly as close to the water as you can. Then we could try and open the door of the plane and hurl the device into the sea."

"No go! Definitely no go!" Gaynor replied. "This is a jet plane, you could hardly open the door at all, if you did succeed in opening it just the slightest, then the door would be ripped off and sucked out and whoever opened it with it. No that is definitely not possible. Got any other plan?
How long do you say we have?"

I glanced at the device. The display showed fifteen minutes.

"I must send out a Mayday call straight away.
Whatever is going to happen will happen over the sea.
We are too far away from land to attempt a landing anywhere.
Would you please think up some other plan. Please."

There was a definite edge to her voice.

"How big is the device?" Gaynor's voice was controlled.
She had finished the Mayday.

"And how long have we got now?"

"Thirteen and a half minutes."

Harry and Treddick had carefully stripped the device down to its smallest size. The timer was attached to a small battery that in turn was taped to the explosive material. Somewhere out of sight was the explosive cap.

In all it was about the size of half a house brick.
And it weighed about the same.
It was safe enough to hold, but inexorably the minutes were ticking by.
There was no way of knowing how to defuse the thing.
It looked disastrously as though the sadistic Chartham was going to succeed in his terrible plan. He had wilfully chosen to destroy not only those who had challenged his fortunes, but Gaynor Morris also.
In her innocence, she had accepted this package from him.
And now along with the rest of us she was going to be destroyed.

"How big is the device?" Gaynor spoke again.

Treddick had the package in his hand, so he went forward to show her.

"There is a slight chance that we might ditch it."

She had seen the size of the device, and was now pointing to the left of the cockpit.

"See there. The direct vision window panel can be opened. You won't be able to just drop the device out though. If you did just drop it, it would probably be sucked up into the air stream and one of those air hungry Turbofans would suck it in, and that would be curtains for all of us.
Someone will have to hurl it up as high as possible, and as straight as possible. Maybe, just maybe, it will miss the engines.
That, I think, is our only chance. So who is going to do it?"

The direct vision panel was used, Gaynor informed us, if the pilot had need of seeing directly what was going on outside, in cases where perhaps a bird had been splattered all over the windscreen, or the forward view had become obscured in any way.

She was speaking in a way that we could understand, using lay man's language, but we knew what she meant.

The panel was on the left.
It opened inwards.
It needed a lefthanded person to be most effective.
The arm would need to be as far out of the little window panel as possible.
Harry was our man. The only lefthanded person available.

"How long now?" Gaynor asked once more.

There was more of a sense of pleading in her voice.
None of us wanted to have the end come in this particular way.
But she, of all of us, was the innocent one.
The anxiety levels were on the rise all round.

"Eight minutes."

Treddick's voice was calm.

Harry had rolled his sleeve up. He was busy rehearsing the sort of throw he might achieve. There was a very serious look on his now perspiring face.
This was going to be a once only attempt. It couldn't be like the throw of a cricket ball. It couldn't be like anything he had ever done before.
Our lives depended on this man's ability to be innovative and strong, our lives depended on him being very lucky!

On Gaynor's instruction he opened the window panel.
There was a rush of turbulence inside the cockpit. The sound level rose.

The four of us were quiet.
My thoughts were mixed. There was the obvious anxiety. But I found myself thinking first of Lara, then of Sam, Michael, Stella and John.
I found myself, not only thinking, but praying.
I glanced behind me.

There too was Treddick, on his face a look of real composure.
His eyes too were heavenward.
For me it was with sudden urgency, but looking at Treddick I could see that he was far more used to bringing the Almighty into his affairs.
There were tears in Gaynor's eyes.

I moved to her side and placed my hand gently on her shoulder.
"Sorry to have got you into this." I shouted the words at her.

I did not know whether she understood what I said.
"Good luck, old man," I shouted to Harry. "Do it for May's sake."

There were three and a half minutes registering on the timer.
Second by second gradually slipping away.
Harry looked at me with a sort of smile on his face that seemed to indicate a 'now or never' understanding between us.
What a friend I had turned out to be.
Here he was about to do the one thing that might save us all.
Gaynor had her white knuckled hands on the controls, not knowing whether she might be needed immediately to cope with shattered engines or who knows what. I guessed that there was nothing in the flight manuals that might give her a clue as to the next procedure to employ if the tail of your plane was blown apart. I wondered, stupidly, whether a flight simulator could be programmed for this sort of eventuality. I was amazed at what was rushing through my mind.

Harry eased his hand out of the direct vision panel. He had a sure grip on the incendiary device. He extended his arm through the opening. I could tell that he was battling to keep control of things.
The air speed was ripping at his arm, wanting to tear it backwards.
A grim look of fierce determination appeared on his face.
There were beads of perspiration forming on his forehead.
They formed and then funnelled down his face.
What was he waiting for?

Gaynor throttled back the engines.

"I dare not reduce speed any further, we're near stalling now."

Harry was peering at the timer.
I too could see the relentless count down taking place.
Fifteen... fourteen... thirteen... twelve... eleven... ten...
Harry contorted himself in one violent upwards motion of his arm, screaming at the top of his voice, hurling the device as high as he possibly could.

We waited.
I was mentally continuing the count down.

Nine... eight... seven... six... five... four... three... two... one...
Harry had his eyes tight closed.
He was gripping the open panel with his other hand as well.
We were still flying.
All we could hear was the rush of air sucking through the opening.
Harry had done it.
We were still flying safely.
Gaynor increased airspeed.
She was unashamedly crying tears of relief.
Treddick came forward with the coffee. As cool as ever. Treddick, that is.
Harry was obviously in pain.
He was unable to get his arm back through the opening.
Try as he may he could not manage it.
He looked at me with a sense of alarm in his eyes.
He was in trouble of some sort.
I moved from where I had been standing next to Gaynor and tried to see what the trouble was. On closer scrutiny it was painfully obvious.
The force of his throw combined with the airspeed was too much for his arm to take. It looked as though his shoulder was dislocated.
How we succeeded in pulling him back into the cockpit, I will never know.
I never knew that he could scream as loud as he did.
It was the only way that he could find to deal with the excruciating pain.
He finally fell awkwardly alongside Gaynor and let out one final scream of agony. The shape of his shoulder in its alignment with the rest of his body was quite grotesque. It was difficult to imagine what we could do for him to ease the pain. Fortunately he fainted, the pain was too much. His brain closed him down.
The cabin was quieter. Treddick managed to close the direct vision window.

"There's morphine in the first aid kit," Gaynor said. "I'll administer it if one of you will just keep the controls steady."

"Gaynor Morris, you are truly an amazing young woman!"

I spoke with quiet admiration for her evident abilities.

"Where did you learn all this stuff?"

"It's all part of our training. O, and by the way, I'm not so young.

I'm just wearing well. I'm on the wrong side of thirty, but who cares?"
Treddick took the controls, whilst Gaynor busied herself with finding the first aid kit. Having found it and opened it she withdrew from its contents a glass ampoule of morphine. She wiped Harry's arm with a sterilised swab. Broke the glass ampoule revealing the sharp needle, and with great care gave the injection that would maintain Harry's pain free journey back home.

She was quickly back at the controls, allowing Treddick and myself the opportunity of lifting Harry as best we could out of the flight deck and back into the cabin area. We settled him into one of the seats, strapped his seat belt on, and found enough cushions to cradle his oddly shaped arm and shoulder, hoping that we had not hurt him too much in the process.

Gaynor was busy speaking to air traffic control at London City Airport. The Mayday situation was cleared up. We could hear her ordering up an ambulance to be there on touch down ready to take Harry on to hospital. She was giving details of what she had done for him.
That conversation finished, she turned back to us.
The look on her face was now completely different.
A cautious smile appeared.
"We should be there in about twenty five minutes," she said. "It's all in a days work. Did I ever get my coffee?"

The Thames was soon beneath us.
Then we could see the Docks.
We were given immediate clearance for landing.
The air ambulance was there, its efficient crew dealing with the situation with great professionalism.
Still out to the world, Harry was taken off to hospital.
I flew with him, and, much to my relief was able to see him attended to with top level priority. The London Hospital was reached in a matter of minutes.
Treddick had phoned on ahead clearing the way.

After Xrays and consultations and painful manipulation was over, Harry with his once badly dislocated shoulder was now in much better shape, sleeping peacefully. The hospital doctor attending him told me that there had been extensive damage to the muscles of the upper arm and shoulder and that there would be some very bad bruising.
It would take time, but everything would be alright.

On his journey to Smettons, Treddick had been able to arrange for a police car to pick May up.
When she arrived I told her just a little of her husband's heroics.
He had saved our lives.
Who was I to understate the part that he had played?
I simply told her the truth concerning Harry's efforts.
All May said was 'fancy that' in her quiet unassuming voice.
She seated herself by the side of his bed, telling me that she would wait until he came round. She fussed at the pillows and took his right hand in hers and kissed him lightly on the cheek.

"You get well, my pet. May's here! Never mind now."

I watched her. It was so easy to know why I liked the pair of them so well.

Harry was still out to the world, so I left the hospital at twelve, telling May that I would go to Smettons and pick up Harry's motor, and would come back for her later in the afternoon in order to take her home.
May found the keys in Harry's pocket and agreed that I should do as I had suggested. She kissed me goodbye with a quiet 'thank you' for making sure he was looked after.
She was thanking me!
Did she not realise that I would be forever thanking her, for being married to such a man as Harry.

Treddick was still at Smettons when I arrived. He had been filling in Michael and the Management with all that had gone on.
Gaynor, after completion of her report at the airport, had also arrived and was being feted as a heroine.
The Chairman had had something to tell Treddick.
That same news Treddick passed on to me.
Whilst we had been on our way back, the Hamburg police had contacted Smettons with the news that the Titians and the other crates of substitute goods had duly caught fire whilst en route to their destination.
They had been totally destroyed.
The driver of the flat bed low loader on which they had been secured had been seen by the following police, leaving his cab and running away whilst the lorry was in a traffic jam.
He had obviously chosen his spot well for the fire services were unable to reach the lorry when his cab exploded moments later, igniting the crates in the ensuing disastrous fire.

That part of Chartham's plan, or was that part Marsters' plan... well whoever it was who had masterminded that particular plan, had almost succeeded.
Apart from the fact that we knew the goods to be fake.
They might have got away with that.
Flatton had been picked up by the police from his home, and, like Moira Brownsmoor, was busy cooperating, telling all he knew of Chartham's plan. Michael had rightly worked out that Flatton was a very small fish in Chartham's organisation. Flatton had told the police of a call from Chartham that he had received whilst Chartham was in Hamburg. He had asked him to check on the status of things at Smettons. It was the answer to that call that had given Chartham the information about the company plane's departure. Flatton had found out from other office personnel that the police and others were searching for Chartham.

So much for security!

Michael had taken the news about Chartham's blatant threats, quite calmly.
There would be plenty of time to worry about that, he had said.
Chartham, he was sure, would take a long time to nurse his wounds, and anyway the police would still be after him.

The value of the two containers of goods that Chartham had got away with was still considerable, some three million pounds worth. The police would continue to be very interested.
They had full documentation of what had been stolen. Chartham would find it very difficult to shift the stuff on the open market.

Michael said again that he wasn't going to worry about Chartham.
Sam was safe, and recovering well. He was back in touch with his family. Everything was going to be all right.

The security risks within Smettons had been identified.
Michael's new 'smart system' had provided a well improved set up that the Management were going to exploit to their advantage. The only untidy end in all of the affair, was Chartham.
He was still out there somewhere. And he had something to settle.
I was not as convinced as Michael about everything being alright.

A number of decisions were made.

By Treddick... first to make sure that Smettons made all information available about Chartham, and then to check with Hamburg the status of things there.
By Smettons... first to give Michael a week off to recuperate and spend time with his family, and then to offer Gaynor a couple of days extra leave which she should take straight away.
By Michael... to go home as soon as he could.
By me... first to pick up Harry's motor and return to the hospital to check on him there and take May back to their home, and then to ask Gaynor for her telephone number. I felt I owed her something, but I didn't know what.

My leaving was prevented for the moment by the Chairman's interesting and challenging comment.

"Mr Grantsman. Michael has been telling us of your unusual involvement in all of this. He has told us that you have no transport now due to a slight accident you had preventing the escape of one of the key players.
I am sure the Company will be more than grateful to you. We will keep in touch. It will be to your advantage. Goodbye Mr Grantsman."

He shook my hand warmly.
I left Smettons having told Michael that I would get in touch after checking how Harry was. For the moment Harry was my chief concern.
I said goodbye to Treddick, knowing that our paths would inevitably cross when Marsters came to trial. It had been good to get to know a man like Treddick, there was something of true worth in him. He had set me thinking at a deep level.

I picked up Harry's motor, noticing the enigma box. I decided there and then that I would give it to Sam, she had helped me with its secret. She had paid a high price for her involvement. She deserved some small reward.

Harry was awake when I arrived at hospital. He was very sore, and I could see the extent of the bruising that was gradually discolouring his upper arm and chest. He was busy telling his story to May in his own inimitable way. We spoke for what seemed like hours, and it was only when a nurse suggested that he really needed to rest that I noticed the time. Late in the evening I dragged May away and made for West London and home. Harry would be in hospital for a couple of days at least.

I decided I would invite myself up to Southwold. Further, I decided I would telephone Gaynor to see if she would like to accompany me.

May was pleased to loan me Harry's van. He wouldn't be able to drive it for some while, she said. And Gaynor, much to my delight, agreed to my suggestion. The following day I picked her up. And we were on our way.
It felt good.
The Southwold home was full of laughter when we arrived.
Sam was definitely so much better.
Canny fussed around me.
Michael had arrived the previous night and the story telling was in full swing. They needed my side, and of course Gaynor's, to complete the story.
There was so much to tell.

I gave the box to Sam, who protested that I should keep it.
But after much persuasion agreed that she had loved it the first time she had seen it and of course she would take care of it.
She would treasure it forever.

"For my birthday then. Tomorrow! St George's Day?
Thank you Michael," she said.

For the very first time in her life she had abbreviated my name.
I was no longer Uncle Michael.

I had become just... Michael.

I looked from Sam to Gaynor.
Quite unexpectedly, I sneezed.
Gaynor's sparkling eyes lit up her whole face.

And she was looking straight at me.

## VII

Alan Marster's trial was a straight forward affair. What with the Berrysford connection through his work, the documented connection with Terry at Felixstowe, the police surveillance at Snape and of course the shoot out at Southwold; all this combined with the prosecution's star witness Moira Brownsmoor's testimony put him away for a considerable term.
The list of his misdemeanors was lengthy, to say the least.

There were disturbing moments brought very much into the public domain as the forensic evidence was revealed concerning the identification of Terry Berrysford's body.
The dental records and the gruesome photograph of the blackened hand that showed that ring were enough and Jack Berrysford once again showed great dignity as he confirmed his personal testimony with the production of a photograph taken at the time of the giving of the ring. The picture showed his own mother, hand in hand with her grandson Terry, their two hands clasped with the ring very evident showing the initials very clearly indeed.

My testimony placed Marsters at the scene of the burning cars, my recognition of his 4.2 being the conspicuous evidence that was drawn from me under great duress, as his barrister insisted that I should divulge the reasons for my certainty in this department.

Gaynor had been there, together with John and Stella, and strangely the pain of the recall seemed to be balanced by a deepening friendship that was developing at what appeared to be an alarming pace between myself and Gaynor. John and Stella were co-conspirators in this as they constantly invited us to be with them on all sorts of occasions.
Treddick had been a constant source of strength at all times through the trial period and we had said our goodbyes with promises made about getting in touch in the future.

It was with great surprise then, that just two weeks after the trial was finished I received a call from Treddick with the disturbing insistence that he needed to see me with some urgency.
He had insisted that he come to my home in his own time.

"Look at those," he said, as we seated ourselves at my now not so clutttered desk, Gaynor's tidiness was rubbing off on me. He had deposited an envelope that on opening contained two photographs, both of which I had seen before, very recently indeed.

"Tell me everything you know about them.
Everything you remember, absolutely everything!"

The photographs were of the ring on Terry Berrysford's hand. The one tenderly held by a doting grandmother and the other the gruesome result of the foul play that had taken his life.

"What do you recall?
Think Michael, and think hard.
Take your time.
When did you first hear anything definitive about the subject matter?"

I was not so silly as to step in immediately with a reply that was painfully obvious. He would not have come so far with a list of questions that were so carefully framed had he not wanted me to go beyond the obvious.

I took my time, twisting the photographs this way and that.
I put them under a magnifier.
The sight of the blackened hand caused flashbacks that quite unnerved me.
Twisting them and turning them…
Twisting them…

"The initials are pointing in different directions, but that's all as far as I am concerned. Is there something that I have missed?"

"Now think again, Michael. Please think again. What was it that Jack Berrysford told us about that ring?
What did he tell us about Terry and that ring?"

I closed my eyes, reaching deep into my so recent memories.
What was it?
It took a while… but there somewhere in the dark recesses of my mind a remembered conversation between Treddick and myself was reforming.

"… that since the day his grandmother had given the ring to him… he had never ever taken it off. He had never taken it off!"

"Exactly, Michael! Thank you for your unprompted recall.
I think Terry Berrysford is still alive.
I think the body the Berrysfords consigned to their family grave was of some other unfortunate, sadisticly made up to cause the misidentification."

"What about the dental records, though? They were exact in every detail."
Treddick waited for a moment before he replied.

"Yes we have a problem there, I know. But not an impossible one. I may have to ask for an exhumation of the body for a further examination to take place."

At the trial there had been no need for DNA tests to be done for the evidence pointed so directly to a positive identification of Terry Berrysford's body. Now that new opportunity was before us I wondered what the Berrysfords would say. I trusted Treddick to approach them with his recognised sensitivity, but who could contemplate or prophesy the outcome?

Treddick stayed on and we enjoyed the immediate updates on the personal side, he had noticed the framed picture of Gaynor that now had pride of place on the same desk that had been spread with those more torrid and newly revealing pictures. I found real joy in the sharing and he spoke of a sense of thankfulness that out of the horrors of the recent past some good had come my way.
He left, having asked for my further cooperation in the future difficult meeting with the Berrysfords.

Two days later we arrived once again at that beautiful home.
Jack, Joanna and Faye were there, the mood was sombre, yet I sensed an air of edgy enquiry as to the reason for our visit.
In pride of place above the fireplace I noticed a simple picture of Terry.
Were we the bringers of some hope for this family?
Would they concur with Treddick's request for the grave to be opened?
Could they be convinced by the slimmest of chances that their beloved Terry was still alive?
Would we be forgiven by them if we failed in our course of action?

Their response to Treddick's carefully worded statement was intense.
Faye collapsed in deep groaning sobs. I moved quietly to her side.
Joanna held her hands to her face to hide the immediate look of fear.

And as for Berrysford himself, he stood erect, his eyes resolute. Grasping Treddick by the hand he said.
"I thought we had suffered enough."

He embraced his wife and held out a hand towards an unseeing Faye.

What more could we do than share their disbelief? What more could we do than encourage a renewed bravery to face the unknown? What more could we offer than the vaguest of hopes?

That they agreed to take the next most difficult step was to their absolute credit and was plainly on account of their desire for truth and closure to be made known. The agonising possibility that Terry could still be alive was to them all only the faintest of hopes.

Once again I found myself demanding that God would somehow do something... shades of Lara's sure faith and Treddick's manly down to earth understanding surfaced in my mind.

The Berrysfords' pain was so obvious... "God help them," was my prayer.

The DNA testing was conclusive...
the body was not that of Terry Berrysford.

Marsters' lawyers started their appeal on account of unsafe process. The whole unresolved story was once again headline news.

Due process takes time so my life settled into a more regular routine. The work process had started. Harry was on the mend. Sam was back to fitness. John and Stella were firmly in my social network again, more as family than before. Michael, busy as ever at Smettons, had not had any contact with Chartham through his devious programming, his cleverness had not yielded any result.

And as for Gaynor... well, we were very much an item.

A phone call from Faye Berrysford interrupted everything.

"Mr Grantsman," she said, with a sense of nervousness in her tone. "I have come across something in one of Terry's diaries that you may find interesting."
Gaynor and I met her two days later at her home.

She looked tired, worn, her face without makeup, she offered coffee, we accepted. I enquired of the older Berrysfords, they were away.
As we drank together in silence she produced the diary.
Clipped to a page of the diary was a well worn, but torn, receipt of some age.

"Could it be some information about that box Dad gave you?"

It was a written receipt referring to a box of some sort.
The tear, and its age, unfortunately made a nonsense of the detail.
There was just visible a faded set of figures, again incomplete because of the tear, 2651483. The words 'Cabinet Makers of Distiction' could be made out in small print at the bottom of the receipt. No address, no other detail.
Nothing more. And nothing of any note on the reverse.

I looked again at the page in the diary to which it had been clipped.
General details of the young man's busy life.
Cryptic detail that would only make sense to the writer.

Faye told us that most of Terry's office equipment; computer, office diary and desk papers had been taken by the police. Why this diary escaped their notice was due to the fact that she had borrowed it the week before he disappeared to check some personal detail and had forgotten its whereabouts as the ensuing tragedy unfolded. As it was mostly just a duplication of what was in the office diary she had not thought to hand it in.

On the Thursday of that week there was written perhaps the least cryptic of the notes.
'Hein'z 'B'eans'.
Besides the writing there was a childish drawing of a can of beans with a telephone number written into the label.

"Any ideas about this?" I asked.

"None whatsoever, it makes no sense at all," she replied.

"Would you mind if I took the diary with me?"

She nodded her agreement, and after a generous time of further innocent enquiry, as to how they were all doing, we left.
Gaynor had done much to smooth the conversation at those points when

emotion got tangled and raw in the sharing of memories about Terry, their wedding, and their hopes and dreams for their future together.

It was mid afternoon when we arrived back in town.
On impulse I opened the diary.
The Heinz Beans number was very obviously meant to be noticed... I dialled.

"Heinrich Zimmermann International.
Can I help you?" was the efficient announcement.

"Sorry, wrong number... sorry to bother you," was my reply, and I put the receiver down.

Who or what was Heinrich Zimmermann International?

The briefest of enquiries on the 'net' gave fulsome detail describing the worldwide corporate interests of Heinrich Zimmermann International.
Shipping, Real Estate, Venture Capital, it was all there.
What attracted my attention especially was the area designated as 'Fine Art and Fortune'.
Heinrich Zimmermann was a man of immense fortune, and his personal interests involved him in the acquisition of, and the public display of the incredible treasures that had come into his possession through a lifetime of collecting. He had bought and sold to his obvious advantage, and his collections were on show in galleries around the world. The current web page indicated that his "A" List was on tour, being shown world wide in twenty five capital cities.

His credentials appeared impeccable.

Had Terry Berrysford made contact with this man? If he had and on the date indicated in his diary, then Zimmermann may be able to supply a further clue as to Terry's whereabouts, or at least his possible movement beyond the time of his appointment.

My letter to Heinrich Zimmermann International was replied to in a prompt manner with a courteous acknowledgement that "... Mr. Terry Berrysford had kept an appointment on the day specified... and that he had refused an offer of employment with the Company... and that sadly they could not help with any further news concerning his whereabouts."

I felt uneasy as I read the reply yet again.

Why had not Zimmermann offered this information to the police regarding the last known whereabouts of the person who had made headline news following a horrific death that had turned out to be a callous hoax.
The Berrysford name could not have been missed.
The credentials of Heinrich Zimmermann no longer seemed to me to be so impeccable. What would Treddick think?

My considered reaction was to ask Michael to check whether there was any way that he could devise whereby a watch could be made on the activities of Heinrich Zimmermann International. Then, hopefully armed with reliable information, I would tell Treddick of the new developments.
Michael's response was predictable.
He would find a route in somehow.

Two days later and we were in receipt of intriguing news.
Michael had easily discovered that Zimmermann, himself, was soon to be in the Danish Capital, Copenhagen.
The "A" list was due there in a month's time.
Zimmerman was to take the opportunity of a very public presentation of a 'major gift of part of the collection' to the Danish Government.
All this was very prominent on the updated Heinrich Zimmermann International website.

My mind leap frogged over the newly presented data and I made a series of crazy links.
The box… fine art treasures… antiques on the move…the burning of the fake Titians… Denmark… Terry Berrysford… Chartham… Zimmermann…

Copenhagen!

Was it possible that all of these had somehow come together?
Was there some insidious link? Were we any closer to finding out more positive news about young Terry? Anxious for the welfare of all the intimates involved, my decision was immediate.

I phoned Treddick. Access to his mobile number gave me direct contact.
"Michael?"

He listened without interruption as I reviewed the current scene.
He made no comment as I spoke of my concerns.

I finished... his silence seemed interminable.

"Michael... you need to be extremely cautious. Do not do anything yet."
His tone was sombre. His advice, as always, sensible. He was busy, but would ring again.

I had said it before on many occasions. 'If only the mind could predict what tomorrow might bring.' But given choices, we have to make decisions.
We were both committed to the outcome, but we were unknowing of the process into which we were entering. We needed to find out so much more.
It seemed sensible to get closer to the action. But how?

Smettons stepped into the equation in a most unexpected fashion.
I received a letter from the Chairman.

Their initiative gave rise to a whole new programme of activity.
For saving their jet, Harry had already been given a substantial sum that allowed him time to recover properly without the pressure of returning to work too soon.
That was so good, he and May were enjoying their time together.
This, they informed me.
But Harry had been quick to tell me as soon as the cheque had arrived.

For myself... the gift of a new vehicle of my choice!
My battered wreck, the Chairman remembered, had been written off!

And added to that... well they made a most interesting offer of employment. 'As I had been involved throughout,' they said, 'and therefore was the person with the most intimate knowledge of all the ramifications of the whole episode... and as I had been partially successful in bringing about some degree of closure... would I be prepared to be further employed by them, short term, to investigate in my own way, the whereabouts of the still missing contents of the empty containers?
All the facilities of Smettons Security Division would be at my disposal via my connection with young Trevough, and travel requirements would include the availabilty, when required, of the company jet.'
Was I being foolish? I didn't know.
Would I refuse? No!

So I was quick to accept, my mind made up that I needed to find the answers... that I would try to find not only the missing antiques, but Terry Berrysford as well. That surely would be the bonus!

When Treddick finally phoned, I told him of the new opportunity. His advice was, once again, of caution. But having shared together so much in recent months he acknowledged that he had recognised a flare for investigation in my approach to life. He would always be available to advise and if necessary to become involved where the international protocol allowed. On the subject of Terry Berrysford... if there was any news... contact him straight away.

"Be careful, Michael, and God help you!"

As ever, he was consistent in his endeavour to draw me to a higher level.
I knew full well that, yes, I would need more than luck.

Luck, good fortune, chance, fate, destiny, coincidence, accident,
or providence; maybe providence should be a part of my thinking.

## VIII

Wonderful, wonderful Copenhagen!

Gaynor put the Smetton's Company Jet down some three hours plus after take off from London City. The Cessna Citation had been held in a stack system for a while but we were now safely on the ground and heading for Terminal Three and the wonderful City of Copenhagen..

Such a different feeling since the last time we had been on board together. My memories of Harry's heroic effort could not be forgotten. There were times on the flight when the re-run of those terrifying moments were uppermost in my mind. Thankfully Harry's recovery was assured.

For Gaynor, it would be a short stop for refuelling and immediate take off in order to comply with her schedule... she was due in Stockholm later in the day and would be there for an unknown number of days waiting for a consignment to be got together for further transportation back to London.
Her life was hectic, and she loved every complicated minute of it.
Part of the complication was our new and developing relationship.
And my new involvement with Smettons only added to the mix.
She would contact me when she was due to return, hoping that the time would be sufficient for me to find out much needed information.

My journey to Copenhagen was occasioned by the news that Michael had found out. Zimmermann was planning the same trip in order to make a lavish presentation to the Danish people. His schedule was public, all on the Company Website. It was going to be a PR masterpiece for him.

So the decision was made easily.
Gaynor to drop me off in Copenhagen... Gaynor to fly on to Stockholm... me to look into the Zimmermann schedule... establish the connection with the lead players in the continuing drama... solve all the riddles... find Terry Berrysford... come back as the triumphant hero... marry the girl... and live happily ever after! If only!

My life had changed for the good, and though there was a dark side to the nature of my journey, I could feel only a sense of well being as to my changing circumstances. Every day now was faced with purpose

and new resolve. Once again I was a contributor to the well being of others.
I was loved, and welcome in the homes of good friends.
Copenhagen was out there.
There was a job to be done.

Bank... to get some Krone.
Car hire... to be mobile around town.
Hotel... to be rested and ready for the task in hand.
All of these facilities were available in Terminal Three, and the Hilton, at which I had stayed before, was five star, and worth it.
And Smettons was paying the bill.
The airport was only twenty minutes or so out of the City and it was always a good place to make your base, mine especially this time, as I would be local and ready for the off once Gaynor returned.

We had said our goodbyes.
I was missing her already.
I was on my own in Copenhagen.

I had been a number of times before, Denmark of course achieving in the twentieth century, true accolades and international renown for great contemporary design. In my early heady days I had shown a number of my designs in some of the provincial design colleges and art institutions.

Modern Copenhagen is the largest city in Scandinavia but it still enables the tourist to feel at home amongst its gabled houses and narrow streets. There is a small town atmosphere about it. A skyline spiked with delicate spires rather than huge skyscrapers. Great areas of pedestrianisation.
And 'green' in every way possible. The guide books were right.
I liked Copenhagen.
There was a peace about the place.

That peace had been broken in recent days, for it had been en route to Copenhagen that the fake Titians had met their fiery end.
The lorry driver had never been caught.
He was just part of the mystery.

The genuine articles were now in place at the *Statens Museum for Kunst* and were being much admired. There had been put in place a tight

security system. Nobody wanted a repeat of the earlier attempt at spiriting them away. I planned to make time to see them once again.
I bought a copy of *The Copenhagen Post*.
Danish news in English with all that was curent around town.
And there, duly advertised, was the event that had brought me these many miles to Copenhagen.

It would be tomorrow at three in the afternoon.

Heinrich Zimmermann to present his generous gift to the people of Denmark.
The venue would be spectacular. The *Tivoli Konsert Salen* had been chosen.
Who would deny that such a place would only enhance the glorious moment?

Was this Zimmermann's only agenda?
Was he here simply to take part in this flambuoyant act of liberality?

The link between Zimmermann International and Terry Berrysford was an
established one. I had had that curt reply... that Terry had refused a job he had been offered by them.

Was there any thing more to this?
There were growing doubts in my mind.
Antiques and big money were Zimmermann's field.

There was Terry's disappearance and faked death.
Then the cryptic note in the diary that Faye had given me.
The link WAS there.

I just wanted to see the man... to make my own judgement.
I would have to wait.
I could not make tomorrow come any more quickly.
So enjoy Copenhagen.
Though the International Festival was over, there was always good jazz to be heard in the many restaurants and sidewalk bars.

Shop.
Buy something special for Gaynor.
Something very special.

How good it was to be thinking in such a way about someone who was beginning to take such a place of prominence in my life. I could not imagine life without her now.
Small bar... good food...
The excellent sound of Copeland played by a young group of jazz enthusiasts. I just loved the trumpet with those muted high pitched notes.
The music was suited to my mood.

The phone... her voice... she was in Stockholm now.
Her time table still unknown... would see me soon... not soon enough!

"Goodnight... I love you!"

Life was so good. I closed my eyes for just a moment...
the dreams so sweet to my recall.



"Mr. Grantsman?"

"Yes."

"Mr. Michael Grantsman?"

"Yes."

"Permit me to introduce myself...
My name is Heinrich Zimmermann.
It is so good to meet up with you at last.
Mr Grantsman you have become a nuisance to me; and that I can tolerate no longer. I must take steps to ease the situation with a final solution that appeals to me intensely.
You will come with me, NOW!"

What I hadn't noticed, was that the music had stopped... the musicians had gone... the bar was empty.
I was on my own, and now confronted by the one I had come to see.
But not to see in this way.
My plan had been a more surrepticious approach.
But now we were full on, face to face.
My immediate thought was... flight, escape.

I looked around and saw two men blocking the entrance doors, another was closing the blinds across the windows.

There was no way out.

I had been stupid.
I had let my defences down.
I had thought that I was in control and that I was setting the pace of things.
How wrong to underestimate the cunning of others whose whole way of life was being seriously challenged.
Who was I to believe that I could do anything about it?
I was a very small fish in a very big and unknown sea and I was being confonted now by a very angry shark.

"Mr. Grantsman. You will come with me... NOW!"

It was not that he was particularly persuasive but rather that one of the two men at the door had pulled a gun on me.
I considered my chances of escape to be poor. So there was no point in committing myself to struggle at this moment.
With no other obvious plan, I quietly submitted.

There was a car at the roadside.
Zimmermann got in and sat with the driver.
I was squeezed between the two heavies in the back.
The car had curtained windows.
No hope of knowing where I was going.

God! What a mess!

The sullen-faced Nordic to my right took out a syringe and without so much as a by-your-leave stuck it through my jacket and into my arm.
I did struggle, but not for long.

Gaynor's phone call to the Smettons Chairman was an anxiety filled one... terse and to the point... there was a sense of deep unease in her voice.

"I can't raise Michael. I phoned him yesterday evening after my arrival here in Stockholm, everything was OK! He was very buoyant.
But today I have tried and there is only a recorded message stating that he is unavailable at the moment... that something had come up!
It wasn't his voice.
Something is dreadfully wrong.
I have tried again and again, still without response.
He would have let me know of any change in the plans he was making.
The Zimmermann presentation was due today and there was a big celebration to follow. Michael was simply going to observe as much as possible.
He promised me that he would do nothing out of the ordinary.
I know something terrible has happened. What can we do?"

To their credit, Smettons advised an immediate return, putting Gaynor's Stockholm schedule on hold.

The 'Grantsman extended family', as they were now known, were got together at Smettons to share Gaynor's anxious concerns. Sam, Stella and John promised their support in every way possible. Michael Trevough's contribution to the plan of action was straightforward and innovative. He reminded his assembled family of the occasion when they were all at home in Southwold and had watched together the infamous "Gotcha!" moment when Chartham had manipulated and closed his money grubbing scheme.

"Do you remember what I said to Michael when I returned his mobile phone?
'Don't lose it,' I said... 'it is a very special phone!' What I didn't tell you all then was that I had inserted a neat little tracker device into it.
It was one of those 'just in case' actions. It was an insurance thing if ever I needed to locate him in the future. Now is that time. It does mean though, that I must go to Copenhagen. The range of the responder was limited."

With Treddick alerted and his willing availability and expertise in organising discreet police involvement in Copengagen promised, the trip was authorised by Smettons and duly started.
Hasty packing by Michael and John. The trip to London City Airport.

Gaynor getting them into the air... her composure professional... but her demeanor on the other hand a lot more tense than usual.
The extended treasures list, that Zimmermann had donated to the Danish people, made headline news in *The Copenhagen Post.*
Zimmermann was being feted around the City.
But where was Michael?

The required computer wizardry was already operational before touchdown. It was very plain to see. For as the map of Copenhagen was enlarged more and more, so the accuracy of the pinpointing of the location became clearer.

A house in *Christiania..*

Treddick knew a little, and expressed real surprise...
The 'WWW' provided further information... much to the interest and increasing concern of Gaynor, and all on board.
And when the group from London had finally got through the landing procedures, the Danish police provided the fullest report on the possible whereabouts of the mobile phone and, hopefully, Michael Grantsman.

*Christiania Free Commune.*

From one Website you read this Mission Statement.

*"The objective of Christiania is to create a self-governing society whereby each and every individual holds themselves responsible over the wellbeing of the entire community. Our society is to be economically self-sustaining and, as such, our aspiration is to be steadfast in our conviction that psychological and physical destitution can be averted."*

When read without further comment by those who know far more of the *Christiania* story, the Mission Statement would convey somewhat of a Utopian hope about the setting up of such a community.

The Danish police, on the other hand were more forthcoming with what they said was the real truth about the place.
One extremely vocal member of the police group who had gathered was forcefully outspoken.
"Squatters... Communists... Hippies... Drug pushers... Low life...
If your man is in there against his will, then he is in real trouble."

Gaynor was visibly shaken by the man's comment.

Treddick's view of the matter was a little more conciliatory.
But he was the visitor, and he could in no way impose his perhaps more measured views on those who were present, especially now, for those present were revealing a pent up anger at the fact that they were becoming embroiled in an international incident that was unfolding right there on their doorstep.

His knowledge of the setting up and development of *Christiania* was a more calculated one. He had at one time in his early career studied many forms of innovative European community living experiments, *Christiania* among them. The outcome of the consequent social interaction, and the continuing history appealed to him. And he still made an effort to keep himself informed, for it was his area of concern and expertise.

Since *Christiania* had been going for over thirty years, its history was ever changing due to the sometimes unnecessary influence of different power groups, good and bad, who sought to dominate. True it was, that the drug culture was high on the *Christiania* agenda. There had been over the years numerous occasions when heavy police activity had determined to stamp it out. But because of the nature of the development of what may have appeared to be a free living, hippie style community, and the skill of those who lived there who controlled the goings on, these clean up operations had always proved difficult to achieve. Over the years, barricades, stone throwers, the effective use of fireworks and even Molotov cocktails, had thwarted the police operations. Unfortunately there had been real violence, shocking headlines and untimely death. Copenhagen authorities were anxious to make changes but not to exercise the iron glove approach.
Things, however, were changing, he knew that the current Danish authority view was far more right wing than previously. This would make progress in the discovery of the whereabouts of Michael Grantsman a lot trickier.

That there was the possibility of the linkage to Zimmermann, an individual currently so high on the social acceptance ladder in the country, and so visible as far as 'banner headlines' were concerned, meant that there would be dire consequences if decisions made regarding the progress of the investigation went disastrously wrong.

Treddick's considered suggestion was that a covert operation be used...

as low key as possible. Ensuring the safety of those investigating was of paramount importance, so communications would be set up with back up in place... but at a distance... and until required, undercover.
There were those within the Copenhagen Police Authorities who were all for a more confrontational exercise. A 'once and for all' effort to stamp out what many thought of as a degrading and unwelcome sore. *Christiania* was a blight on the community landscape.
A social nuisance that should be got rid of, finally.
The old Military Area, that had been over run for all these years, should be reclaimed and redeveloped for the good of all.

Thankfully the more covert approach, having been debated for a long and sometimes tedious length of time, prevailed.

Treddick, two officers of the Danish Police, Michael with his computer knowledge, and Gaynor, to make the group a little more mixed and social, would go in as a visiting tourist group. They would explore innocently, search out and discover as much as possible, and hopefully come across at least the whereabouts of the mobile phone (it was still operational and still giving the same recorded message). John would stay back and act as liason with the waiting undercover group.

It took a while for Treddick to convince the authorities to accept the involvement of both Michael and Gaynor. But on the point of knowing who they were searching for, and involvement in the previous history, there were no two better qualified people to be a part of the Team.

Journey on!

In at Badsmandsstraede, through *"Christiania City"* (as it was affectionately known), passing the amazing buildings, shops, bars and alternative dwellings, and on to the more leafy, rural setting.
The map, that Michael was cautiously watching on his 'hand held', was leading them out of the settled areas. The tell tail pointer alerted him to the required change in directions.
To maintain the pretence of being unknowing site-seeing tourists, Treddick took detour after detour to make sure that any observer would be at ease with what they were seeing.
What was so fascinating to those of the party who were seeing all this for the first time was the amazing variety of style, colour,and design of the properties passed along the route. Graffiti heaven you could call it.
Once adjusted to the way things were presented, and setting aside the

complicated nature of their journey, it could easily have become an enjoyable experience.
"We have just passed it," Michael whispered to Treddick. "I didn't say immediately in order not to draw attention to the fact."

They had reached a tree-lined clearing, and there in the middle was a most unusual house. They stopped, in order to determine what the next move should be. They were alone. The crowds had been left behind them as they had walked on through the wooded glades.
Gaynor spoke up with the most natural of suggestions. She could ask for help at the property, explaining her need for a toilet facility.

The ringing of the bell brought no one to the door. However, the door was not shut, and through the opening could be heard the distant strains of music of a most ethereal nature. Gaynor beckoned them all to join her.

"Hello!" she said, entering through the open door, "is anyone at home?"

From a hallway that was deceptively large there were stairways that went both up to first floor level, and down to the floor below to what appeared to be a large basement area. They all stood in the hallway waiting for someone to appear. No-one... nothing other than the music to be heard. But to those who knew, the aroma was a give away.

Treddick made a deliberate move towards a low table situated by the stairs that led down to the basement. On the table were the obvious contents of someone's pockets. Money... English and Danish, wallet, diary, comb, watch, and mobile phone.
Michael, noting Treddick's discovery, nodded an affirmative that this was indeed the mobile they were after. Could the owner of the phone be close at hand? Was it 'Mission accomplished?'

"Can I help you?"

The words were spoken slowly... distinctly... by a uniquely apparelled young man with long flowing hair and patriarch beard. There was no hint of surprise in his voice, no anger at the intrusion. No fear... no suspicion.

"Gustaff Madsen... may I welcome you... please share my peace..."

The young man descended the stairs slowly, deliberately, one hesitant step after the other. He held the carved banister to help his downward progress.
"You've come to see Carl? He is not very well I'm afraid."
Still his speech was slow, there was a determined effort to make his words as clear as possible. Treddick, and the Danish police with him, knew the signs so well. The young man was communicating through a haze of induced stupor. He was sadly, a victim of the worst that *Christiania* had to offer.

Something altered in the young man's approach. His voice and delivery changed. He became distinct and communicative. In a much higher pitched voice he spoke as though addressing a crowd of interested visitors.
We were very interested but for very different and personal reasons.

"The table..." he said, "an unusually low Chippendale single-drawed lowboy, with especially ornate handles. 18th century."

He advanced slowly towards another piece of furniture, this time, a chest of drawers. And again in that high pitched deliberate voice he spoke.

"1755... Queen Anne figured maple. Chippendale period. Note the fluting on the columns... a good example. And the chair over there..." his voice quickened, the pitch was noticeably higher, "Dutch circa 1680, its strength is in its Continental design, graceful... see the legs... forerunners of the cabriole style... forerunners of the cabriole... cabriole... cabriole. See the legs... forerunners of the cabriole style."

He began to cry.
To all present it was disturbing.
After a short while he stopped his tears.
It did not seem to matter to him that we had witnessed his distress.

"The Master says I will soon be ready. I long to be of service to him."
His tone had reverted to the slow deliberation of his earlier communication.

Treddick spoke.

"And Carl? Where is he?     Gustaff... show us where Carl is, please."

"He is downstairs... I don't like going downstairs.
I don't like to hear him when he is in pain.
He wont mind you going down, he hasn't had any visitors today."
Gaynor, fearing what she knew to be the truth, was first to discover the whereabouts of the one Gustaff had called Carl.
She was at the foot of the stairs... across in the corner of the large basement room... a bed... and on the bed...
It was Michael...
Tied up, seemingly unconscious.
Heavily bruised about the face.
His mouth covered with tape.

She cradled him in her arms.
Her tears were full flow.

"Michael!"

Treddick took control. Eased the tape away.
Untied the constraints that held him powerless to move.
Slowly sat him up.

Michael groaned.
Then screamed!

"Michael! Wake up!   Michael! Gaynor and Michael are here.
Michael we've found you. You are safe now."

Michael would not wake. Alive he was, just... yet dead to the world.

The critical question was how to get Michael to a place of safety without alerting the whole of the *Christiania* community to the rescue operation.

Who had done this?
Whoever the previous visitors were... where were they now...
how imminent a return might they make?
What should they do with Gustaff Madsen?

In discussion with the two Danish police officers, Treddick, ever the clear thinker, suggested that they contact the backup group and get a couple of them in on *Christiania* bicycles. They could smuggle Michael

out at least. Those big wheeled carrier boxes enabled residents to move everything they needed from one place to another.
*Christiania* bicycles were well sought after machines.
Upstairs, Gustaff had started again on his descriptive understanding of every piece of furniture in the place. His words were hesitant, he became unsure of what he was saying.

"It's time for my medication.
I'm getting so confused.
Please would you help me?
You will find it all on the table by my bed."

The policeman who found the medication recognised it as one of the mind altering, psychotropic drugs favoured by a number of the residents.

Allowing, and watching the self-administration of the drug, the officer knew he could be in trouble. He knew also, the inevitable result.
Within minutes Gustaff was sound asleep.

Gaynor was so unsure of letting Michael out of her sight.
Treddick took a while convincing her that they as a group would have to exit *Christiania* in exactly the same manner as they had entered… as tourists.
The entry of strangers was sometimes logged by residents anxious about infiltration by the authorities.

She needed to trust others now.
She picked up Michael's belongings.

"Thank you… special mobile phone," she whispered, as she kissed it.

She busied herself finding blankets and cushions.

The bicycles arrived.
The one was loaded up with the deeply sleeping Gustaff.
The other was loaded up with the deeply unconscious Michael Grantsman.
The return journey to safety was started without delay.

"Please God. Let the pair of them remain silent." Treddick voiced his prayer.

Silent they were.
Safe they were.
And securely hospitalised, with a strong police guard.
Treddick, John and Michael Trevough returned to England with Gaynor. But with Smetton's approval and authority, Gaynor was the constant return visitor to Copenhagen. Michael's recovery was painful, but swift. His injuries were mostly physical, he had been severely beaten. Each time, on her return to the hospital, Gaynor would hear more of his story. Their love deepened.

The police in Copenhagen were loathe to pursue the Zimmermann link.
He had returned to London unquestioned.
They had yielded to obvious pressure.
All went quiet on that front.

For Gustaff the journey back to life was very different. Questions needed to be asked. Was he a willing participant in the damaging mind changing process? Or had he too been forced against his will into that ugly scene?
The police made discreet enquiries.
No-one came forward as either family member or friend.
What was all that clinical detail on antiques all about?
Why was he so possessed in being correct in his descriptions?

When Michael finally left the hospital with Gaynor, he found Gustaff in the secure ward and wished him well in his recovery. Gustaff was still ill at ease.
Michael couldn't help noticing, as they shook hands in saying their goodbyes, that Gustaff's hand was badly deformed.
He had a finger missing on his right hand.

"How did you lose that?" Michael asked.

"Do you know what… I can't remember," was Gustaff's reply.

"Goodbye, and good luck!" And with that, Michael and Gaynor were gone..

But there was something that Michael couldn't get out of his mind.
He didn't know what it was.
He was obviously deeply disturbed by what had gone on.
That was not the point. He must see Treddick when he got back.

The 'Bingo!' moment came just as they were landing at London City.

"Gustaff is Terry Berrysford! Terry Berrysford! Gaynor... I'm sure that Gustaff is Terry Berrysford."
Each time he said the name he became more sure of the truth of what he had said. Gustaff was Terry Berrysford. He had after all looked at the photographs of the young man so carefully when he was at the Berrysford's home.
He had looked into the young man's eyes... the eyes had it.
He was Terry. The long hair and patriarch beard had hidden the truth.

Michael phoned Treddick immediately... The truth must be discovered. There needed to be verification of Michael's amazing conjecture.

Treddick's handling of the situation was impeccable. The police still held the DNA details that had been used to prove that the body buried in Terry Berrysford's name was not Terry Berrysford. It was straightforward then to use this evidence in the reverse direction to prove that Gustaff was Terry Berrysford. Treddick authorised the intervention necessary to get to the truth.

The DNA results were positive.
The family was informed. Their former despair now turned to hope.
Could the impossible be true? Treddick counselled caution.

The police guard on Gustaff... Terry... was increased.

Measures were taken to organise the return trip for continuing hospitalisation in England. There was still a long way to go in Terry's recovery programme.
It was unknown whether Faye would get the husband she knew and loved back again. His mind was so mixed up.
Would the Berrysfords regain their son?
Time, always of the essence, would play the most important part.
Jack and Faye Berrysford accompanied Terry back.
Hospital, first. For how long they did not know, and then, hopefully, to home.
A new journey had started for all of them.

For the sake of justice, there were scores to be settled.
Zimmermann and Chartham were still out there.
Marsters... his new trial booked, would surely be put away for a long time.

For Terry's sake. For Sam's sake, justice must be done.
For the Berrysfords and the Trevoughs.
For Harry, May and Gaynor, all so intimately involved, they needed closure.
Sadly, there were still so many loose ends.
Michael once again, made a solemn resolve. He would see it through.

## IX

The medics working at Terry Berrysford's recovery, were at a point where nothing more appeared to be happening. They were at a loss to know how else they could bring him to a moment of full release. He would regress so far to a point in time and then withdraw deep within himself.
There was no way forward. All they surmised was that something cruelly traumatising had broken him in his recent past.
His relationship with Faye and, of course, with his parents, was beginning to develop. He was accepting of their offered love. But still distanced himself from them. It was heartbreaking for Faye, all she wanted was some recognition of what their relationship had been. All the recent history was replayed… their wedding photos… their crazy home videos… they listened endlessly to their favourite music. She would cook his favourite meals.
He would occasionally smile as though remembering, but then the withdrawn state would once again take hold.
Faye feared that she would never know him again as once she did.
On the medics advice Faye had moved in with Terry's parents, the suggestion being that there would be many more memories associated with that home rather than the limited memories built together in the short time that the pair of them had been married. Terry was now back at his home. He and Faye shared his former bedroom, and they shared the same bed, but there was little that spoke of intimacy.

Michael and Gaynor visited as often as possible. They began to observe the growing nature of the frustration that at times turned to anger. Jack and Joanna Berrysford were at a loss to know what they could contribute, and Faye was increasingly tired of daily routines that produced no good result.

The medics had still prescribed a diminishing drug regime for Terry.
This gave times of peace for all of them.
But this was definitely not the answer.

They rehearsed together all the known facts leading up to Terry's strange disappearance. All they had was the bizarre note in his diary. They were sure that the connection was Zimmermann. But that Terry had refused a job offer from Zimmermann, was all that they knew.

Had the trauma that gripped the poor boy been experienced by him there?

How could they test the possibility of that?
An opportunity did eventually arise as a result of an interesting telephone call made between the Michaels.

"Uncle Michael. You will be interested to know that Smettons are about to make a legitimate delivery of an extremely high value George III Pembroke table... to the headquarters of Zimmermann International in London.
The table was bought for £40,000 at a Country House auction last week. The scheduled carriers were, at the last minute, unable to make the delivery due to the sickness of their driver, so they contacted Smettons to get them out of a hole. We have it in storage and are planning to deliver it on Monday. And do you know what? Zimmermann is out of the country. He is with his "A List" tour in Madrid."

"Thank you, Michael. It may be just what we need. Let me think about it for a while... I will contact you later"


An opportunity for what!


What could be more innocent than making a delivery of a piece of furniture?


The plan seemed straightforward enough. Harry was fit, willing and available, and very keen to get back to work. Treddick was supportive and also available if necessary. Michael T. would also be in on things in order to keep the Smetton's link legitimate.

Terry could be in on it as well. His strength had returned but he was still in a distant world as far as recognition and memory was concerned.
Maybe, just maybe, a visit to Zimmermann's might do the trick.
There were enough on the job to make sure that he was OK with things.

A return call was made by Michael to Smettons and the details of the delivery were confirmed. Monday it would be. Michael and his 'Team' would take the place of the Smetton's regulars. It was, after all a straightforward delivery of a piece of furniture.

Early Monday morning saw the Smetton's van arrive at the London Office of Heinrich Zimmermann International.
All was in order.
The removal 'Team,' now smartly attired in their Smetton's uniform jackets, put their plans into action smoothly and efficiently.
The securely wrapped Pembroke table was manoeuvred into position and then lowered to the ground on the tailgate of the lorry.
Whilst Harry was supervising this procedure the others were grouped around him in a protective circle. It would have been obvious to any critical observor that they were all quite on edge.
Young Michael took the opportunity of telling them that he had secreted a little something in a hidden recess of the table that would enable him to track forever the whereabouts of the table.
'Added security', he told them. And 'no... it would never be found!'

Terry turned to face the entrance of the building. His look was quite disturbed. Memories were kicking in at an alarming rate. Surprisingly, he took off his Smetton's jacket, returned to the passenger cab and redressed himself in his own very smart jacket. He was in a world of his own.
Without so much as a by your leave, and without looking back for approval, he walked resolutely in the direction of the entrance.
The others were all, unfortunately, involved in some way in the procedures of either closing the back of the lorry up, or taking up their carrying position, or sorting out the paper work they had brought with them, so no-one was in a position to stop the inevitable happening.

They were too late!
But had they been able to see Terry's face, they would have seen a marked change in his usually sullen features.

Terry reached the front doors of the building and went straight in.


"Mr Gustaff! It is so good to see you again."

It was the cheery voice of the receptionist.

"The Master told us that as you had finished your contract with us, you wouldn't be coming back again... Anyway I am pleased to see you. Mr Chatham is downstairs, is he expecting you?"
Terry, calmly walked towards the lifts.

"Good morning, Jean. You say Chatham's in? O well! No, don't bother to ring him. Let it be a surprise. O, by the way, there is a delivery coming in.
They tell me it is a Pembroke table... presumably for the Collection. Would you show them down with it straight away."

The summoned lift arrived. The doors opened. He entered. He pressed the button for Basement 2. Reaching that underground level he alighted and waited patiently in that coldly clinical area. He thought for a moment then with determination made his way along the brightly lit corridor.
The huge bronze doors were before him. He punched in a well remembered code... the doors opened slowly. He entered... the doors closed.

Terry called out.

"Chatham! Chatham! Chatham... or should it be Chartham? Jean told me you were here. There is a delivery coming down."

There was a voiced cry of disbelief that sounded quite faraway in the massive room that housed Zimmermann's private Collection.

Chartham was plainly disturbed by all that he had heard, he was unsure of his next move. The warning bell interrupted his thinking. There were people waiting to be let in. He kept silent.
Terry entered the code and pressed the enter button and the doors opened to allow the 'Team' to bring the table in.

"Alright, Jean, you can leave us now."

She left. The great doors closed again.

Terry's breathing was becoming laboured and obviously painful for him. There was a change happening to his demeanor. The determination and resolution that had given him some hidden strength to achieve what he had in the last few minutes, was now visibly draining from him. He sank to the ground and began to weep inconsolable sobs. The sound echoed through the vault-like interior. Unknowing of the imminent danger, his friends left the table and came to his aid. Terry struggled to tell them of the peril they were in. The words would not come. Terror haunted his eyes.
Chartham appeared... he stood at a distance, gun in hand.

"O, the stupidity of it! Terry, what did you think that you could do? Don't you remember what happenend right here? Can't you feel the pain of it again? Can't you hear your screams? Go on, listen to that sickening crack once more. Can't you remember Zimmermann's sadistic pleasure?"

Terry groaned. His agony increased with every word that Chartham was throwing at him. The memories were flooding back.

"And you Trevough, your arrogance amazes me... it seems that I have you at my mercy at last! I will certainly make you cry! You have caused great personal loss to me, and such nuisance to us all.
And you Grantsman, you have interfered for the final time. I told Zimmermann that he should have got rid of you when he picked you up in Copenhagen. But he was too protective of his public image. Too vain. Too stupid for his own good.
And you others, well... I'm so sorry that you have become involved. Over there... all of you!"

Harry was anxious not to leave Terry. It was self-evident that he was in dreadful distress. His breathing was laboured. He was groaning fitfully.
But Chartham insisted that they all move to the side of the room.
Though he was in control of the situation by the fact that he was armed, it was obvious that he was wanting to access the telephone that was on the opposite wall. Presumably to summon help.
As he passed the spreadeagled Terry there was dramatic movement, Terry lunged at Chartham's feet in a desperate effort to prevent his progress.
Given the unexpected opportunity, all four of the 'Team' made their effort to change the odds in this particular setting.
In the scrambling that followed Terry's crazed attack, a shot rang out, its echo in the vaulted room, increased the volume to deafening proportions.
Treddick fell to the ground. The fight continued till thankfully they had overpowered Chartham. Harry wrestled the gun from Chartham's flailing hand. Two more shots rang out in random directions. The fight was over. Harry had the gun and trained it menacingly at Chartham.
They stood still for a moment.
A sickening pool of blood was spreading from the fallen man.
Michael felt for a pulse.
There was none. Treddick was dead.

What came to Michael's hand was a heavy brass candlestick.
He struck Chartham just once.
Treddick's killer fell soundlessly to the floor.
Michael had no feelings of remorse for his act.
He hoped that Chartham was dead as well.

The three still standing stood lifelessly, unspeaking, unheeding of what next should follow, unknowing of what they should do.
The scheduled task for the day that had sounded so simple in their earlier discussions had now brought them to a place of abject sorrow.
Terry was collapsed at their feet, now silent in his private despair.
Treddick was dead.
And Chartham…

They needed help. How much of what had happened had been heard above?
Were they in imminent danger of discovery? Who might be waiting for them outside those huge bronze doors?
Michael tried his phone… no signal!
The only point of call, it seemed, was the wall-mounted phone that Chartham had been trying to reach. But who would be at the other end of that?

The activation of the bronze doors, they could see, was through the coded key pad on the wall. Only Terry knew the sequence that could release them, and he was collapsed and unfit for the task in hand. They were trapped.

"Terry! Terry! We need your help."

It was Harry tenderly trying to ease some understanding into the poor boy's mind. He held him in his huge arms and nursed him as though a baby.
Terry groaned and woke with fright once more. His screaming deafened the ears and tore the hearts of those who looked on.
They too were helpless in their own despair.

Terry woke again and for a moment focussed on the scene in hand.
He looked, with tired eyes, at each in turn and recognised them one by one.

"Terry we need your help.
The code number for the doors. Can you remember it?

It took an interminable length of time. Terry stirred and spoke... still without the ability to share the code that would enable their release.

The phone on the wall rang. They knew that they should answer it. Michael took the handset from its place.

"Hello, you down there," a cheery voice said. "It's me... Jean up here."

The voice was uncomplicated and jaunty, and without interruption went on.

"The police have just called in to ask if you could move the delivery van... the morning traffic is building up... is that OK?  Bye for now."

With her message speedily delivered, and without waiting for reply, she disconnected and busied herself with her daily routine.

"Terry... the number... please tell us the number."

Harry's gentle insistence finally brought recognition of the need. The number was forthcoming.

The question then was... how should they make their exit.
They must remove Treddick's body, but still retain the semblance of truth about their original purpose.
An old oak coffer was the answer. Harry was quick to move it into position enabling it to become for Treddick a forerunner of the inevitable coffin that would be his final resting place.
They lifted his body. They felt the dead weight in their hands.
The trio worked with gentleness, their trashed emotions laid bare as they completed the task.
Terry got up slowly and moved towards the doors.
He entered the code. The doors opened.
Before they left, and unknown to the rest, he pressed a further button.
The immense doors closed behind them and soon they were in transit carrying the coffer towards the lift.
The ascent achieved. They moved towards the entance.

"You going too Mr Gustaff?" It was Jean again.

"Yes Jean," Terry replied, "I need a little air. I'm not feeling very well."
They were safely away. It was observable that Terry was back with them, his mind and actions under greatly improving control.

"I need a phone," he said.

Michael's was offered.

Terry dialled. There was no response.

"A message for you, Zimmermann. This is Terry Berrysford." He spoke with deliberation, wanting each word to carry weight. "Be sure to listen carefully. There is damage limitation required here in London."

He handed the phone back to Michael, and travelled in absolute silence for the rest of the journey.

The state of shock that all were experiencing probably contributed to the trail of questionable decisions they now made. They all agreed that Terry needed to be back at home, for the trauma of the day had changed him dramatically.
And they persuaded themselves that they should return Treddick's body to his home turf, so they drove on to Chelmsford knowing that the terrible outcome to their day's activity would land them all in trouble.

This was, indeed, the case.

The Chelmsford police, a little more understanding than their London counterparts, set in order the due process to cover the death of Treddick. Intense investigations were commenced. Scotland Yard were furious at the delay and had the trio of unwitting participants back down for questioning immediately. The only thing going for them was that Treddick had left explicit notes about the scheduled journey, and its hoped for outcome.

Treddick's only relative was an older sister. She was informed of his untimely, but brave death in the line of duty. She would have to wait until further investigations had been completed before a funeral could be arranged.

The police entered Zimmermann's London Office in force.
Jean, first in line, calmly told her simple story.
All she knew, she related with accuracy. 'Early this morning Mr. Gustaff had returned. There was a delivery of a table for the Collection, Mr Gustaff had gone to the vaults, Mr Chatham was already down there, an oak coffer had been removed, and Mr. Gustaff had left, not feeling too

well. She had not seen Mr Chatham return, he and one of the delivery men could still be downstairs. Although they could have come back up the fire escape at the back of the building. If they had done that she would not have known.
People have come and gone as they usually do all day. Zimmermann's is a busy place, you know! And we are about to close up and go home.'

When asked; she gave directions to the basement.
The Police, armed with the entry number given them by Michael, went quickly to their task.
At the huge vault doors they stopped.
A sign was flashing a message at them.

    AIR FLUSHING PROCESS COMPLETE

By this time the House Manager had appeared. He was unaware that a 'flushing' had been completed. Unaware that it had been ordered. It was only usually done once a year on Zimmermann's authority, and it certainly wasn't due. The handful of people who had right of access to this part of the building were few in number. He very rarely came down this far.
It was safe to go in. The toxic 'bug control agent' would be out of the system by now. There was a built in safety element to the timing device. Yes, he insisted, it would be safe to go in. The so-called 'bug control' killed off any insect infestation in any new antique acquisition brought in to the Collection. It was the cleanest place he knew.

The vault was empty... none of the expected treasures as described by those still held in custody, were there.

Treddick's spilt blood was there.
Chartham's body was there.
Strangely contorted in death.
His hands clutching at his throat.
He had breathed his last.

"And Mr Zimmermann?" the police enquired. "Where is he?"

"Madrid." The House Manager replied. "He is with his "A" List. He is on tour showing some of his finest treasures all over the world."
The police call to the Madrid Gallery where the "A" List was on show, gave them a simple answer to the whereabouts of Zimmermann. He had

left in a hurry that morning and had flown in his private jet back to London.
He should have checked in at the office already.

The police asked Jean if Zimmermann had returned. To her answer 'No,' she added. 'He doesn't always come in the front entrance, he has his own private entrance through the car park in the basement.'

But having paged him for some time it was obvious that he was not there.

Crime scene forensics experts were left doing their developing investigation in the vault at Zimmermann's, whilst the other officers returned to continue their questioning of the only suspects they had.

Michael G. and Michael T. and Harry were still in trouble.

"Only part of what you have told us is verified.
Treddick's blood all over the floor. Yes!
The body. Yes! You did not say that it was a dead body.
But the vault was empty of any antiques.
So what is your story now?"

Each in turn told the truth as he knew it.
It came as a tremendous shock to Michael when he heard that Chartham was dead. He had not thought at the time that he had hit him that hard.

Inevitably the police were loathe to believe that the three of them were innocent in the matter. One of their own had been shot dead.
A further individual was dead at the scene of the crime.
Antiques, that they were told were worth many millions of pounds, were missing. There were too many loopholes and unknowns.

Michael Trevough, when it was his turn, informed them of the 'bugged' Pembroke. There was a way to locate, at least, that one piece of furniture.
And there was a remote chance that all of the antiques had been removed to a single safe storage area.

On this information they needed to act at once. Michael was released under supervision and set to work back at Smettons to find the table.
Treddick was sadly out of the picture, the police were so angry at his death.

It was confirmed that the one single bullet fired at such close range, had ripped through his body severing his aorta.
He'd had no chance.
With his killer dead as well… cold justice had been partially served.

What Zimmermann's role was in all of this, was still to be established.
That he was in it up to his neck, was beyond doubt.
How to prove it was the seeming impossibility.
Terry held the key to the unlocking of Zimmermann's involvement.
Deep down he knew the condemning facts.
But would they be forthcoming?

Treddick's files were helpful for they were meticulous in their detail.
In studying them, the link was easily made with all that had gone before regarding the Trevough family, the Grantsman association, Smettons and the Berrysfords. When those facts were known, all hostility towards those still in custody was removed. They became contributors in the continuing investigation. They were free to go, but they must stay in touch, and let the police know of any further development.

As for Terry Berrysford… the police would wait till he was well enough, before listening to his side of the story. The stopping point in his recovery had been dramatically overcome by facing the trauma of whatever took place at Zimmermann's. Those who remembered his inconsolable sobbing, were well aware that a deep place had been reached.

For Terry, his homecoming was the start of a gentle restoration of relationships with all who loved him dearly.
At their meeting, Faye held out her hands for his touch, and in that special, well remembered way, she knew that Terry was hers once again.
She was impatient to know the full story.
She promised herself to wait, however long it took, knowing that if he felt he could, her Terry would tell it all.

At Smettons the work was going well.
The technology did it all in a clinical and thorough way.
The tracker searched for the bug.
The bug rsponded to the tracker.
The whereabouts of the Pembroke table…was discovered.
Unbelievably, the location showed the Zimmermann Headquarters building to be the hiding place. The police, still there, were examining every inch.

Forensics were still there.
Laboratory tests were showing that Chartham had traces of the 'bug control agent' in his lungs. The fact that he had been discovered, his hands clutching at his throat, proved that he had died a dreadfully painful death.
Who had killed him?
Who had started that poisonous process? No-one knew.
The question nagged away at the 'Grantsman mind-set,' after all, he was the one who had struck Chartham to the floor.


Treddick's calming influence was missed at every level.
The friendship and trust that had developed between him and Michael, in particular, had secured for them all a deep sense of respect, right from the beginning. Respect not only for his much admired professionalism, but also respect for the way he lived his life.
There had been a tangible peace when he was around.
His obvious dependence on all things holy was never intrusive.
He was good to be with.
The care that he had shown to the Berrysfords had been so gentle.
He had had such difficult information to give to them.


It was Harry's straightforward logic that jerked them into action once again.

"Terry phoned Zimmermann in Madrid. OK.
We heard him mention the fact that damage limitation was needed in London. We know from the contact with the gallery in Madrid that Zimmermann had then left hurriedly to come back to London.
We know that the 'bugged' Pembroke table is back somewhere in the Zimmermann building in London.
Terry seems to have had a strange relationship with the Zimmermann organisation under the name of Gustaff.
Jean easily recognised 'Gustaff' and fully accepted his authority.
Terry knew his way around the building.
Zimmermann must be there.
So. Terry is the only one who can find him!
So. Terry must go to London"
The police reluctantly agreed that it seemed the logical thing to do.
They further agreed that Terry should be supported by the trusted presence of good friends. Decision made.

Faye was angry at what she thought to be an unnecessary intrusion into their life. Terry had come home to her. He was feeling safe and secure. Why should he be exposed so quickly to the possibility of renewed trauma? She took some convincing, but with Terry's promise 'not to do anything silly,' and Michael and Harry's promise to look after him, she let him go.

Each of the four had a recognised role... Michael T. to fine tune the search for the Pembroke table... Michael G. and Harry to provide support for Terry... and Terry, hopefully to locate Zimmermann.

The plan of action had been decided.
First... Michael would make his sophisticated electronic sweep. If there were clear indications of the table's whereabouts, then Terry would be given the opportunity to develop the search as he thought fit.

The successful sweep gave an answer that was intriguing. The table was there but somewhere much deeper underground. Much deeper in fact than the vault that had housed the Zimmermann "B List." Terry had told the police that part of his story when he had realised the stolen nature of a number of the articles that he had seen. The probability that many more articles in the "B List" Collection were of the 'stolen' variety was obvious.

Terry took them all to the underground car park.
Adjacent to the lift that gave access to the rest of the building there was a private car lift that gave direct access to the road at the back of the building.
It was for Zimmermann's private use. He shivered as he remembered, he knew that he had been brought in this way before, but only down to this level.

Michael's electronics said deeper.

The lift controls were simple.
Two buttons, each with an arrow, one pointing up, the other pointing down.
Set apart from those basic controls was another panel, with a button marked in red, 'Emergency.'
This pressed... they started their descent.
Down... down... down.

Deep underground... they stopped.
The lift doors opened.

The area before them was crammed full with what was obviously hastily deposited furniture. Priceless items were carelessly stacked one upon another.
Statues, some fallen and broken. Paintings leaning precariously.
Frames touching canvas causing irrepairable damage.
Terry recognised what was before him.
The "B List" had been ingloriously deposited in haste. The total lack of care was something that proved the frantic nature of what had happened.
No-one in his right mind would have done such a thing.

The police, now extremely cautious, explored the full extent of the bunker.
For bunker it surely was. The chaos was everywhere.

In the wall at the far end of the vast room was a single door, slightly ajar.
An armed officer pushed it open. There was no sound from within.
It was a small entrance hall to what appeared to be a continuing suite of rooms that were beyond.
What met their eyes, on entry, was appalling.

Four bodies on the floor.
Each with a single bullet wound between the eyes.
It spoke of execution.

Terry recognised three of them.
One, the driver of the car that had brought him to this place those months before. Two of them, the heavies who had held him as Zimmermann had administered the drug that had changed his life so much.
Number four though, he did not know.
Michael Grantsman also recognised three...the same three... they were the ones who, with Zimmermann, had trapped him in Copenhagen.
Michael Trevough, on the other hand, recognised the one remaining...
a member of the staff at Smettons.


"Gustaff? Is that you Gustaff?
Please come in. I want to show you something very special.

Bring your friends in as well. I shall be pleased to meet them"
Terry, still calm, knew who it was.
Michael, now very much alert, also knew who was speaking to them.

Zimmermann! Yes it was Zimmermann.
There, in the centre of the room, sitting on a magnificent chair.
Zimmermann!

"Be careful, all of you, the place is rigged to blow!"

He held in one hand a gun and in the other a control set of some kind.

"I've put on a little show for you all… do please sit down."

A video screen on the wall above him came to life.
The lights dimmed.
The picture sharpened to its point of focus.

There was Terry with Zimmermann, they were talking of the offered job.
Terry's refusal was clear for all to hear.
A scene change was announced with a dramatic title.

'HE NEEDLED ME WITH HIS REFUSAL…SO I NEEDLED HIM!'

They watched the sudden violent event that followed.
The opening of the wall safe.
The removal of the stainless steel box.
The removal, and the filling of the syringe.
The moment when the drug was injected.

But the point at which Terry began to vomit was quickly cut.

The next scene was titled. 'A CLEAR CUT OPPORTUNITY.'

Even the most hardened officers, who watched, drew breath when they saw the next clip unfolding.
It was obviously at a different time, and in a different place.
But there in front of them they watched as Zimmermann got Terry's diamond ring by surgically removing Terry's finger. They heard the crack as the surgical cutters broke through both flesh and bone.
Way above the sound of that was the sound of Terry screaming.

Zimmermann had turned the volume up at this point and had added to the sound with his own sadistic laughter. The tape had been edited to repeat the action and the sound over and over again. He became hysterical and stood before them watching it in seeming triumph.

Unbeknown to Zimmermann, and fortunately covered by the darkness in the room, Terry moved closer to the officer who still held the gun. He wrestled it from him, and in one quick move had it in his hand. He levelled it at Zimmermann and fired expertly.

The control set flew from Zimmermann's shattered hand.
The laughter turned to screaming.
The show was over.

"Terry... the gun please. Give me the gun."

The senior police officer was eager to take control.

Terry fired again...

Zimmermann grasped his knee and collapsed unconscious to the ground.

Michael spoke up.

"Terry! It is over now. Remember what you said to Faye."


In remembering all that spoke of love.
In remembering deep commitments he had made.
In remembering lasting values shared with friends.
In remembering all the hopes for future life and destiny.
In remembering...

The situation was redeemed.

It was over now. Michael's job was done.

# Post script

## Terry's story.

Zimmermann's obsessive interest in Terry Berrysford had been sparked by the occasion when Terry had forced Zimmermann to spend more than he had expected at an auction. His enquiries had led him to believe that Terry was the right man for a job that he had in mind. He needed a brilliant expert.

When the generous job offer was refused, Zimmermann was forced into playing his hand in a very different way. He had been so sure of Terry's acceptance that at the initial interview he had shown him the extent of the Zimmermann "B" List Collection.

Terry's knowledge of some of the antiques in the collection made him aware that Zimmermann had a dark side unknown to the general public. Chartham, an associate of Zimmermann, was first of all an occasional supplier to Zimmermann, later drawn more closely into the alliance he devised a plan that would enhance the Collection considerably.

Zimmermann's ruthless plan was to persuade Terry in another way to come into his employ. He was not going to lose... nobody ever refused to comply with his will. Terry's death was staged, some poor unfortunate was killed off to take his place. Mind controlling drugs were administered over weeks in order to change Terry's understanding of who he was. Gustaff was born.

The new character of Gustaff replaced that of Terry. Zimmermann's new creation grew in his knowledge of the antiques in the Collection... but, sadly things began to go wrong. Gustaff was shipped off to *Christiania* for supposed rehabilitation.

## Treddick's funeral.

A gentle affair, filled with respect and full honour. His only relative, a sister, knew the calibre of the brother she was burying. Her love for him all through the years had enhanced his life. Their shared faith in God, developed over many years in their upbringing, was never questioned.
He remained a believer to the end of his days.
His stedfast witness to the reality of the presence of God in his life was a challenge to all who met him. Michael Grantsman had learned a great deal from the man and he counted him as a dearly loved and respected friend. Through him he had learned to pray.
Michael and many others would miss him greatly.

## The seven digit number on the torn bill of sale for the box.

At a social event at the Berrysford's lovely home, well in to Terry's recovery period (he had sadly suffered a relapse due to the strain of the final events at Zimmermann's) everyone was present to celebrate a marked improvement in his health and also to congratulate Faye and Terry in that they were now expecting their first child.

Harry and May were there. Michael and Gaynor and all the Trevoughs were there, all the Berrysfords and Bertie Bantock as well, they made a great extended family. They had dined well.

Following the meal the subject was brought up of the beautiful box they had given to Sam. Sam had brought it in order to show Terry the way to open it.

It was the box that had started all this incredible sequence of events.

They performed, very theatrically, and with great laughter, the intertwining and the eventual opening routine. Terry was impressed.

Michael asked about the torn bill of sale... and that seven digit number... Michael had returned it to Faye with Terry's diary, did Terry know any more?

Terry was sure that if it were like others he had handled then it wasn't anything to do with the bill. Rather it should be a code used in connection with the contents. Maybe there were more secrets to be found. Faye found the diary, and sure enough the torn bill of sale was still attached. 2651483 was the number, it was obviously incomplete, but the paper was torn at this point.

It couldn't be an opening sequence for that they had discovered by chance in that 'all together' way.

Jack Berrysford suggested that it may be a further sequence to be followed once the box was open. There were eight Wyverns. Seven digits in the code. The number seven was missing. They had already noted way back when first they had discovered its secret that the Wyverns were different in size.

Together, they deduced that they should press them in the stated order in descending size, from the largest Wyvern to the smallest. 2651483... 7.

A most satisfying click followed... equally followed by a gasp of surprise uttered by all who watched. A hidden compartment had opened and there revealed was a brilliant diamond, and by its side a small scroll of paper. Written on the scroll

"ECCE SIGNUM"

Jack Berrysford spoke out slowly, and in a grand manner.

"BEHOLD THE TRUTH."
Michael looked at Gaynor. She smiled.
"If you want the truth.
We have something to tell you all."

But there was no opportunity for them to say what they wanted to say. For all had chorused… 'you're getting married!'

## The wedding. The church at Blythburgh

There is a time in the year when the sun shines in to the Church at Blythburgh in a most delightful way. Those standing at the communion rail are bathed in a shaft of light. On this day and in that light Gaynor and Michael were wed.

The diamond on her finger, the very one that Jack Berrysford had revealed.

## The car

After the reception at the Trevough's house the couple set out for life together in their new car. Their 1.9 CDTi Vauxhall Vectra suited them very nicely.
The Wyvern on the back said it all.